STRICKLAN
Strickland, AdriAnne,
Wordless /
33090023114954

MAIN 12/15

...ary real-world implications ... Brilliant."

—Chelsea Pitcher, author of *The S-Word*

LONG BEACH PUBLIC LIBRARY
101 PACIFIC AVE.
LONG BEACH, CA 90822

33090023114954

Praise for Worldless

"A fast-paced blend of sci-fi fantasy with s

ADRIANNE STRICKLAND

WORDLESS

flux®

Woodbury, Minnesota

Wordless © 2014 by AdriAnne Strickland. All rights reserved. No part of this book may be used or reproduced in any manner whatsoever, including Internet usage, without written permission from Flux, except in the case of brief quotations embodied in critical articles and reviews.

First Edition
First Printing, 2014

Book design by Bob Gaul
Cover design by Lisa Novak
Cover image: iStockphoto.com/1569366/©Atropat

Flux, an imprint of Llewellyn Worldwide Ltd.

This is a work of fiction. Names, characters, places, and incidents are either the product of the author's imagination or are used fictitiously, and any resemblance to actual persons living or dead, business establishments, events, or locales is entirely coincidental.

Library of Congress Cataloging-in-Publication Data
Strickland, AdriAnne.
  Wordless/AdriAnne Strickland.—First edition.
     pages cm
  Summary: "After helping Khaya, the Word of Life, escape from her prison, seventeen-year-old trash collector Tavin Barnes joins her on the run, attempting to prevent Khaya's captors from using the Words for world domination"—Provided by publisher.
  ISBN 978-0-7387-3966-3
[1. Runaways—Fiction. 2. Sanitation workers—Fiction. 3. Literacy—Fiction. 4. Identity—Fiction. 5. Fantasy.] I. Title.
  PZ7.S91658Wor 2014
  [Fic]—dc23
                                                    2014010786

Flux
Llewellyn Worldwide Ltd.
2143 Wooddale Drive
Woodbury, MN 55125-2989
www.fluxnow.com

Printed in the United States of America

For Lukas,
who is the Word of Support, Patience, and Love

ONE

I'd heard the story when I was a kid. Everyone had, even wordless nobodies like me who had never set foot in any of Eden City's cathedrals. The story went something—no, exactly—like this:

Two Nameless Gods created the earth just by speaking. Twelve Words was all it took. Then they made their Words into flesh, giving twelve people the powers of creation—people who could bring darkness or light, harness the earth or air, spark a fire or raise a flood, shape things from the clay and breathe life into them. Or kill with a touch.

Old Man Drey was killing me with the story right now. I hadn't even leapt off the back of the garbage truck before he'd stepped down from the driver's seat, leaving the truck rumbling like a neon-green beast against the curb, and walked around back to continue lecturing me about the Nameless Gods and their Words, like I hadn't heard it a hundred times before. He acted like he belonged behind a podium, not the wheel of a garbage truck, somehow managing to look dignified even in those goofy green overalls.

As for me, I jumped down onto the gray cobblestones and straight into a pile of dog crap. I slipped and almost ate it—literally. So much for dignity.

"Damn it." I glared at the bottom of my boot and scraped it on a rare uneven cobblestone. The stain wouldn't be there for long, once the street sprayers got to it.

"Tavin, language," Drey reminded me. "Now, where were we?" He stepped into an alley nestled between two four-story buildings.

He didn't mean in our trash-pickup routine. He meant the story, which he'd started telling when the sky was still dark. Now a pale blue light frosted the frilly stonework decorating the buildings on either side of us, making even the alleys in this section of town look better dressed than we were. Not that many people were up and around this early. Usually it was only us, cleaning the city before everyone else awoke.

"The Words have to live in the flesh of man, inscribed into skin like ink in the pages of a book until the flesh becomes the embodiment of the Word," Drey continued. "Or else the Words would lose their spark, that special something—the breath of the Gods."

I dragged my foot as I followed Drey's voice, both to clean it off and because I was none-too-eager to hear the rest of what he had to say. But I didn't complain. Instead, I listened to him over the coos of the pissed-off pigeons we'd awoken on the wrought-iron fire escape above our heads. I listened because Drey was the only one who ever bothered to teach me anything. And because he was the reason I had a job, not to mention the reason I was alive enough to work in the first place. So what if he got repetitive sometimes?

That didn't stop me from looking at the sky, to better dodge pigeon crap and to imagine what it would feel like to fly up and out of this alley. It was depressing that even a stupid pigeon could manage such a feat, but not me.

Drey kept talking in his lofty way, like he was a God in the heavens instead of a garbage man in the alleys of Eden City, even as we picked up the trash bags waiting for us by back doors. "The Words must be sustained by a man's breath. Or a woman's," he added, glancing at me over his shoulder as if he was trying to keep up with the times and failing by about a century. "Or else the Words would die and we would lose the power of the Gods forever."

"Uh huh," I said, throwing in a nod for good measure even though, to me, the story seemed like a bigger load than the trash bags I was hauling back to the truck.

Sure, there were Words—nine that were still around. There was picture proof right in front of me on the giant flat-screen TV across the street: an image of the Word of Earth, smiling smugly with his muscular arms crossed. He was the poster child for Eden City and its diplomatic mission to bring peace on earth through worldwide cooperation. The Word of Life appeared next, her face as unsmiling as always but equally stunning. I was downright sick of seeing them.

Not that I ever saw any of them in person. They gave public service announcements that appeared on our video phones, reminding us to be good citizens, and posed on billboards and posters. But the Words Made Flesh were as distant from me as the world outside of Eden City. Only the glowing TV screens that Drey and I passed on our daily route proved the existence of either: the various Words—young and beautiful, as poised and perfect as the city they controlled—shaking hands with the heads of various far-away countries like China, Russia, and America, or greeting the leaders of our much-closer but equally inaccessible neighbors like Switzerland and France.

The Words might have been far above people like me, but that didn't mean they let us forget they were there, as much as I tried.

Yet I just didn't buy the crap about the Nameless Gods. That part of the story was way too up-in-the-clouds, not meant for normal people down on the ground—or knee-deep in garbage.

"Tav, I can tell you're bored," Drey said, making me start with the guilty realization that I'd been tuning him out. "But I'm telling you this again because it's relevant." He heaved the black trash bags, bunched in his hands like giant sagging funeral balloons, off his shoulder and into the gaping maw in the back of the truck.

He could always sling them more accurately than me, even though he had grizzled stubble on his chin and a frightening cough, and I now had bigger arms than him and was "at the peak of youth"—which was Drey's fancy way of saying he didn't know exactly how old I was. Or how old I'd been when he'd found my nearly dead infant body in a trash container about seventeen years ago.

"I want it fresh in your mind," Drey went on, "and I thought it best that it came from me. Unless, of course, you want me to drop you off at a cathedral...?"

"No, no!" I said quickly. "But how the hell—I mean, how is any of this relevant now?" *Or ever*, I thought.

Drey looked at me seriously. "I came from the Athenaeum before picking you up at the garage this morning."

"Right," I said. Not only would that mean he was up earlier than any sane man would be awake, but no one— especially not the garbage brigade—just *went* to the Athenaeum. That was where the Words were, not the wordless. The Gods would have to come down from their clouds to personally vouch for people like me and Drey before we could ever set foot inside.

Or at least that was what I thought until Drey said, "I think I got you a job there."

"*What?*"

Right then one of my bags tore, spilling empty wine bottles and—my favorite—rotten fish onto the curbside. We were next to Bodine's, one of the nicer seafood restaurants in Eden City, but what came out of the back end of something was never as pretty as what went in the front. Drey hadn't even taught me that; I'd learned that lesson on my own.

That was when I spotted the fur in the pile of refuse. "Aw, hell."

I dropped to my knees and lifted the small body in my

gloved hands, cradling its head and trying to glimpse some life in its half-closed eyes.

A puppy. A dead puppy. This day just couldn't get any better.

Drey didn't even scold me for my "language." He just looked down at me, a sad expression on his face. He probably knew why I liked to save anything alive we found—the only thing that separated my fate from that of the tiny body in my hands was the cot in the back room of the garage that Drey let me sleep on.

That was me, Tavin Barnes, able to relate to dead puppies. Drey's sympathy only made me more embarrassed to be on my knees.

I cleared my throat. "Weren't you saying something completely insane about getting me a job in the Athenaeum, before—" I waved at the mess.

"Part-time. You start tomorrow."

"What? Why? How?" My words grasped at the situation as clumsily as my hands, which were now trying to scoop everything back into the torn bag. A fish head fell back into the gutter, and a man in a crisp black suit with a matching briefcase gave me, not the fish head, a disgusted look as he walked by.

Drey bent down to help me. He never had to do things like that—I mean, technically, he was my boss, and the boss of our district garage—but he always did.

"I already told you what," he said. "As for why ... I think you should try to move up in the world, Tavin, and not just rot on the street with this trash. And me."

"But—but I can't read!"

That was only the first of many reasons why I could never set foot in the Athenaeum. The wordless survived at the bottom of the food chain, far beneath the rich and influential. Eden City was the richest of all self-governing city-states, a haven for the über wealthy because of its favorable taxes, and the Athenaeum was the hive at the heart of it, swarming with those types of people: not only the Words and the City Council—who, together with the Words, ran the city—but the politicians, diplomats, and businessmen that flocked around them. It was the center of government, international relations, and power. The wordless were the nobodies of Eden City, the lowest class, treated like the trash we cleaned or the dirt we scrubbed from floors.

"That makes you a more desirable employee." Drey chucked the torn bag into the trash compactor. "You don't pose a threat. You can't read the Words and use their power, even if you were standing right next to one."

I didn't understand how on earth someone could "read" a person—Drey called this kind of reading "godspeaking"—but he was right, as usual.

"So instead of being the young thief who's broken into the sultan's harem, I'm more like one of those servant-guys who's had his balls chopped off." I flashed Drey a shit-eating grin.

"Those 'servant-guys' were called eunuchs," he reminded me with a scowl. He didn't like being reminded that he'd told me that story, which had veered away from my history lesson into fantasy. "Here I want to give you a good education, and that's the sort of thing you remember."

Maybe because I often felt about as impotent as if I'd been neutered. Impotent—a great word for a wordless guy like me.

"I'll never be educated," I said, finally pitching the rest of my trash bags into the back of the truck. My lack of education wasn't Drey's fault. He couldn't read either, so he couldn't exactly teach me. I didn't want to make him feel bad, so I changed the subject. "And I still don't know why the hell they'd want me. What can I do?"

Drey pushed a button and the green steel jaw of the compactor began to whine shut, devouring bottles, fish heads, and dead puppies alike. It sounded impolitely loud on the quiet street. "Someone needs to clean up after them."

"So," I said with hefty skepticism, "I'm going to collect trash . . . for the Athenaeum?" There were some things that simply didn't fit together, and "trash" and "Athenaeum"—the colossal, shining pyramid rising at the north end of the city like a glass mountain trying to reach the Gods—were two of them. Did they even generate trash there like normal human beings?

"They sure don't clean up after themselves," Drey said.

And that made sense. Because garbage really didn't have anything to do with them—only with people like me. Maybe the Words liked to take credit for Eden City being so clean, as if one of them was the Word of Trash Removal, shooting sunbeams out of his ass to scour the streets . . . but no.

"Fine," I said, grabbing a handle on the back of the truck

and assuming my precarious perch above the cobbled street. "But you never answered this question—how? Who did you even talk to, to get me this job?"

Drey gave me the smile that meant I was being a shithead but he didn't mind. "'Whom,' you mean—'to whom' did I talk. And I have connections."

"You have connections?"

Maybe I'd gone too far with that one, because his tone was stuffier as he said, "I don't need to remind you that I'm your manager."

Sometimes I did need reminding. He often didn't act like my boss, always driving a trash route with me and only me. He was more like a protective uncle—the closest thing to a parent I would ever have.

"I wasn't always in the business of garbage," he continued, much more softly.

Now that was curious. If Drey had connections to the Athenaeum, what the hell had he done to get thrown out here—to rot, as he'd called it?

"And it's none of your business," he added, right as my mouth opened to ask him. "I'm dropping you off at the Athenaeum tomorrow morning, and I'll pick you up when you finish at noon. Maybe other opportunities will open up for you in such a place."

He leapt into the truck and gunned the engine with a roar, leaving me hanging off the beast's backside.

TWO

Drey made good on his word, coming to the garage even earlier than usual to tip me out of my cot and shove a cup of coffee into my hands. It looked and smelled like he'd brewed it out of old truck tires.

I blew on it, sitting on the side of the cot, and took a sip. "Mmm, even tastes like tires."

"I want you alert this morning, Tav. This is important," he said, scooting aside a box of spare earplugs and gloves to lean against the metal desk across from my cot. He used to use this room for storage and still put a few boxes in here, but I didn't mind. He was letting me live here for free, after all. Before moving in here, I'd lived with him in his tiny studio apartment—a total bachelor pad—until we could no longer stand the proximity. That was when I was about six.

"I know it's important," I said. "If the Athenaeum's garbage doesn't get collected, they might realize it exists."

"Tavin."

"I'm listening." I got up and padded barefoot across the concrete floor to the mini-fridge that I hoped would contain breakfast.

"You're an intelligent, handsome, hardworking kid, Tav. This is an important opportunity for you ... to be noticed."

I froze. "I'm handsome?"

Drey scowled like he usually did when I was ridiculing something he said, but this time there was no ridicule. I couldn't remember the last time I'd looked in a mirror. I'd grown a lot in the last year, my arms thickening to the point where other guys at the garage joked they needed to start working out to catch up to me, but that was about all I'd noticed.

"You can still do something with yourself. Don't squander your life," Drey said, reiterating what he'd told me yesterday.

And like yesterday, I still had some serious doubts, even more now that he'd thrown "handsome" onto the list of my imaginary attributes. "Thanks for the pep talk, but it's not like I'm going to climb to the top on the strength of my trash-hefting muscles." I peered into the fridge. "Especially with no milk to put on my cereal." Captain Crunch was my favorite American import—there was a flow of goods across the borders, just not people—and I tried not to go a morning without it.

Drey sighed and raised a brown paper bag that had been resting behind him. It had grease splotches on it, which was always a good sign. Unless that was engine oil and not butter. "I got you a pastry," he said.

He'd gotten me two. With chocolate filling. I started in on the first one as I trailed him down the narrow aisle between the trucks and a wall of tools. The smell of diesel fuel and ripe trash didn't bother me as I inhaled the pastry like a starving man. I was used to those things.

It was so early that the other guys hadn't yet arrived to take the second truck. Still, Drey didn't give me time to shower in the weeny stall in the garage, which was there for the sake of anyone who'd gotten doused in garbage juice. And he raised a hand to stop me when I reached for my usual neon-green overalls and jacket.

"They gave me a different uniform for you," he said, opening the door of our truck to toss me a plastic-wrapped package from under the seat.

I tore it open to reveal a white long-sleeved jacket, almost like a doctor's.

"What, am I going to a hospital?" Before Drey could answer, I added, "Do they even know what we do? *White?*" White clothes and trash were two more things that didn't mix well.

"We're an independent company," Drey said, getting in the truck. He waited until I'd climbed in the other side before continuing. "But you still have to report to the head of the Athenaeum's janitorial staff. So try to look sharp. She'll tell you where to go and what to do, though I know you'll be collecting trash from small sites around the complex and then driving it to the main containers outside. We'll empty those when I come to pick you up, and then we'll finish our usual run through the city."

"Did you say 'drive'?" I asked as Drey started the engine. The volume of our voices adjusted to be heard over the roar.

"Yes, you'll get your own vehicle. A small one, nothing like these"—he was backing the great rumbling monster out of the garage—"which you already know how to handle."

I was going to be trusted with my own vehicle? It was too good to be true. "I still don't see why they would hire me," I said, rubbing the white jacket between my fingers as if it were made out of silk. "Don't they already have someone for the job?"

"Nope," Drey said tersely, looking straight ahead into early morning traffic. The city was already waking up in this section—the poor section—where buildings were tall but made out of concrete instead of stone, like a prison block. "Buckle your seat belt."

I grumbled under my breath and put on my jacket and my seat belt. I was intrigued, even though I had no illusions about my "future opportunities."

We approached the Athenaeum from the south, crossing a bridge over the Nectar River as the sun officially crested the horizon. Golden light bounced off Lake Eden in the east and raced along the river, a glowing slash that cut the city in half. The colossal fountain on the lake ignited like a pillar of fire, and the massive glass pyramid lit up like a lantern. As big as it was, the Athenaeum would have to be a lantern that belonged to the Gods. And I was about to go inside.

We drove around to a back parking lot. I spotted the trash containers against the outer base of the steeply slanting glass walls, next to a gate just wide enough to allow a vehicle to pass: a service entrance.

When I jumped down from the truck, Drey came around to inspect me. He reached up to flatten my mussed brown hair with fingers that were disturbingly crabbed. And either I was still getting taller—which was pretty damned tall already—or he was shrinking. I often called him "Old Man Drey," but now it struck me like a sucker punch that he *was* an old man.

"You need a haircut again," he said. "It's falling in your eyes. And that jacket's a little tight across your shoulders and short in the arms."

"Thanks, Dad." I didn't want to call him "old man" ever again.

Drey suddenly looked uncomfortable. I didn't know whether he'd liked me calling him Dad or not, even sarcastically. I'd taken his last name, Barnes, but only because it had been the only one around to give me. I sure looked nothing like him—my skin alone was several shades darker.

We were both about to say something, probably something awkward I didn't want to say or hear, when the small gate slid open, discharging a compact truck that was more like a cart with a trailer bed attached. It parked a short distance away, and then a woman in white stepped out and approached on foot, flanked by two people in black who'd followed her from the gate. Their rooster struts screamed *power-tripping security guards* louder than their official-looking uniforms and badges...and guns.

And the woman was walking the same way, even in heels and a tight skirt.

"Uh, see you later, Drey," I said as he broke away. "In a few hours, right?" I was suddenly afraid he wouldn't come back for me.

"Of course. Remember what I said, Tav." He hopped in the truck, which sounded like a metallic avalanche as it took off.

The woman marched up to me without pausing or smiling, her heels clicking sharply on the asphalt. "You're Gustav Barnes, I presume?"

"Tavin. Or Tav," I said with a wince. Drey and his stupid names.

She held up an electronic tablet without acknowledging what I'd said. "Look here. Open your eyes wide and hold still."

I stared into what looked like a camera lens on the back of the tablet and didn't blink, like a good boy, until she lowered her arm and tapped at the screen.

"Retinal scan complete." She detached a stylus from the tablet and held them both out to me. "Sign here."

I balanced the slim device on my arm and pinched the stylus awkwardly in my fingers. The screen, which for me would usually have shown a video recording of someone giving instructions, was full of little black symbols that meant shit to me.

"Uh, where?" That was the first of my problems. The other would be writing my name.

"Where it says 'name,'" she responded.

"I don't know where that is."

She smiled a smile that had nothing to do with kindness. "Good, you're wordless. We wouldn't want you claiming to be someone you aren't, hmm?" She snatched the tablet and stylus back from me, signing the screen herself before doing an about-face. "Right this way."

I followed the pinched lady as she marched toward the small truck. Her strut *was* somewhat inhibited by her skirt—she walked like she had a stick up her ass. That, along with many other things about her, cancelled out the positive effect of her nice legs. I tried to pretend the security guards weren't there, positioned on either side of me like they were escorting me into prison. We stopped in front of the truck.

"Here is the vehicle you will be using," she said, handing me the key. "It will be parked inside the gate every morning. I assume I don't have to explain your duties, as they're rather simple. If you'll excuse me."

"Wait," I said as she strode back toward the gate with the security guards. "I don't know where to go."

"You have brawn," she said, giving me a backward glance like I was something she'd accidentally speared on one of her stiletto heels. "But try to use your brains. Follow the signs. They're mostly in pictures, but scan them with your video phone to get an audio prompt if you still can't understand. You *do* have a phone, right?"

Even the homeless had phones, never mind the wordless who needed them to function. "Uh, yes. Ma'am."

She nodded and turned back around. "Don't wander, or you'll be fired immediately."

All I had to say to her involved a string of expletives, so I let her vanish inside the giant structure without another word. I slipped into the truck to follow and was amazed when I barely heard the engine turn over. It was electric, like probably all the vehicles in the enclosed space of the Athenaeum—no exhaust. The garbage truck was the only vehicle I'd ever driven. Drey was right: next to that, this little pickup handled like a silent breeze.

I drove up to the gate, where the security guards were waiting with no-nonsense, brick-stupid faces. They let me pass with another retinal scan, even though I kept expecting them to stop me.

What I saw inside made me forget them instantly.

The Athenaeum was a city of its own—the pyramid was just an outer shell. Roads and sidewalks cut through landscaped gardens that lined the inner wall of the pyramid before diving between buildings that rose as high as the slanting glass allowed. The buildings climbed like shining staircases until those under the highest point, at the center, were literally skyscrapers. Somehow, there was a breeze, and sunlight shone through the glass like I was outside.

After driving around for ten seconds, I discovered that most of the signs were in pictures I could identify: a silhouette of a running man who needed to piss—okay, maybe that was an exit; a fork and spoon for restaurant locations; the outline of desks for offices, color-coded for different sections of the complex; and, lo and behold, a two-dimensional trash can with a crumpled wad of paper being tossed into it.

It struck me that you had to have a lot of paper to be able to throw it away like that.

There was even a sign I recognized from outside the Athenaeum: a serpent twisting up a staff. Why the hell would they need a hospital when there were three outside? Maybe they didn't like sharing.

At this early hour, there were only a few other electric cars and early risers—joggers, mostly, with only a couple of people in suits. It made the Athenaeum feel sparsely populated. But there were obviously many people living here with the Words, more than I'd ever imagined. The trash can signs, and the trash cans themselves, were mostly along the widest roads, clustered among swanky hotels and embassies that displayed flags from around the world. But sometimes the signs led me down narrow, canyonlike streets so deep I could hardly see the sky, into tucked-away parks shared by sprawling private apartments.

This made me wonder whether I should collect the trash in these more private areas...plus, the people who'd been strolling the streets had all vanished. But there hadn't been many "strollers" to begin with, since everyone had acted like ants on the march, and I hadn't seen any signs telling me these streets were off-limits.

Besides, I was still finding trash to collect in these residential areas. The cans led me, like crumbs leading a street rat, to a group of ritzy apartment buildings with fancy windows encased in ornate wrought-iron bars. Probably to keep people like me out.

Soon I couldn't shake the feeling that I was an intruder,

no matter what, and I figured I should probably head back—until I spotted trash bags in an alley between two of the apartment buildings.

The alley was gated.

Curiosity killed the street rat. But I couldn't help it. I left the truck to investigate on foot, looking as purposeful as possible in case anyone saw me. They probably already had, I realized when I saw the security camera and the eye scanner next to the twelve-foot spiked gate.

I don't know why I did it. Maybe for the same reason I grinned at security guards—my impetuousness, Drey always called it. Or maybe because there was trash behind the gate, and I was the Athenaeum's new trash collector.

I waved at the camera, leaned in, and put my eye up to the scanner.

A small yellow light on the scanner began to flash, as if it was thinking. It thought for a long time, as if scrutinizing not only my retina but my entire life story: *Abandoned orphan. Charity case. Lowly garbage boy.* Any moment, I expected the light to turn red and alarms to sound.

But instead, the light turned green and the gate popped open with a soft click.

It had to be a mistake. I stuck my head tentatively inside and slunk into the alley. I was pretty sure I didn't belong here—especially considering what I did next.

Rather than take all the bags to the truck at once, I left one in the alley. When I returned for it, I picked it up but didn't stop there. Moving quickly, I followed the alley toward the lawn I'd spotted at the other end. I just had to see who lived in places like these, these boxes within a box, and who somehow felt they could control the lives of the rest of us.

I burst into a grassy courtyard, which was surrounded by an elegant building that rose to the sky like an inverted tower. There was nowhere to hide the fact that I was trespassing here, and the pinched lady's warning not to wander echoed helpfully in my mind.

I turned to hurry back through the alley to the truck— and stopped dead.

On a balcony several stories above me, a girl leaned against the railing, gazing up at the distant sky with longing— or maybe with only what I imagined was longing, because that was how I looked up at the sky from trash-filled alleyways. Like I wanted to sprout wings and escape it all. Her viewpoint might have been better than mine, but at least I didn't have to look through massive panes of glass to see the clouds.

Still, this wasn't what I'd been expecting. The trash bag slipped from my fingers and landed in the grass with a clunk.

She glanced down. The new angle revealed her features better: she was about my age, with dark-chocolate hair parted in a long, wavy curtain around a smooth, medium-toned, mind-blowingly beautiful face ... a face that briefly registered surprise as she saw me, then nothing.

I recognized her then.

She straightened abruptly, as if she'd heard my thoughts. She turned, vanishing inside, but not before the odd, backless cut of her black shirt confirmed what I already knew.

She was lined with markings so black they stood out

against her honey skin, covering her from the nape of her neck to her slender waist, and probably even farther but her pants blocked my view. That would have been unfortunate in other circumstances, but here, now, I'd seen enough. More than enough.

She was one of the Words. The Word of Life; the one I never saw smile on TV.

I didn't stick around for an introduction. I snatched up the trash bag and ran like hell.

three

When Drey picked me up at noon, I didn't tell him I'd seen one of the Words. He didn't need to know how close I'd come to getting into deep shit—or fired—on my first day. I wasn't positive, but I imagined people like me weren't supposed to stare slack-jawed at the Words on their private balconies, let alone come within a thousand-foot radius of them. I'd been told not to wander, and that was probably why.

The security guards didn't bar the gate when Drey dropped me off for work the second day, and I breathed a sigh of relief. As weird as the Athenaeum was, this job was definitely something different, and I didn't want to lose it quite yet.

The early morning sun soon grew bright outside, but the greenhouse effect that I expected to develop underneath the pyramid never happened. The place was apparently the biggest damned sun umbrella in the world. The glass panes took on a tint as the morning wore on, which should have made everything dim, but even that was counteracted by enormous lights ringing the peak of the pyramid. They were as bright—but not as hot—as small suns. Probably the work of the Words of Darkness and Light.

These people hadn't just created a city-within-a-city; they'd created their own little universe, as if they were the Gods themselves. The Athenaeum was like a fantasyland for the Words and their entourage. It was hard enough to get a passport into Eden City; living in the Athenaeum must have required a passport plated in gold.

I still couldn't believe that this job had just landed in my lap, like a gift from the sky. This strange, shining place sure had some nice wrapping, but I didn't know what it really held inside. The best presents I'd ever gotten—which were all from Drey, since he was the only one who ever gave me presents—came wrapped in black plastic bags and utility tape.

I went about my day as I had the first, retrieving my truck from a parking lot inside the gate and driving nearly the same route, making a few adjustments for efficiency's sake. In fact, I finished earlier than I had the day before, and in the same place: the heart of the pyramid. Continuing down the road would take me back to the exit, while a quick right onto a side street would take me to the alley and *her* courtyard—if the monitored gate let me pass a second time. I tapped the steering wheel in indecision.

Maybe today was too much like yesterday, because I found myself turning right and driving toward the alley, like some other force was in control of the little truck.

It was like poking at a candle flame when I knew I'd

get burned, just because it looked warm and pretty. I was secure enough in my masculinity to admit that the girl—the Word—had scared the piss out of me, but I also wanted to see her face one more time, maybe to convince myself she wasn't as lonely-looking as I'd thought. Nor as hot—hot enough to melt my brain to gooey stupidity with a glance.

At least she wasn't the Word of Fire. Because then she really could melt or burn me—to skeletal ash, according to the rumors.

When I reached the gate, I slammed on the brakes harder than I meant to. I must have lost my mind. No girl's face was worth getting fired.

Then I saw it, through the bars of the gate and the narrow gap between buildings: a black trash bag on the grass underneath her balcony. There was no way into or out of the courtyard other than the alley, so it had either been carried there deliberately... or dropped from above, as if someone wanted to get my attention.

Something about the best gifts being wrapped in black plastic came to mind.

I leapt out of the truck with a silent command for my common sense to shut up, received a green light after my eye-scan, and arrived in the shade under her balcony like I had the previous day: in a nervous rush, all the while trying to appear calm and purposeful.

I didn't know what I'd been expecting. The Word to be waiting? She wasn't, but maybe she would still come. I looked up, eagerness and impatience bouncing me on my toes.

Here I was, trying to talk to one of *them*—and probably about to get caught.

No one appeared on the balcony, and I was getting more anxious by the second. Eventually I snatched up the trash bag—it was surprisingly light—and took off, not quite as fast as the day before. After all, I was just doing my job, carrying garbage.

Only after I'd returned to the truck, the bag tossed hurriedly next to me instead of into the back, did it occur to me to look inside it. The bag rustled like it was full of dead leaves as I opened it.

Not dead leaves. Crinkled wads of paper, pristine white as though fresh from the factory. Someone had deliberately crumpled up about a hundred brand-new sheets, just to make a trash bag look like it was full of trash. *What a waste. Unless...*

I unfolded pieces of paper in a flurry, tossing each creased sheet on the floor as soon as I saw it was blank. It took half of the bag before found it: a sheet that wasn't entirely blank.

Not that I understood the situation any better because there was writing on it. Two short words printed in neat lines. It had been written by hand—a rare sight these days, even if you weren't wordless.

I crammed the sheet into my jacket pocket since I didn't know what else to do with it, and stuffed all the other pieces of paper back into the bag. I knotted and swung the bag through the cab window, into the back of the truck with the other trash. The tires left behind some rubber as I drove away.

Drey probably wasn't even waiting for me yet, so I eased

off the gas, trying not to drive like someone who'd just robbed a bank. Because then I would look guilty. And I wasn't guilty.

Right?

I smoothed the worry from my face as I turned toward the service gate that would take me out to the trash containers. Just in time. The two security guards were standing outside their booths, blocking my exit.

I mustered a grin as I slowed to a stop and stuck my head out the window. "Hey, boys."

"That's 'officer' to you, *boy*," the closest guard said.

"Fair enough." I shifted the truck into park. "What can I do for you, *officers*?"

"I've been instructed to give you something. It came from security headquarters."

Security headquarters? Cold sweat broke out on my forehead as he turned to his booth. I thought of the locked alleyway, its security camera and the Word I'd seen. *Shit.* Had she reported me? But then why would she slip me a message? Maybe someone else had finally realized I was nosing around where I didn't belong. In any case, I was probably about to receive orders telling me not to bother coming back to work tomorrow. Or worse, orders for my arrest.

The guard returned and passed a manila envelope through the window. But he didn't move out of the way. He obviously wanted me to open it in front of him. The city was visible through the gate, and for once I wished I could be out there instead of in here.

I unfolded the top flap of the envelope and shook a card out into my hand. Instead of just having a barcode for me to scan with my phone—how messages usually arrived—this card was laminated. It did have a barcode stamped on it, but also a shield and some words I couldn't read.

I fumbled for my phone and almost dropped it as it came out of my pocket. I scanned the card with shaking hands.

"A message from Athenaeum Security," a polite female voice intoned.

My phone's screen immediately came alive, showing a young man wearing all black, from his high-necked, long-sleeved shirt down to his ass-kicker boots. I knew this person—just like I knew his clothes were hiding something. And not just his muscular physique.

They hid the Words on his skin.

I'd only seen this Word once in a while on TV, and whenever I saw him, he was smiling like the others. But it was a smile that raised the hair on my arms, like now. He should have been my favorite Word, especially as a kid when I was still trying to see myself reflected in strong, cool people. Both his eyes and hair were about the same shade of brown as mine, as was his tan skin, but that was where the similarities ended. It was easy to imagine him lunging out of the picture to kill me. He could kill with a touch, after all—in any way imaginable.

I guessed it made sense that the Word of Death would be the face of the security department. His pinky finger had more power than any gun.

But then a white man with gray-streaked brown hair and a gray suit—an expensive-looking suit—replaced the Word of Death on my screen. The man blinked, and I realized I was seeing a video recording instead of a picture. The time signature told me it wasn't live.

"Greetings," the man said. "I am Dr. Swanson. Your name and employee file was forwarded to me for clearance permission at approximately eleven-hundred hours yesterday morning."

Which was right about when I'd first shown up outside the locked alley. I was definitely screwed.

Dr. Swanson continued. "Your position in the janitorial and maintenance department allows for this level of clearance, as did your background check. Please take this badge, indicating your new clearance level, for wherever eye scanners are unavailable. Be aware," he added, almost as an afterthought, "that with your higher level of security clearance, it is now your responsibility to report any suspicious activity. Feel free to report to any member of our security team or even to me personally. Remember, help is never far away."

To me, "be aware" sounded like *beware*. And despite his distantly friendly tone, the rest of his speech had come across as something like "I'll be watching you."

The screen went dark.

I was breathless, both with relief and with renewed fear. Was this a test? Was I supposed to report the strange note that I'd found, a note that was probably from the Word of Life? But she was one of the nine Words who ran the city. Why the hell would I need to report her? Was *she* testing me? I had no idea what to think. And I wouldn't know until I'd deciphered her message.

I felt like puking, but I grinned again at the security

guard. "Can I go, now, officer? I have a higher level of clearance, after all."

The guard scowled and punched, rather than pushed, the button to open the outer gate.

I almost forgot to empty the bags into the containers outside after I passed through the gate, and to leave the keys on the driver's seat for the security guard. And I nearly failed to stop myself from running instead of walking across the sun-baked parking lot to our garbage truck.

"Are you all right?" Drey asked as soon as he laid eyes on me. "You sick?"

I jumped in with only a shake of my head. I kept silent while he maneuvered the truck's beefy mechanical forks to lift the containers, tipping the contents into the compactor. If I started talking about what was happening, I wouldn't be able to stop myself from admitting I'd sneaked into the Word's courtyard and found her note. This job had been a favor from Drey, an *opportunity*, and I was most likely screwing it up spectacularly. The crumpled paper felt like a lead weight in my pocket. Never mind the laminated card in my other pocket.

I finished up the rest of our collection run without saying much. The old routine was colorless and boring after the excitement—too much excitement—of the Athenaeum. I was all but jumping out of my neon-green overalls with impatience, and maybe something closer to panic, by the time the day was over.

I closed myself in my room as soon as we returned to the garage, telling Drey I felt sick—which was actually true. As soon as I locked the door, I tore the piece of paper out of my jacket pocket and hurled it onto the metal desk like it was a live scorpion. Maybe it was even more lethal; I wasn't sure, and I didn't have an easy way to find out.

I spread the sheet flat on the desk. The near-perfect handwriting was still visible through the wrinkles. The page looked out of place in the room; Drey didn't keep much paper around. Part of me just wanted to get rid of it, and fast, like it was incriminating evidence. There was a lighter underneath my cot, which I'd used for smoking a couple of times before I'd lost interest in making my mouth taste like a garbage incinerator. I *could* burn it.

But what if the message was important? What if it was meant for me? What if it was from her and it wasn't some sick test of my loyalties to my new employer?

Maybe I needed to get rid of the paper, but not the message.

There was a postcard taped above the desk, the only decoration on the concrete wall. Drey said he'd found it in a trash container long before he'd found me in one. *Matterhorn, Switzerland,* the letters over the picture apparently said—Drey had asked someone who could read before he gave it to me. It showed a craggy mountain and a more wide-open sky than I'd ever seen. As much as I'd stared at the front of it, wishing I could be there, I knew the back was blank.

I tugged open one of the drawers in the desk, cursing when it protested with a shriek. The thing needed to be oiled—not that now was the time. Drey might be wordless, but he knew numbers and used to scribble down simple calculations for the garage, back before he started using his phone. My fingers scrabbled past a broken calculator for a dirty nub of a pencil that looked like it hadn't been used in a decade. I certainly hadn't been using it.

I slapped the postcard face-down next to the glaring white page and hunched over both, studying the incomprehensible message, the pencil gripped in my hand like a knife.

The first letter looked like scaffolding with only one shelf in the middle. I carved it as delicately as I could—though my dexterity was definitely lacking—into the postcard. The second letter was a little more difficult: a vertical line with three shelves sticking out to the right. The third was easy: a right angle like the square ruler out in the garage, which I almost wished I had for this project even though it would be unwieldy. The last letter of the word was like a hatchet standing upright, with a rounded blade facing to the right.

I paused to look at my handiwork. The scratchy pencil marks only vaguely resembled the original letters. Good. They were close enough ... and different enough, especially on the yellowed back of the postcard that would soon be facing the wall again.

The second word was short, only two letters. The first looked like two pyramids, linked in the middle with no bases. The last was one I'd already copied—the second letter of the other word.

When I finished, I crouched in the corner with my lighter and the white piece of paper. Before long, there was nothing but flaking ash, which I stomped into the concrete.

But there was smoke, too.

"Tavin?" Drey said, his voice as sharp as the sudden pounding on the door. "I smell something burning. And why is your door locked?"

My own feet tripped me up in my hurry to get to the door. I didn't often lock it, and I never failed to open it after he knocked. I cursed after smashing my knee into the metal chair and whipped the door open to find him frowning up at me.

"What's going on, Tav?"

No doubt my face looked too guilty to deny everything. "I was ... I was smoking."

Drey sighed. "You know that's bad for you. And if you don't, take it from an old man."

"You're not old," I said.

He smiled—but then he sniffed the air. "That doesn't smell like a cigarette. Or dope. What on earth were you smoking?"

He sidled into the room before I could think of anything to say. I tried not to look at the greasy smear of ash in the corner. Fortunately, the concrete floor was already pretty grimy.

But Drey wasn't looking at the floor. He was looking at the desk, and only then did I remember that I hadn't re-hung the postcard or closed the squeaky drawer, which was open like a mouth shouting the truth.

"What's this?" Drey asked, picking up the postcard with the message scratched into the back. The pencil sat nearby, looking like a murder weapon at the scene of a crime.

Before I could invent some excuse about pretending to write—which would have worked, since Drey couldn't tell the difference between real or fake letters—he asked in a tone of utter surprise:

"Why does this say 'help me'?"

Four

H-E-L-P M-E

So that was what those letters meant. The news was nearly as shocking as the fact that Drey could read.

"How do you know what it says?" I demanded.

"I . . . well . . ." Then his surprise, which had obviously lowered his guard, vanished. "Never mind! What is this doing here? Did you write this? And what was burning?"

I folded my arms, not caring that I looked—and sounded—like I'd reverted to the age of ten. "I'm not telling until you tell me how the hell you've been able to read all this time! Why didn't you ever say anything? Why didn't you teach me?"

The hurt was audible in my voice—yep, definitely ten—and Drey's expression turned regretful for a second. Then his grizzled jaw hardened. "That's none of your damn business. I don't owe you any explanations. But you're in my garage, so *you* owe me an explanation of what's going on in here!"

He'd never before drawn a line between his and my territory, always treating me more like family than an employee. I dropped onto the edge of my cot without saying anything. I didn't think I *could* say anything without embarrassing myself. My throat was too tight.

The letters that apparently said *Matterhorn, Switzerland* stared at me from the back of the postcard in Drey's hand. He'd told me that he'd asked what they meant, but now I knew he hadn't. He'd read them himself.

"I kept it secret for your own good," Drey said in nearly a whisper, putting a hand on the desk almost like he was steadying himself. "And I still can't tell you anything, so don't ask. No one knows I'm not wordless. Please don't mention it to anyone. Forget this ever happened."

I was looking into my hands, not at him. Pencil smears darkened the tips of my fingers. It all made sense now, why he was so smart and knew so many things. All of those legends and histories—I'd assumed he'd heard the stories from other people, but who around here could have told him? Anger melted the lump in my throat.

"If I have to forget you can read, then you forget you read those words," I said. "Forget you smelled smoke. I'm not sharing secrets if you won't."

Drey looked tired, more tired than I'd ever seen him. He hesitated, studying the postcard he'd given me years ago that now bore an ominous but cryptic message, as though wondering if my secret was worth trading for.

It apparently wasn't, because he left the room, taking my view of the mountain with him.

That didn't make me angry—I was already angry enough. Besides, I didn't need the copied message anymore, now that I knew what it said. Not that I knew what I was going to do about it.

All I *did* know was that she—the Word of Life—had asked for help. She was the only one who'd spotted me with a trash bag in that courtyard. No one else had been in there; I'd been on the lookout, seeing as I'd been sneaking around. And she was the only one who could think I was stupid enough to help her, probably from the way I'd gawked at her.

The message had to be from her. For me.

But why the hell would she need my help? What could I even do? I was impotent, and she was one of the most powerful people on the planet.

Maybe she *had* been looking at the sky with longing. But why? Perhaps that place was somehow a cage for her, even though she was powerful. Or, rather, *because* she was powerful. Maybe she had to pose for so many TV clips and posters that she didn't have any time for anything else. Maybe the other Words, like Death, were using her.

Or maybe my imagination was running away with me again. Maybe she was the one using me. But I had to find out.

Drey had always told me that anger makes a man lose his head, and he was probably right. Because I was going to try to help her. Even if I was a sucker, at least I would be doing *something*. Whatever it was. The only plan I could think of was to hang out under her balcony until she either turned up or dropped another clue on my head.

The object in my other pocket weighed me down again, and I slid the laminated card out. I leaned back on the cot, resting my sweaty shoulders against the cool concrete wall, studying it, even though the typewritten letters made no more sense to me than the Word's secret message had.

Dr. Swanson had said that it granted me higher clearance. Maybe I could use this card to get into the Athenaeum outside of my scheduled hours. But anything I did outside of my usual work routine would draw unwanted attention. If I used the card to get in, I couldn't just drive around in the truck, losing myself in the streets until I could sneak back to the courtyard; the security guards would expect me to report to them or go straight to Dr. Swanson, who would expect the same thing if they let him know I was there—which was likely. Then they would be looking for me.

Deciding to go back to the Athenaeum wasn't difficult. Waiting until my next shift the following morning was the hard part. I sat on my cot, staring at the cracks in the wall now that my postcard-view of the outside world was gone. Maybe, I thought with relief, she only wanted something little from me, like smuggling something in for her—maybe she couldn't get Captain Crunch in the Athenaeum. I sure had plenty of that to give her. Because what else could I do?

Realistically, I knew it had to be something more than that. Maybe much more, and I didn't know how far I was willing to go. I didn't want to lose my job—or worse. Picturing the Word of Death and his lethal touch made me swallow butterflies, and not normal-sized ones, but monster butterflies careening around in panic, trying to break out of my stomach with their flapping.

I lay down on my cot in my clothes, giving sleep a try, but the train of my thoughts was racing too fast to let me get off and rest. Eventually, I got up to shower in the middle of the night and was still awake when Drey tapped on my door almost timidly a couple hours later. I was already dressed, buzzing with nervous energy, and I didn't accept the rank-smelling cup of coffee from him this time.

Drey was quiet, offering none of his usual stories as we suited up, me in hospital white and him in our usual green. It was like he was sorry. But he didn't apologize, or tell me why he wasn't wordless, as we made our way to the truck and out of the garage. I kept my end of the pact of silence and didn't say anything about my crazy plan—or lack thereof—to try to help one of the Words.

We pulled up behind the shadowy pyramid with the first rays of morning light peeking over the forested mountains ringing Eden City and the lake. Drey cleared his throat, but I opened the truck door anyway.

"I don't know what you might be up to," he said, as softly as possible over the growl of the engine, his hands on the steering wheel and eyes straight ahead, staring across the empty parking lot. "You're a smart boy—a smart man, even. Just be careful, okay, Tav?"

"I'm always careful." I hopped out onto the asphalt, failing to mention that I was planning on being a hell of a lot less careful that morning. I slammed the heavy door without another word and immediately wished I'd said something nicer—*warmer*, maybe, or at least a goodbye. But I didn't want to reopen the door only for that, and then Drey was driving off.

My little white truck was waiting in the same spot. I didn't grin or even acknowledge the security guards this time. The palms of my hands were already coated in a film of sweat when I got into the truck and started the engine, my body reacting to what my brain knew: I wasn't headed off on my usual pickup routine.

I collected a few bags of trash, enough to look busy and avoid suspicion, but then drove straight to the gated alley between the still-quiet apartment buildings. The sun was barely lighting the peak of the pyramid as I turned off the engine and slipped out of the truck, leaving the door cracked to avoid the slam of closing it. There was no sign of even a stray person wandering at this hour, though the other days I'd seen joggers not much later than this. Haste would be necessary if I didn't want more people to start cropping up. The security camera and retinal scan were bad enough, as far as discreetness went.

At least the gate popped open without a wait.

I speed-walked down the alley and into the courtyard, grimacing as my shoes squeaked over the grass. It was wet, as though it had just been watered, clear drops beading on the blades and on the plants in their beds. At least I wasn't tiptoeing through sprinklers—if this was even the work of sprinklers and not the Word of Water. They probably didn't do anything like normal people here.

I didn't let myself think about who I was trying to help as I stopped underneath the darkened balcony. She was just a girl. Just your average all-powerful, insanely beautiful girl.

My thoughts weren't calming. My heart was thumping as loud as a jackhammer at the crack of dawn—which was about what time it was, sunlight trickling down from the peak of the pyramid, turning the world to gold.

Would she even be awake? In my eagerness to help her, I hadn't really considered the possibility that she wouldn't be. I almost wanted to laugh.

Then, out of nowhere, something hit me like a pile of bricks, so heavy it flattened me on the wet grass.

Not a something—*someone*. A person, sprawled on top of me. A girl covered in blood.

She breathed against me, her hair in my face, so at least I knew she wasn't dead. A blow from her elbow to my head had dazed me, but I was pretty sure I'd heard a snap when she landed. I wasn't hurt, and I'd only partially broken her fall, so it must have come from her foot or leg as it met the ground. I wondered where all the blood was coming from until she tried to lift herself off of me, pressing against my chest.

The thumb of her right hand was missing. The gaping wound glared at me, weeping red all over my white jacket. White obviously didn't go well with trash *or* blood.

I yelped at the same time she gave a stifled cry of pain. She must have somehow forgotten her thumb was cut off when she'd tried to use her hand. She almost fell on me again—albeit from a much lesser height than her balcony. I grabbed her wrist to steady her. My hand was now wet with her blood, but I hardly noticed as I pushed us both upright until we were seated in the grass facing each other.

There was no mistaking that face, scattered strands of wavy brown hair sticking to her tear-streaked cheeks.

It was her. The Word. She was definitely as beautiful as I'd previously thought, if not more so, but that was beside the point. I'd wanted her to show up or drop another clue from her balcony, but she'd done both in one go.

"If you're here to help me, stop staring and start moving," she said. Her dark eyes were focused, looking right at me, her voice and breath ridiculously steady for the amount of pain she had to be in. "But don't pull that bracelet off yet or we're both in trouble."

After registering that she had a husky voice I would have found sexy on any other occasion, I noticed that my hand was still around her wrist, encircling it along with a black plastic bracelet.

My fingers were sticky when I pulled away. Though her tight black shirt and pants hid most of the blood on her, save for what was on her hands, they couldn't disguise the horribly wrong angle of her ankle.

"Did you hear me?" she said calmly, maybe even coolly. "My ankle is broken. If I try to move and cause myself more pain, my heart rate will spike and they'll notice." She nodded at the bracelet, now mostly red instead of black as she held her arm upright, blood running down her wrist. It amazed me that she wasn't trying to staunch the flow with her other hand, until I noticed what it held.

Her severed thumb.

"Gods," I said, involuntarily leaning away from her. "Don't you want to … don't you need … a doctor or something?"

She smiled grimly. Rather, she gritted her perfect, pearly teeth and followed my stare to her thumb. "Anything but," she said, then took a deep breath. "I can reattach it myself, but only after I take off the monitor. That's why I cut it off in the first place."

"You cut off your thumb?" My voice came out higher than I would have preferred.

"Yes!" she said, suddenly impatient, gritting her teeth again. "That's the only way I can get the monitor over my hand. And the longer you wait, the sooner I bleed to death, since they'll know the moment I take it off—and the location. So I can't heal myself until it's gone, and I can't get rid of it until we're moving. Go!"

"Where?" I asked, leaping up and looking around, as if the flower bed might hide a first aid kit or a splint.

"To your truck! You have spare black bags in there, yes? Bring four of them."

"Four? Why?" Plastic bags weren't very absorbent or very structural, as far as mopping blood or splinting a broken ankle went.

"Because one bag would tear. You're going to use them to carry me. You have to get me out of here, out of the Athenaeum." Desperation was offsetting the steady tone of her voice. "You have to help me."

Her words hit me like another blow to the head, and I couldn't think to argue; I simply reacted. I turned and ran, slipping across the grass and down the alley until I reached the truck. I wrenched open the door, cursing as I left bloody streaks on the white paint. Thank the Gods the truck was blocking me from the security camera so they couldn't see what I was doing.

A roll of paper towels flew out of the glove box as I ripped into it. I wiped as much blood as I could off my hands and face and the door before I tore four bags off the roll in the back of the truck and quadrupled them into each other. After taking the laminated card from my pocket, I stripped off the not-so-white jacket, leaving myself with an undershirt that was mercifully dark blue. I threw the jacket and the bloodied towels into the beefed-up bag and even ripped open one of the actual trash bags, grabbing a few handfuls of crumpled wrappers and plastic cups and takeout boxes to stuff in there too, filling it about a fourth of the way.

It occurred to me that I could still drive away from the insanity at this point, throw away the bloody evidence tying me to the scene like any other trash. But it was only a passing thought. I was already dashing back the way I'd come.

Five

When I returned to the Word, she was crouched over her ankle on the lawn, muttering under her breath with her eyes closed, her right hand still held aloft. She looked like a dark goddess in the shining golden grass, a piece of night shoved out of the sky by dawn. Blood continued to flow from the place her thumb had been, but her ankle—she'd straightened the bone. I hadn't heard her scream or even make a noise. I'd broken my wrist falling off the garbage truck when I was twelve, and when the local doctor straightened my arm, you could have heard me shouting from the other end of Eden City.

"My ankle isn't healed yet," she said, and I realized she was talking to me now, whereas she'd been mumbling words before—had they been *Word* words? "It's better, but I'll be too tired if I go all the way. Lost too much blood. I need to save energy for my thumb."

She looked up, blinking at the layered bag slung over my shoulder and the roll of paper towels in my other hand.

"It already has something in it?" she asked, looking at the bag.

"My jacket and some ... trash." I wondered if a Word would be offended by the thought of sharing a bag with garbage. "To hide your shape."

"Smart." She sounded surprised by her assessment, and almost sleepy. She stood slowly on one foot. "I'm Khaya," she said, meeting my eyes in a heavy-lidded way that made my heart lurch in my chest. "The Word of Life."

I already knew who she was. What I didn't know was why the Word of Life would want to escape the Athenaeum. And I didn't have time to ask, because she fell over.

I dropped the paper towels and caught her before she hit the ground. She was easy to hoist with even one arm, her head lolling only as high as my shoulder, her frame warm and light and soft against my chest in ways I didn't want to think about. I didn't quite know what abilities the Word of Life had—aside from giving life, obviously, and healing, apparently—and I hoped mind-reading wasn't one of them.

She smelled good, too, not like the trash bag I shook open with my other hand.

"You sure you want to do this?" I asked, doubt creeping into my tone—the one sane voice among the decision-making committee in my head. "You're not doing too well. We can still find a doctor."

In response, Khaya half-knelt, half-slid down my side, tipping sideways into the bag. Once in, she curled into a ball, wrapping her left arm around her tucked knees, trying to brace her ankle while still clutching her detached thumb. She held her disfigured hand upright as I ripped a small hole through the four thin layers of plastic: an air hole.

When she waved her raised arm at me—the arm with the bracelet—I realized she was doing more than trying to slow the bleeding.

"Do you see that drain next to the flower bed?" she asked, her voice muffled by the plastic but still firm. "Slide the bracelet off my wrist, quickly, then drop it in there as fast as you can. It will be sailing around in the sewer system after that. It will confuse them."

I was confused myself until I made sense of what I should have minutes before. The bracelet was a tracking device—a very sophisticated one, if it also monitored her vital signs and could only be removed by chopping off a thumb, not by cutting the bracelet itself.

What the hell...? But there wasn't time to ask.

Another wad of paper towels soaked up the blood that had found its way back onto my arms and hands. Then I dropped it, with the rest of the roll, into the bag with Khaya. I clamped my fingers around the bracelet, eyed the metal grill set in the gutter several yards away, and positioned my feet.

"Ready?" I asked, almost more to myself than her.

Khaya gave a short nod from within the bag, her shadowed eyes showing a hint of fear for the first time.

"My name's Tavin," I said.

Then I whipped the bracelet off, ignoring her gasp as it brushed over her wound. I sprinted for the gutter and rammed the bracelet into the drain, like a starved nicotine addict racing to get a coin into the slot of a cigarette machine. I skinned my knee and jammed a finger, but I didn't care. The bracelet was gone in about two seconds flat—but not before I saw a little red light embedded in the material begin flashing angrily.

As if she'd seen it, Khaya hissed, "Hurry!"

I arrived back at the bag, knotted it, and slung it—slung her—over my shoulder before she could say anything else. She was heavier than a normal load of trash, but not too heavy for me to march back to the waiting truck. I probably could have run, with the amount of adrenaline pulsing through my veins, but running would raise suspicion and not be too comfortable for someone with a broken ankle and a severed thumb.

Her body shook against my back, low sniffs punctuating the words she was whispering too quietly for me to hear. I would have been howling if I'd chopped my own thumb off, yet this was her greatest show of pain, even with the monitor bracelet gone. She *was* posing as a bag of trash, but still, I wondered if her subdued tears weren't just to keep up her disguise. This was the Word, after all, who never smiled or showed any emotion. So I tried to ignore her reluctant, semi-private display, along with the less-subtle feeling of panic crashing over me.

Where the hell was I supposed to go now that I had a bloodied Word in a bag over my shoulder?

Out. She'd said she needed to get out. Who knew *why*, but I focused on that goal as I reached the truck and deposited her gently but hastily in the back among the other identical black bags of trash, avoiding looking at the security camera as I did so. I made sure the air hole was unrestricted and wiped my hands on my pants to clear any remaining blood before I leapt in the truck and turned the key.

I didn't hear anything. Then I remembered how quiet the engine was, muttered another curse, and threw the truck into gear.

I was too anxious to worry about going slow. The slight hum of the engine rose until it became a high-pitched whine while the apartments and buildings flashed by my window in quick succession. Luckily, there was hardly any traffic. My eyes were half on the road and half on the lookout for anyone coming—coming to arrest me, in particular.

Or to kill me.

No one had stopped me when I reached the main road out of the Athenaeum, but as I flicked on my blinker like any good driver who hasn't just been going sixty miles per hour, I realized something was wrong. The security guards were standing outside their booth again, not lazing in their chairs, and both were talking on portable radios. And then a siren sounded, echoing among the distant central buildings under the peak of the pyramid. It was so loud that I didn't need to roll the window down to hear it, but I did anyway.

It must have been because Khaya was no longer wearing the bracelet. I didn't know what else it could be.

I made the turn and drove at a measured pace for the gate as if I hadn't noticed the commotion, trying not to think about the bloodstains darkly visible against my brown pants, my missing white uniform jacket, or the black bag with the air hole sitting in the back of the truck within plain sight of the security guards now that they were out of their booth. All I could do was take a deep breath, like Khaya had done against the pain of a severed thumb and a broken ankle.

The truck slowed to a halt when one of the guards inevitably raised his hand for me to stop. I tried to roll down my window only to discover that it was already down. *Deep breaths.*

"You've finished early," the guard nearest my window said, his radio still halfway to his mouth. "Thought you were done at noon." He didn't even look at me, his eyes on the source of the siren, emanating from the heart of the Athenaeum.

"Part of my contract agreement on … Wednesdays." I needed to grope for the day of the week. When I found it, I realized I actually had a good excuse. "It's garbage barge day for us, so I have to cut my route here short." Only the second part was a lie. The barge left at night, so I would have had plenty of time to finish up all my routes.

"I wasn't aware of that," the guard said, more grouchy than suspicious. "And we have a situation, anyway, so I'm afraid you'll have to sit tight before you're clear to leave."

"But I could lose my job." My hands rubbed the steering wheel, stress edging into my voice. I noticed a splotch of blood on my finger and dropped my hands into my lap.

"Not my problem." The guard still wasn't looking at me, missing all the details that were screaming as loud as the siren, trying to give me away. He obviously didn't imagine I had anything to do with the "situation." How could he? I was a garbage boy. He was being a bastard to me because he could, not because he was trying to catch me out.

I forced a superior smile, adopting a tone to match. "But it is your problem, officer. Dr. Swanson is well aware of our agreement. We arranged it specifically, which is why he granted me a higher level of clearance. Don't you remember that?"

He finally cast me a glance. "Yeah, but—"

"Well then, you'll remember he gave me this card that says I can come and go as I please." I ignored the other security guard, who'd stepped up to the passenger door with his hand on his hip—or, more significantly, on his gun holster. I passed the card out the window with clammy hands, breathing a silent thanks to the Gods that there was no blood on it. "Dr. Swanson wouldn't be happy if you cost me my job for breaking the terms of my contract. I thought he made that clear."

The guard snatched the card from me and squinted at the words on it, under the barcode. There was a good chance he couldn't read any more than I could, but he wouldn't want to admit it. I hoped that was the case, because the card probably said absolutely nothing about me coming or going "as I pleased."

"See?" I said. "I'm allowed to go now. You could call Dr. Swanson to double-check, but he probably wouldn't appreciate having to repeat himself so soon."

The guard thrust the card back at me with a scowl. "Fine, runt," he said, even though I must have been a foot taller than him. "I don't know why Dr. Swanson gives you the time of day. I certainly wouldn't. Now get out."

"Yes, sir," I said, too relieved to be sarcastic.

I showed more restraint than I thought I possessed by not flooring the gas pedal as soon as he raised the gate. The limits of my restraint were reached, though, when I made it to the middle of the parking lot without being stopped or followed. I screeched out into traffic like a wild animal bursting from a cage, forcing a car to swerve widely around me. The little pickup was far more maneuverable than the garbage truck and I zipped between lanes of expensive vehicles, swearwords leaving my mouth in a rush to match my driving.

"What the hell were you thinking, Tavin? What are you doing with her, huh?" Apparently I not only cursed but talked to myself when I was in a state of near-hysteria. "Where the hell am I even going? Oh man, Drey is going to kill me ... if the Word of Death doesn't kill me first. Hey, but I'm okay, because I have the Word of Life to save me—in a *garbage bag* in the back of a *stolen pickup!*"

My tirade ceased when I eventually slowed down with the flow of traffic, no longer careening around other cars like I was in a high-speed chase. The only time I'd come close to feeling this way was one evening after Drey and I had gotten in our worst fight ever, and I'd stolen a hundred in cash from him along with the garbage truck. I'd felt unleashed— in a bad way—but I'd ended up only driving a few blocks and spending ten bucks on candy bars at a twenty-four hour convenience store. Drey hadn't even been mad at me in the end, even though I'd returned at three in the morning.

I figured Drey would be pretty mad at me now, so that nixed heading back to the garage as a possible answer to the "Where the hell am I going?" question. I had no idea where in Eden City I could possibly take Khaya in her gruesome condition and not be turned in by people who might not even recognize her. And if they did recognize her, they might kill me *before* turning me in. The Word of Death wouldn't even have to get his hands dirty—or his fingertip.

I had to go someplace where no one would expect to find her ... without powerful or power-hungry people ... where anyone who saw her would ignore her.

Then I had it. Just the place. I'd been heading toward the mountains, deeper into the hillier, richer section of the city, but I made an abrupt turn and headed downhill toward the Nectar River.

I took narrow backstreets to get near the waterfront, which were blissfully vacant at this time of day. These types of streets were busier under cover of darkness. I parked well underneath the Old Bridge—not the oldest bridge, but the shabbiest alongside grander, shinier counterparts—and didn't even have an audience as I hopped up into the back of the truck to tear Khaya out of the trash bag.

The ladies under the bridge worked at night, and the sun was now officially up.

A few years ago, after having one too many drinks one evening while keeping me company at the garage, Drey had told me about these ladies—women who wore scooping shirts and short skirts and leather boots that made my brain melt to mush. I mean, I'd seen them as a kid, but never really *seen* them until Drey's story; and, after a couple more drinks, he'd told me exactly what they could do and for how much. But then he smacked me upside the head when I jokingly asked him for a hundred bucks.

Funny thing was, I had gone to see them. But Drey was with me, and we went for lively conversation, nothing else. We saw them usually in the early morning—the end of their "day" and the start of ours. People like us, who were only one step off of the streets and still worked on the streets, often only had people of like status for company.

Khaya looked barely alive as I knelt and pulled the black plastic away from her, her long hair and sticky blood all over. But she still somehow managed to look beautiful. Even crazier, her thumb was reattached, though there was still a sharp red line around it as if she'd glued it on. It was pretty amazing.

"Don't touch it," Khaya snapped before I could even lift a finger. "It's not fully healed. I need to sleep first."

I jumped up, loose trash falling off me. "You're welcome," I said before I could restrain myself. My restraint reserve was about bone-dry.

She looked around for the first time, blinking at the gray underside of the bridge as if she was having trouble focusing. She damn-near looked drugged. It wouldn't cast me in a good light if some law-abiding citizen were to see us. But I was betting on the likelihood that none of those would be here.

"Where am I?" she asked.

"Under the Old Bridge. There's a roll of paper towels in your bag there. You might want to clean yourself off before you leave the truck."

She fished around awkwardly in the garbage for the roll,

avoiding the use of her right hand. Fumbling to tear off a paper towel, she ended up only ripping a sheet in half.

"Don't just stand there, help me!" she said with audible frustration.

I stared at her over folded arms. They probably looked more intimidating than necessary, especially since they were bare, but my white jacket was wadded up underneath her. "Maybe you're used to having everything handed to you in the Athenaeum, but I just risked a shit-ton to get you out of there. I'm still taking a risk, as far as I know. And I'm not even sure why, but have I demanded answers? No! So the least you can do is give me a simple please or thank you with *your* demands."

She looked up in surprise, her eyes shining more than usual before she went back to studying the paper towel roll. "Thank you. I've been so absorbed in the larger situation, I overlooked..."

Me. Instead, I said, "Common courtesy? Better yet, deep gratitude?"

Her voice went cool again. "I said thank you."

And I hadn't demanded answers—yet. "You're welcome. So, what exactly is the 'larger situation'?"

"I can't tell you right this second. Just...please, help me. I can't even see where I have blood, and I can't..." She gestured with her Frankenstein hand. Drey had told me Dr. Frankenstein's story, and of course it was one I'd remembered.

I sighed, then sat back down in front of her and took a few towels in my hand. I paused after lifting them to her perfect face. "I'm going to have to touch you, just so you know."

"Really," she said flatly.

"I'll try to avoid jabbing your thumb and ankle, but I make no promises."

Of course, I wiped her off as gently as if she were one of the creatures I found left for dead. Maybe too gently, because she had some stubborn patches of dried blood on her cheek. I held a towel to her full lips, trying not to think about what it would feel like to kiss them.

"Spit," I said.

She stared at me. "What?"

"Spit," I repeated. "Unless you want *my* spit on your face."

Looking skeptical, she spit barely enough into the towel to suffice, which I rubbed into her cheek.

"That's disgusting," she said as I scrubbed.

"No, it's useful in a pinch. Let me guess, you don't have spit in the Athenaeum."

She opened her mouth to say something that probably wouldn't have been friendly, but before she could, we heard a voice echoing under the bridge: "What is going on here?"

Thank the Gods I recognized the voice. The woman it belonged to certainly wasn't law-abiding.

"Chantelle!" I said, vaulting out of the back of the truck. "It's me, Tavin."

Chantelle stood in front of me, wearing a leather jacket over a red miniskirt and heels. Not that I really noticed; at least, not in *that* way. She was old enough to be my mother, and usually acted like a mother whenever I stopped by to talk to her, telling me to eat well and stay out of trouble—and to stay away from the younger ladies. She was as bad as Drey.

She'd come out of what had been a utility room under the bridge, which was now sort of a communal break room used by all the ladies. "Tavin! What are you doing here, honey? Shouldn't you be on your route with Drey?"

"Uh, I'm doing something different today." Which was an understatement. I didn't know how to elaborate, so I tried to change the subject. "What about you? You're up late."

She rolled her heavily made-up eyes. "Yeah, well, business ran late. Don't you hate those last-minute—who's that?"

I turned. Behind me, Khaya was trying to climb down from the truck—unsuccessfully, by the looks of it, with only one hand and foot at her disposal. I grabbed her before she could fall, lifting her the rest of the way down. She leaned unsteadily into me, which would have been nice if it didn't make me look shady. At least her messy hair was shadowing her face and her gory hand was tucked behind her back.

Chantelle raised her thin, penciled-in eyebrows. "She doesn't look too good. She on something? Tav, I never thought you were one to take advantage—"

"No!" I said quickly. "I, uh, found her on my morning route...in an alley. She's hurt, see, but she didn't want to go to a hospital. It's, you know, a touchy situation, I think. I didn't know where else to take her, since Drey didn't want her at the garage."

Chantelle brightened. "Well, honey, you've brought her to the right place. I can see why Drey wouldn't want to get mixed up in anything, but here, we're all mixed up!" She patted Khaya's arm. "There's a cot in our little 'office' over there—no business ever done on it, of course, only napping.

You're more than welcome to it for as long as you like, and a cup of coffee. We'll get you feeling better."

"Gods, thanks, Chantelle," I said, while Khaya nodded weakly, keeping her head down.

"It's nothing, sweetheart. I'll go put some hot water on." The clicking of her heels rebounded underneath the stone bridge as she strode away.

"Perfect," I whispered, guiding Khaya over to the wall to use as support. She could only hop on one foot. "You can stay here for a little bit. I need to go—"

Her good hand tightened on my arm as she watched Chantelle's retreating figure. "Don't leave me here. I can't stay—I need to leave the city!"

"First, I need to take back the truck. Then we can figure out—"

"You can't go back to the Athenaeum," she said, interrupting me again. "It's too dangerous."

"No," I said, my patience wearing thin. "It's dangerous if I keep the truck. They'll know I'm involved with all of this if I steal it! Maybe you don't have to work, but I still need my job." She shook her head but I ignored her. "You'll be safe here. Later, we can figure out a way to get you out of the city, if that's what you really want. Drey might know a way—"

"You have to leave, too."

I felt like she'd slapped me. "What?" I asked, staring at her.

Khaya didn't have her usual aloof look as she sagged against the wall. Her eyes were wide, as if she was almost afraid to break the bad news. "You have to leave or they'll kill you. They'll find out you did this. There are cameras every-where in the Athenaeum—too many to monitor constantly, but it's only a matter of time before they locate the footage they need to identify you… if they haven't already."

Of course they would have more cameras than the one at the alley gate. And how could I forget that Dr. Swanson was already watching me, suspecting me of a crime I hadn't yet committed? Actually, I hadn't forgotten. I'd been vigor-ously *trying* to forget.

"They'll come after you," she added in a low voice. "Hunt you down, even in your home."

Home. The garage. *Drey.* The facts locked together in my head like nuts and bolts, constructing a thought that was pretty unpleasant.

"Drey," I said out loud.

"I need… I don't think I can do this on my own," Khaya said, squeezing my arm tighter. "I've never been so weak. Whenever I accelerate the usual biological process to heal a living thing, it exhausts the one being healed. I'm exhausted. I've never been hurt this badly."

"Drey," I said again.

"Tavin, listen to me." Not only did she say my name for the first time, she shook me. "Even if you won't do it to save your own life, you have to help me get out of here. You don't know how important it is for me to—"

But I was gone before she could finish, dashing for the truck. I left her leaning against the wall, shouting my name a second time.

SIX

The ride back to the garage passed in a blur. I considered sneaking up on it, but if something had happened to Drey, my own safety didn't really matter anymore. So I barreled straight there, driving like a maniac until I screeched to a stop in front of the garage.

I hoped he would be out driving the usual city route without me, but one of the wide, rolling doors was open when I arrived and Drey's truck was already parked inside. He'd probably come back to look for me after I didn't meet him outside the Athenaeum. Or at least that was what I told myself as I leapt out of the pickup and raced up to the open door.

There I stopped. It was too quiet. Of course, the other guys were out driving the second truck, but still, something wasn't right.

Maybe because there was a trail of blood snaking from the driver's side door of Drey's truck toward the back of the garage, the red as vivid as the bright yellow walls. Drey had chosen that paint because he said I needed more sunlight in the garage.

My foot took a mechanical step forward. "Drey?"

There was a groan from within. I broke into a run down the aisle between the wall and the truck, and then whipped around the front bumper.

I would have stopped dead in my tracks, but a puddle of blood made me slip and fall to the floor—near Drey, who was seated in the center of the mess, his back against some shelves.

My hands and knees slid on the wet concrete as I crawled over to him. "Gods," I said, looking over the ragged red hole in his shirt, which burrowed right into his stomach. I had a hard time catching my breath. "Oh, Gods. Someone shot you?"

Drey opened his mouth to speak, then coughed his usual frightening cough—except this time, blood bubbled on his lips. "Herio," he said. It took me a second to remember that Herio was the Word of Death. "Surprised me while I was waiting for you. Athenaeum security blockaded the parking lot, but they were no match for the truck." He coughed again. "The only reason they haven't followed me here now is because they're probably using me as bait. You have to leave."

So a bullet hadn't made that wound—the Word of Death's finger had. How Drey had managed to drive himself back to the garage in this condition was beyond me. He could hardly move now, his lips pale and bloodless where they weren't bloody.

I pulled my phone out of my pocket, but Drey clawed it out of my hands and smashed it against the ground. He groaned at what the effort had cost him. "Don't use that. They'll trace your number here."

I didn't care. I scrambled away from him, tracking red handprints across the concrete, then launched myself at the video phone in the corner of the garage. I practically hammered on the emergency button Drey had programmed years ago, leaving red prints on the screen.

"Idiot," Drey murmured from his slouch. "They'll definitely know you're here if you use that."

I didn't hang up when someone answered, or even bother hiding from the video camera since my voice was more than enough to identify me. I just gave our address as quickly as possible and added, "Drey Barnes has been shot, and he's...he's...hurry!" before I hit the button to end the call.

"They know it was you who took Khaya," Drey said. "They want her back."

"But why did they do this to you?" I crawled back over to him, my hands and legs feeling almost too weak to support my weight. The slippery floor didn't help. "Everything is insane! Dr. Swanson watching me, and now...this. What do you have to do with these people?" The question came out forcefully, almost like an accusation, maybe because the words were getting caught in my throat.

Drey took a ragged breath. "Because I used to work there...for Dr. Swanson."

"Wait...what?" I halted, leaning over him. I wasn't sure what Swanson had to do with it all—I didn't even know what his official position in the Athenaeum was. But the fact that Drey had worked there... "That's why you're so smart. And that's why they hurt you. They thought you put me up to this!"

Drey smiled, and blood dribbled from the corner of his mouth. "You're smarter than me—too smart for your own good."

"I'm an idiot!" I shouted, tears finally overflowing my eyes and running hot down my face. "I sneaked a Word out of the Athenaeum and they did this to you! Aren't you even mad?"

He shook his head, more of a single jerk against the shelf. "I understand why you did it. Believe me."

"But look what I've done…look at you…" I glanced down at his stomach, then back up at his face as soon as possible.

"You can't save me, boy," Drey said, still managing to sound gruff. "I'm old and I have lung cancer, anyway. You know it, so don't look at me like that. I could have gone to the Words for a cure—maybe Swanson would have helped me, after everything—but no, I don't think we should have the power of the Words. Not meant for us. Only for the Gods."

"Then why did you get me a job there?" I demanded.

"I wanted you to see…he needed to see…" Drey's voice grew faint. His eyelids fluttered.

"What?" I lifted a hand as if to shake him, but I left it hovering over his shoulder. "Who needed to see?"

"They're probably coming…" His focus drifted, his eyes wandering up to the garage's high ceiling. "I always thought of you as my son, not…"

I'd never noticed quite how blue his eyes were before, like

the sky in that postcard he'd given me. Blue as the sky over the Alps.

Those eyes snapped back to me, suddenly as sharp as they were clear. "You need to run. See this shelf, right behind me? To the left you'll find a backpack strapped underneath. Yes, there it is. Don't open it now. Use the back exit out of here. Get to the river, to Jacques. You know Jacques, the captain of the trash barge."

I knew, but I didn't move from my knees as I clutched the brown backpack in my arms. "Khaya. Khaya can heal you."

He didn't acknowledge what I'd said. "Promise me you'll stay far away from Herio."

It actually hadn't occurred to me to do otherwise. I couldn't do a thing to the Word of Death, but maybe I could still help Drey. "I can bring Khaya here—"

"Don't even think it. That's exactly what they want."

"But—"

"No!" Drey shouted, shoving me with one last burst of strength, toppling me over backwards. "Go, get out of here! Now!"

I stumbled upright and leaned against the front of the truck, shaking from head to foot.

His blue eyes were almost angry as he stared at me. "If you ever wanted to do anything for me, son, do this. It's my last wish. Now get the hell out."

His head dropped back against the shelf, eyes closed.

"Goodbye, Drey," I said. Like I hadn't said the last time I'd seen him.

I still didn't move. Here was the man who'd raised me,

who'd taught me everything I knew, who'd made me the person I was, and I couldn't think of anything more to say than *goodbye*. No wonder the Gods had made me wordless. At the time I needed to say the most, words deserted me.

Drey deserved better. I turned back to tell him everything I felt and had never said. But I stopped when I saw his slack face. He couldn't hear me anymore.

But I could still hear his last wish:

Get the hell out.

He was probably right—they were coming.

I was a worthless, powerless nobody who couldn't do or say anything to save the closest thing I had to family. But I could run, like a coward. I could get the hell out of here, for Drey.

I swung the backpack over my shoulders and left the garage by the back exit, into a narrow alley, and was soon lost in the twisting and turning maze of alleys. I wasn't even sure how I was moving; I could barely feel my legs. My life felt like a bag of trash with the bottom torn out, spilling its contents behind me as I ran and leaving me oddly weightless, empty.

If the drive to the garage had passed in a blur, I could hardly remember the winding trip back to the waterfront. I was suddenly there, standing in a daze in the shade under the bridge until Khaya poked her head out of the old utility room, spotted me, and let out a gasp. I vaguely remembered I was covered in blood again—not hers, this time—with a backpack on my back. And then I was aware of hands on my shoulders, turning me and guiding me to the door.

It took me far longer than it should have to realize it was

Khaya doing this, and she was hopping on one foot. As soon as I was inside, she locked the door behind us and pushed me down on a cot. I fell over on my side and lay there, staring without seeing.

She said something to me, but I didn't hear what. It didn't help that I hadn't slept the night before, but something else, too—the weight of it all—pressed my eyes closed. I shut out the entire world, along with her, and fell into a deep, black sleep.

SEVEN

When I woke up, I thought I was on my cot back in Drey's garage. Then I remembered everything that had happened, and that I was actually on a strange cot in an old utility room under a bridge. I hoped I was still asleep, since my life couldn't actually be this nightmare. But it was, and there was no waking up.

For a while, I lay in the darkness without moving. I must have been crying, since my face was wet when I eventually stirred and rubbed my eyes.

There was faint light from the crack underneath the door. As my sight adjusted, I made out Khaya's profile sitting on a metal folding chair, her head in her arms on a table, along with a coffee press and a microwave. A small mountain of wrappers sat next to her arm. An empty box lay at her feet, with a dim picture of a cookie on the front. She'd devoured enough for a team of hungry people. Maybe her hunger had something to do with her healing, like her tiredness.

I couldn't remember the last time I'd eaten, but it didn't matter. I never wanted to eat again. Even the sight of the wrappers made my stomach twist.

I sat up and two things happened: I discovered I was in my boxers, and the cot creaked, cutting through the thick silence. Khaya jerked upright, her hand shooting for the light switch. The blinding glare didn't bother me. It let me cover my eyes and shut out the world a little longer.

"You're awake," Khaya said from behind my hands. "What happened? You can talk. Your friend ... Chantelle ... is gone. She went home to sleep right after you left."

"Drey's dead," I said, without further ado.

"Who's Drey?" she asked, with her characteristic lack of feeling.

"My dad." I hesitated, not wanting to clarify. "Close enough, anyway."

"I'm sorry," she said.

"Not your fault," I responded automatically.

"I didn't say it was."

I dropped my hand and squinted at her. "I never thought I would be the one to say this to anyone, but you could really work on your people skills. It wasn't the bracelet keeping you from showing any feeling. It's just you. So leave me alone right now, will you?"

She almost looked hurt—more hurt than when she'd had a missing thumb. "When I said I'm sorry, I meant that I can relate."

"*You* can relate to *me*?" My scoff turned into a hiccup. "How?"

"My dad is dead too." She looked away, at the wall, where the concrete surface was covered in an oriental-patterned cloth. The room smelled like heavy incense to match, overlaying a slight hint of mildew. "He was a Word, the same Word as me. He died when he gave it to me. I was five."

I couldn't really process what she'd said and I didn't feel like asking why he'd died. But I didn't need to.

"Since Words are carried on the breath of life, it takes a life to pass the Word on to the next person," she continued. "Someday it will cost me my life to give this Word away."

She drew her knees up to her chest, like she was cold. Her long-sleeved black shirt was off, her black tank top leaving her arms bare. From this angle, I could see the dark letters at the beginning of her shoulder, vanishing around her back.

"Who knows," she added. "Maybe the Gods gave their lives to give the Words to us."

"Well, I wish they hadn't. I wish the Words didn't exist." Now that I knew it was possible to hurt her, it was like I wanted to. As soon I realized this, I felt terrible. More terrible, anyway. "Sorry. I don't really mean that. But the Word of Death—Herio—killed Drey."

"He's good at that," Khaya said quietly. "He can kill you however he wants, as long as he can lay a hand on you—quick or slow, messy or clean. That's all he's good at." Even quiet, her voice was hard. And colder than ever.

Such enmity between the picture-perfect Words might have made me curious at another time, but I didn't want to know about them anymore, or even why my shirt and pants were folded on the table instead of on me. I wished I could go back to the way things were, before I'd gotten Drey killed, before I'd even met Khaya. Well, maybe not that far. But I wasn't particularly enjoying her company at the moment.

"Your clothes had so much blood on them, I figured you wouldn't want to get it on your friend's cot," she said.

"You can read minds too, can you?" I wondered how the hell she'd gotten my clothes off while standing on one foot, and I didn't know if I liked or disliked the idea of her undressing me while I was dead asleep. Then I hoped she couldn't read that thought.

"No. You were looking at them, on the table."

I reached for the backpack that I'd apparently been using as a lumpy pillow and opened it, just for something to do other than talk to her. Still wanting to know her made everything even worse, as if I'd somehow wanted Drey to die—like I'd traded his life for hers. Maybe I had, helping her and killing him in the process. She might be beautiful and powerful and important, but I didn't even want to look at her. I looked in the backpack instead.

Everything was in plastic bags—waterproofed. I wondered when Drey had packed this; not recently, based on the number of things inside. There was a compass and a map; a flashlight with batteries; matches and a lighter; a first-aid kit; a packet about the size of my fist with a silvery, folded sheet inside; a water filter; food bars; a pocketknife that really deserved to be called a pocket-toolbox; and an envelope stuffed with euros, Swiss francs, and Eden City bills. A lot of them. The envelope also held the Matterhorn postcard.

I turned it over, not wanting to look at the blue sky that reminded me of Drey's eyes, expecting to find the message I'd copied from Khaya on the back. But there was something else instead.

"What's this?" I demanded, holding it out to Khaya, who'd been intently, almost eagerly, watching me unpack the bag.

She leaned forward in her chair, her dark eyes scanning it. "An address... but not one in Eden City. It's outside, in Switzerland. There's also a message. It says, 'You must go here.'"

"Drey had an address in Switzerland?" I asked out loud, even though Khaya couldn't answer that question. "So he was there—the place in the picture. He didn't find this in the trash. He wasn't wordless. He probably wasn't even really a garbage man!"

And then I was angry at Drey's lies all over again, like I'd been when I'd found out he could read, except much, much angrier.

I thrust my hand into the backpack again—the escape pack—to make sure I hadn't missed anything. My fingers encountered cold metal beneath waterproof plastic. I pulled out the last bag.

A gun sat inside, heavy and dark, along with an extra clip.

"Gods," I whispered.

Khaya didn't say anything, but she didn't look eager anymore. Her intensity had turned to something closer to hatred as she stared at the gun.

I didn't feel hatred. With a gun, I could actually *do* something. With a gun I could blast a hole in Herio's stomach like he had Drey's—Gods, what was I *thinking*? How could I even imagine taking on the Word of Death?

I hurled it back in the bag, followed by everything else in a jumble, zipped the whole thing closed with a jerk, and put my head in my hands.

Khaya didn't say anything for a while. She still didn't wait long enough.

"We really should be moving," she murmured. "We've slept almost the whole day, but at least night is better cover. If we don't leave the city now, they'll find us. I need your help—"

I held up a finger without looking at her. "Don't. Not right now. For once, stop thinking about yourself."

"I'm not thinking about myself." She didn't explain, and I didn't ask her to.

I didn't know what I wanted to do. Well, I did. I wanted to eat an enormous bowl of Captain Crunch and go back to sleep.

Basically, I wanted to do nothing.

I'd rescued Khaya once already, but that was before I knew I was getting myself into a long-term thing. The legends never mentioned what happens *after* the hero saves the lady, especially if neither of them has anywhere to go. Well, sometimes they get married, but I sure as hell didn't want to do that, and I was pretty sure Khaya would gut me if I even tried to kiss her. She only wanted me to take care of her, like her nursemaid, until she got better.

Problem was, I might be killed in the meantime.

I was all of seventeen years old—maybe—and the responsibility of having someone depend on me was some hefty shit. I couldn't believe what Drey had done, taking me in when he didn't have to. He'd had enough to worry about, if he'd been hiding from the Athenaeum. He could have left me where he'd found me. Just like I could leave Khaya now, taking the backpack with me. Part of me wanted to go off on my own and part of me didn't. I wanted to be responsible, but I didn't want *this* responsibility. Not when I wanted to curl up in a ball and sleep for the next year, then wake up to someone taking care of *me*.

It struck me like a kick to the gut that Drey would never again wake me up with bad coffee.

His words suddenly came to mind, like he was talking right next to me: *It's always easy to start something. The hard part is following through.*

Yeah, well, if Drey had been so wise, maybe he'd still be around to help me follow through.

"Why should I keep helping you?" I asked, dropping my hands and startling Khaya in her chair. "You haven't been the nicest person on the planet. Convince me."

She blinked at me, as if I'd awoken her as she'd been nodding off. "What else can you do at this point?"

I stared at her.

When I didn't respond, she answered my question with yet another one, which was even more infuriating. "Don't you trust me? If you didn't, there's no way you would have come this far."

"You make me sound like a brainless idiot, and yourself so all-knowing. You didn't know anything about me, either, when you threw yourself on top of me." Her eyes narrowed, but I kept going. "In fact, you knew less about me than I knew about you, since you're a Word. How could you have been so sure that a total nobody-stranger would risk his neck for you?"

"You helped me, didn't you?" After she got only silence in response to yet another one of her question-answers, she added quietly, "I trusted you, too."

"Why?" I was glad I got to ask the question first, since my answer to her would have been something like, *Because you're the most beautiful girl I've ever seen.*

"Because you're beautiful," she said. "That was my initial reason, at least."

I gulped, choked on my own spit, and started coughing my lungs out.

She kept talking. "You were almost beautiful enough to be one of us—a Word. Yet you were free, like I wanted to be."

I didn't see how her description could apply to me, but my throat was burning too much to comment. Mostly I wanted to put my clothes back on.

"But, of course, that would be impossible," she said. "The Athenaeum keeps very good track of all of us." She lifted the hand that no longer had the bracelet. The line around her thumb was now only a tender pink. "Plus, your nose is slightly crooked"—from a fist fight with a street kid when I was thirteen—"and there's a scar on your forehead"—from yet another spill off the garbage truck. "Words don't have flaws."

I was oddly grateful for my imperfections. They were like protection from that other stuff she'd said, the crap about being beautiful, which was distracting me from what was actually important: that she *had* been trapped in the Athenaeum, with that monitor bracelet like a collar.

I still didn't understand how it was possible. She was an all-powerful Word.

"It was such a coincidence to see you outside," she continued, "when I'm so rarely allowed to see anyone. Then I saw you with a trash bag, and I realized you had access to a disguise no one would ever expect...and a way out. I had to seize the chance, ask for your help in secret, wait to see if you came back, then get rid of the monitor. I didn't have much time to plan, and of course I'm always being watched, so I had to take a leap of faith. Literally."

I cleared my throat. "How did you chop your thumb off, anyway?"

A wince flickered across her face like an involuntary twitch. "An axe. There's one for fire emergencies in the hallway of my apartment. It would never have been there if they thought I would actually use it for that purpose. In fact, they'll probably get rid of all the axes in the Athenaeum just to keep the others from doing the same thing."

Normally, the thought of someone hacking off a thumb with an axe would have made me pause, especially since I'd seen the results, but I had too many questions. "So, *all* of you are like...prisoners, with these monitor bracelets? The other Words would want to escape, too?"

"Not all of them." She seemed to be holding something back.

"Why you, then? What made you jump out of your apartment, aside from my irresistible beauty? Or, better yet, *in spite* of my flaws?" Maybe I shouldn't have sounded so sarcastic. Beauty seemed like any other measurable quality to her, not a compliment to others or vanity on her part. It was just a fact—not that I agreed with her when it came to me. I took a deep breath. "Why should I keep helping you?"

She leaned back in her chair and put her hands in her lap, regarding me with level, dark eyes. "Because you'll keep the world a free place by helping me escape from here. Or, as free as it is now. Trust me—it could be much worse."

"Oh," I said, scratching my bare knee. Nothing she said could really have touched me through my numbness, but that came close. Because, for some reason, I *did* trust her. "The world, huh? I guess that changes things."

I looked around the room. There was only myself, Khaya, the backpack...and my clothes. I stood up, making sure my boxers weren't gaping, shook out my stiff pants, and stuffed my legs into them. Then I tugged on my dark blue shirt. All of the encrusted blood made my chest itch. "You ready to go?" I asked.

"Now?" she asked, leaping up from the chair. She sucked air through her teeth as her ankle hit the ground, then put her weight on it more slowly and was able to stand on two feet. Apparently she'd only needed sleep to heal—and maybe a shit-ton of cookies. One day's rest had been far more recuperative for her than it had been for me.

"Good. You can walk, at least," I said. "You can tell me your story about the world on the way. It sounds important, but that means leaving is more important."

"That's what I've been trying to tell you." She snatched her shirt from the table and turned away—shyly?—to pull it over her head. "Where are we going?" she asked, her voice muffled.

The incomprehensible letters shifted over her shoulders before they were covered. They looked almost alive in her skin. Guess that made sense, for the Word of Life.

I smiled, but it felt hollow. "I hope you liked your trip in the garbage bag."

"Why?" She jerked her shirt all the way down.

"Because you're about to take a ride on a garbage barge."

eight

Before we left the old utility room under the bridge, Khaya pulled a crumpled ivy leaf out of her pocket.

"What's that for?" I asked, cracking the door to peek out into the dusk. A couple ladies had arrived to start their "day," but luckily they hadn't yet noticed us in their usual space. They were too busy standing around outside, chatting in the brazen tones I always admired, bejeweled hands on their hips.

"A diversion. Both for the women outside and for anyone hunting us. I picked it up while you were gone." She crouched down in front of the cracked door, careful of her ankle, and set the leaf just outside. "Which way are we headed?"

"West, downriver. We need to get to the dock."

"Isn't the dock all the way upriver, on the lakeshore?"

"The one for yachts is. We're trying to catch a *trash* barge, remember? You think rich people want to share their dock with garbage?"

"Oh, right," she said, sounding embarrassed. And then she started whispering to the leaf.

I couldn't hear what she was saying, but the leaf sure as hell must have. It sprouted a vine that went snaking out of her hand, and then—zip!—it took off out of sight, racing as fast as a lit fuse. Except this fuse was growing, not shrinking. Which made me wonder what would happen when it reached wherever it was headed.

I didn't have to wonder for long, maybe a minute. One of the ladies outside gasped, and then they all were crying out in amazement.

Khaya and I slipped out of the utility room, crossing behind the ladies, hugging the river. Their backs were to us as they pointed and stared at a group of buildings to the southeast.

Even in the twilight, it was pretty obvious that the buildings had turned green. They'd been stone a minute before, but now they were completely covered in ivy.

I was tempted to point and stare too, until Khaya's fingers clamped around my wrist and gave me a tug in the opposite direction.

"You … *grew that*?" I hissed, starting down the cobbled waterfront road, still eyeing the explosion of green over my shoulder. "From a leaf?"

"Yes," Khaya said simply, limping alongside me, keeping her head down. She could walk, but her pace was pretty slow.

"That's thousands, hundreds of thousands of square feet of ivy! It didn't make you tired?"

"I told you, I only get exhausted when I heal myself. Making other things live and grow is no problem."

"Oh," I said, casting one last glance behind. Without the shelter of the bridge over us, the hissing echo of the Nectar River had become just a murmur on the evening breeze, which smelled like algae and piss in this neighborhood. I felt exposed.

And that reminded me why I was running. Of the life—and death—I was leaving behind. I was still numb to it all, and I didn't want that to change. If I thawed, I might fall apart again. *Focus*, I told myself. *Get to Jacques. Fast.*

Without thinking about the consequences, I put my arm around Khaya's shoulder as if to support myself, but then brought it down around her back, gripping her side and hoisting her up. She gave me a startled look and opened her mouth—maybe to ask what the hell I was doing—and then closed it. She'd realized that walking was easier this way.

"It might help if you slouched more," I said, trying not to think about how good her perfect posture looked. "Act drunk, even. No one searching for you will expect to find you stumbling around down by the river with some low-life." I scanned the darkening frontage, not on the lookout for the usual crooks and creeps, but people in uniforms instead. Or a young man wearing all black.

Khaya's cool voice made itself heard this time, as if she was offended at the thought of even pretending to be drunk. "You know, they won't want to publicize the fact that I'm missing. I doubt it's widely known *within* the Athenaeum, let alone out in the rest of Eden City. So if people are searching for anyone, it will be you."

A tremor of fear rose underneath my frozen calm, like an earthquake deep underground, but I ignored it. "Huh, and acting drunk by the river won't disguise who *I* am. To do that, I would need a tuxedo and ... well, someone like you, I guess, so this helps."

"You're not often down here with a ... lady?" Her tone sounded more casual than cool.

I halted mid-step, making us stumble, before I continued walking and speaking in a rush. "You mean—you don't mean, one of *those* ladies? No! No, Drey and Chantelle never let me—I mean, not that I wanted—I mean, I *have* had girlfriends before, but not—"

I abandoned wherever I'd been going with that, using the slightly more populated street we'd come to as an excuse to shut up. A two-lane road rose perpendicularly from the waterfront lane, where a few small convenience shops and a Chinese restaurant were, then met up with the much wider, busier street at the top of the hill above the Nectar River, where a giant video screen perched above a corner supermarket. I couldn't hear what was being broadcast from so far away, but I could make out the face currently on the TV, filling the whole screen, glowing against the near-dark sky.

Mine. The white jacket was visible on my shoulders, so the image must have been taken from one of the Athenaeum's security cameras.

"Shit," I said.

"I don't care," Khaya said, probably thinking I was still

talking about the ladies under the bridge. Then she followed my stare to the bright screen on the hill. "Oh, shit."

At any other time, I would have been surprised to hear a Word curse. Instead, I turned my face away from the street, suddenly interested in the inky ripples of the river. My fear spiked, becoming much harder to contain, sort of like a panicking beast in my chest. It didn't help that helicopters were now hovering around the ivy-covered buildings, spotlights shining through the night sky. At least they were distracted.

"We have to walk faster," I said. "The barge leaves after nightfall on Wednesdays and Sundays. We should make it in time, but the earlier the better."

"And they'll let us on?" Khaya asked, her voice particularly low and husky as we passed a guy walking the other direction, his hands in his pockets and his head down. Luckily, he looked like he wanted to be noticed as much as we did.

"I know the captain. Well, Drey did, mostly." I had to swallow. "We dumped off our garbage at his barge. His name is Jacques, and Drey said he'd help us. But if he's seen my face on TV . . . " I swallowed again. "Can you finally tell me why I've let myself become a wanted fugitive? Gods."

"I can," Khaya said. "It's complicated, though."

"Remember, I'm not a brainless idiot. Not totally. Or maybe I am. But go on."

She ignored my rambling, limping faster alongside me, probably at maximum speed and discomfort. Out of the corner of my eye, I could see that her face was a smooth mask. It was only what she murmured that betrayed anything of significance:

"You know that Eden City is a highly influential force within the rest of the world, and the Athenaeum is the hub of that power, housing not only the Words and the City Council but the Godspeakers?" *Godspeaker* was the word I didn't understand, but she didn't pause for a question. "Eden City is the 'peacekeeper'—a bully, in actuality, who strong-arms the rest of the world into cooperation with us. It's for our own benefit, of course. We use trade agreements, embargoes, and the threat of retribution from the Words. Still, we let the other world powers feel included, which makes their compliance easier for them to swallow. We let them contribute to the creation of the Words, to the very power that manipulates them."

"How can they contribute?" I already knew some of what she'd told me, about all the bowing and scraping from the heads of other countries, but nothing much about the Words' role in all that. And especially not their "creation," which made them sound like they were manufactured in a factory. Drey had told me a lot of stories, but those were only legends, never involving recent generations of Words. And yet, if he'd worked with Swanson...he must have known about them.

I ignored the twisting pain in my chest at the thought of Drey. It felt like my heart was getting wrung out like a rag.

"All Words have one parent who was the Word before them, whether a mother or father. As for the other parent, the Athenaeum considers bids from other countries, accepting only their brightest and most beautiful individuals—basically, their best stock—otherwise known as the donor parent. They're chosen from particular countries for political reasons too, of course."

"Wait," I said, halting on the sidewalk before Khaya tugged me back into forward motion. "People are sent here from all over the world to be bred like animals, and they *compete* for this? What if the Word doesn't like the person, and they have to—they have to—"

"It's not like that," she interrupted, shooting me a chilly glare as if it were my perverted idea. "They use a process of artificial insemination, extracting genetic material from the father—whether he's the Word or the donor parent—and inserting it into the mother."

"How romantic." I nearly tripped over a stray cat that hissed at me and bolted into an alley, which made Khaya stagger. She gave me another glare, but probably not because I'd tripped her; she must have been born as a result of such a "union." She'd said her father was the Word of Life before her, so that meant her mother had been one of these donor parents. I wondered which country donated her, but figured now probably wasn't the best time to ask.

"It's not about romance," Khaya said. "It's about power. So, the Council and the Godspeakers arrange for the creation of a new generation of Words, every thirty-five years. All the births occur within a year of each other. This keeps the Words isolated in a single age group, and also always keeps them young—easier to control."

"So the Words *don't* run the city!" I lowered my voice with another glance around the waterfront. This was yet another way my entire world had been turned upside-down in a day:

the almighty Words, the smiling face of our government, were just … puppets? "You aren't the ones in charge, even though you have the power?"

"And you call yourself a brainless idiot." I couldn't tell if she was complimenting me or making fun of me for stating something that probably would have been obvious to anyone else.

"How do they make you obey, other than those bracelets?" I asked. "I've heard only a little about godspeaking, which I guess has to do with someone reading those words on your back…"

Khaya stiffened, leaning away from me as we walked.

"Don't worry," I said hurriedly. "Even if you didn't have your shirt on, I wouldn't be able to read them. I'm wordless."

My clumsy—and probably crude-sounding—attempts to put her at ease seemed to work.

"I wondered what you would see," she said, sounding thoughtful. "The Words are always changing. The language even changes, depending on who's looking, but if you can't read…"

The Words seemed even more like living things to me— the breath of the Nameless Gods, kept alive in her body like a parasite—and I pictured them crawling around under her shirt, in her skin. I almost leaned away from her like she had from me. At least we were nearly to the dock. I could see the lights only a few blocks away, the glow rippling on the Nectar. Boat masts and exhaust stacks painted a dark silhouette of a geometrical forest against the night sky.

"I'm sorry," Khaya said, somehow sensing my discomfort.

"I don't mean to trivialize the fact that you're wordless. Keeping the lower classes illiterate is a tradition the Words started when they took over this city several centuries ago, to create a safe environment. How ironic, since it was the upper class who took control away from us anyway."

I was relieved she hadn't guessed what I'd really been thinking about. "I don't care," I said. "I mean, I'm used to being wordless. But you're the one with all these people trying to read your back. Now *that's* uncool."

This time, she didn't shy away at the mention of her back. I even caught a flicker of a smile under the first streetlamp leading up to the dock, which made me way happier than I had any right to feel.

Encouraged, I asked, "So the Words used to be in charge?"

"Yes. Before we all came together in one place—Eden City—we ruled as kings and queen in other parts of the world for millennia. We thought joining together would make us stronger, but it actually made it easier for the Godspeakers to take control of all of us soon after. They like us to believe the change was for our own good, that we're better with their *guidance*, but for one group to have so much power..." She trailed off, her eyes on the sidewalk.

"How does that even work? Godspeaking, I mean."

"It's like reading a book out loud," she said. "When someone reads the Words in my skin, those Words temporarily become their words. It gives their voice strength that it could never have on its own—the strength of the Gods. Hence, they're Godspeakers."

I imagined it was sort of like putting on brass knuckles

to punch someone, but I didn't say that. Khaya didn't need any more reminders that I was raised on the back of a garbage truck. Not that Drey had raised me poorly. He'd tried, with what he had … and apparently he'd had a lot more than I'd realized.

… Drey. I didn't even know who he'd really been.

"So," I said, to think about something other than the fact that Drey was dead and I was running—walking—for my life, "anyone can read your back and make things come alive?"

She shook her head. "It's not that easy. I'm a Word, which sounds simple—singular. But a Word from the Gods carries so much potential, like a seed, or that ivy leaf, and you saw what came from that. All the facets of the Word of Life are written into me, and each idea builds on the last, leading to more and more complicated possibilities. I use my power intuitively, but Godspeakers have to do it the hard way, navigating the path from my back. They have to know what they want to do before they try, almost like they need to know what they're reading before they read. They devote their entire lives to studying the Words, and they still don't understand us well. So we're not that easy to control."

"Then why was all the thumb-chopping necessary?" I asked. "Can't you say no when they tell you to do something you don't want to do?"

Khaya's voice was soft, distant, as we took our first steps onto one of the steel ramps leading down to the dock. The place was practically empty at this time of night. We had a good shot at sneaking up to the barge. Our footsteps rang more loudly against the grating than I would have preferred, louder than her voice, but there was no one to hear.

"If we say no, they just read the Words instead. Even if they can't do exactly what they intend to, I become a tool when the Godspeakers use me. I can't move. I'm like a body possessed—a gauntlet on their hand, bending the way they want."

It sounded surprisingly similar to my brass knuckle theory, though I still didn't mention it as we stole between boats, keeping our heads down. Her words were only a whisper along with the gentle lapping of the water against the steel pilings around us, with only the occasional hollow echo of the wooden planks beneath our feet.

"Tools that we are, we still know how to do things that the Godspeakers only dream about. And there are things we have the potential to do that they've only begun to realize. But some of those dreams are nightmares...nightmares that the Godspeakers want to see come to life."

I didn't have much time to think about what those nightmares might be, because she stopped in a dark stretch between two looming fishing boats, pulling me up short.

I heard voices in the distance, now: the crew, preparing the barge for departure.

We continued on, falling silent as we drew nearer to the voices, creeping between boats until our section of dock connected to the commercial area. As I expected, the barge sat in the water at the end of the jetty, wide and heavy with heaped garbage under the dock lights and its own deck lights, the five-man crew scurrying along the gunwales and down the gangplank like rats. They looked about ready to go, but they weren't casting off.

Because Jacques, the captain, wasn't onboard. He was still standing on the dock, talking to six people who were lined up in front of him. They looked like a police squad of some sort, wearing black uniforms and caps, but the badges on their arms weren't from Eden City's force. The insignia was a gold pyramid, stitched on black—the Athenaeum's.

All of the men were carrying guns. Big guns.

nine

Khaya and I froze when we saw the men. We hid in the shadow of a fishing vessel's expansive bow, peering out of what I hoped was indistinct darkness. Neither of us dared to breathe.

It wasn't hard to pick out Jacques's voice echoing around the dock, bouncing off the boats and water, his French accent sounding harsh rather than sophisticated. "Well, you searched us. Now can we go? I may only be delivering trash, but I've got a schedule to keep."

One of the men in uniform put a hand to the side of his head, and I realized his ear was equipped with a transmitter. "All clear at the downriver dock. No sign of Barnes."

How had they known where we'd go? But then, this was an obvious place to check. They knew what Drey and I did for a living, that we had connections to the trash barge. It would be a simple way for us to escape the city. But they didn't necessarily know Khaya and I were trying it, otherwise more than six men would have been here. The Athenaeum's forces were probably spread throughout the city, searching as many places as possible ... including a few random ivy-covered buildings, thanks to Khaya.

"Yes sir, the barge is leaving now, and so are we," the man added to the invisible listener, then nodded at the other men, who slung their rifle straps over their shoulders, holding their weapons in a more relaxed manner. Not that any of them looked laid-back.

When they turned to leave, the leader looked at Jacques one last time. "Remember, captain, if the kid turns up, you call us immediately. This is a matter of the city's security. Don't let him fool you into thinking otherwise. He's smart and he's dangerous."

I might have taken that as a compliment if I hadn't had to swallow bile first.

Jacques didn't comment. It wasn't clear if he believed them or not. He only stood there, his steely arms folded across his broad chest, which was covered by his usual thick canvas overalls.

Khaya and I shrank farther into the shadows as the men marched away. We were already crouched at the edge of the dock, and kept ourselves from toppling into the black water only by holding onto the side of the fishing boat. Thank the Gods the men took the main way out, straight up to the biggest ramp leading to the waterfront street. Otherwise they would have walked right by us.

"Come on, crew," Jacques hollered, turning back to the

barge. "Stefan, take the helm. The rest of you, prepare to cast off."

"We've got to run for it," I whispered, glancing at Khaya. All I could see was the glint of her wide eyes in the darkness. "The barge is only a few feet from the dock and only a couple feet higher. We have to jump."

I made sure the backpack was secure on my back, then seized her hand without waiting for a response. I took off as Jacques started up the gangway, hauling Khaya behind me as fast as I could. We ran through shadows toward the stern of the barge, where the stretch of dock was darker and the deck lights couldn't quite reach over the mound of garbage. When I hit the end of the jetty, I leapt without hesitation for a shadow-lined patch of trash, hoping Khaya would be able to follow.

So I was surprised when she landed, catlike, on her hands and knees a few feet beyond me. She'd even avoided crushing her ankle in the garbage.

Of course, one of the crew noticed us boarding as he untied the barge's stern from the dock. He let out a shout, but Jacques silenced him with a sharp wave of his hand. The captain met my eyes from across the deck as he stepped onboard, the gangplank retracting behind him. I didn't see anything recognizable in his gaze. His light brown hair was spiked straight up, as usual, from the wind. He was probably only forty-five, but he looked ten years older with his silver-lined beard and the deep lines that etched his weathered face. Working hard outdoors did that to a guy—I'd witnessed the same with Drey. I only hoped he wouldn't act as tough with me as he looked.

Jacques made another gesture and the deck lights winked out, leaving only the powerful spotlights in the bow to navigate upriver to the lake beyond. The barge pulled out into the rippling black water, the current carrying us away from the bright wharf lights and anyone watching us.

Moments later, Jacques strode across the deck, then along the outer edge of the main trash hold. He stopped, standing above us in the dark with his hands fisted at his sides. His arms were bigger than mine, a lot bigger, a rare size to see even in the trash-hefting profession.

"Tell me why I shouldn't throw you overboard right now, Tavin Barnes," he said quietly, "or call those pricks on the dock to come get you." His hard eyes flicked to Khaya. She was crouching in the trash with her head down, her messy hair partially curtaining her face. "And who the hell is she?"

"We need help," I said hurriedly, not answering his last question. "Drey said you would help me."

Jacques gave me a dubious frown and folded his massive arms. "Drey and I made a deal, yes, that I would get you and him out of the city if you ever needed it. But that was a few years ago, before I knew you were a wanted criminal—a thief, so I hear—trying to escape with something you stole." He again eyed Khaya, who was now staring through her hair at him in wary silence, like a cat ready to flee. "Maybe some*one*. She some higher-up's daughter? Wife?"

"Uh, not really," I said, hoping that would satisfy him. Not even he could imagine I would do something as insane as take off with one of the Words. Good thing he still hadn't recognized her in the dark.

"And I don't see Drey with you," he added, as if I hadn't spoken. "Where is he?"

My throat knotted. "He's dead." I went on as if my voice hadn't cracked. "He was mixed up with Athenaeum some-how, and that's exactly why he wanted us to have a way out, in case we ever needed it. Those guys with guns you were talking to, people like that killed him." I didn't mention Herio's role, since I didn't want Jacques to be any more reluctant to help us than he already was. Not that he looked afraid in the slightest.

In fact, he growled, "I would have strangled those bas-tard sons-a-bitches if I'd known, so it's probably a good thing I didn't." He paused, his eyes softening a fraction as he looked out over the river, then back at me. "Damn, he's dead? Really?"

I nodded, unable to say anything else. I felt a soft touch on my wrist where my hand was buried in trash and jerked away before realizing it was Khaya, not a rat.

Jacques hadn't noticed our odd exchange. He was looking at the night sky, his head thrown back. "Gods." He sighed. "I've known Drey forever. Well, if there's one last thing I can do for him, it's to get you out of here like I promised, no ques-tions asked . . . no more than I already have. The deal was for two." He glanced at Khaya—the closest thing to an invitation she was going to get—and then back up at the stars. "I know he cared for you, kid."

He was honoring Drey's last wish against his better judg-ment, like I had. But maybe my first impulse should have been more like Jacques's—to kill the bastards. Yet I was powerless against a force like the Athenaeum, armed with Words and guns, so I didn't know if I was smart or cowardly to be running. Then again, it wasn't about me anymore. I was helping Khaya. Or maybe I was only telling myself that so I didn't feel like a chickenshit.

I could almost feel the cool weight of the gun through the backpack.

Jacques's eyes dropped from the sky, sharpening again as they found us. "Keep your heads down. They already searched the barge for you, so they likely won't again, but we still have to get through the city and out into the lake. We'll reach it in a few minutes. But even once we do, someone is bound to notice I'm not headed for the incinerator."

"Where are we headed?" I asked.

"Drey's designated drop point—where the lakeshore is less populated, around the bend and into France." Then he strode away toward the cabin without waiting for thanks.

I sagged as he left, and noticed that Khaya did too. Even though we'd slept during the day, it was past the usual time I hit my cot. And Khaya had been healing herself. I didn't know about her, but I was so tired I could have curled up right there and gone to sleep with my face mashed in a rotting banana peel.

Khaya fell back against the mountainside of refuse, leaning against something that could have been a used diaper. Then she sniffed and sat up straighter.

"It stinks," she said.

I actually hadn't noticed. "Beggars can't be choosers, as they say."

"I'm not complaining. Well, I am, but not in the way you think." She stared off the stern, at the inky river rippling in our wake. Eden City's lights were passing by on both sides of us. "They're going to have dogs. The smellier we are, the easier we'll be to find. We'll have to rinse off, probably in the lake, wherever the captain drops us off, and follow streambeds from there."

I hadn't thought that far ahead and didn't want to, especially now that dogs had entered the picture. I liked puppies, but fully grown dogs always chased me as I was hanging off the back of the garbage truck.

"You never really finished your story," I said, changing the subject. "You said something about nightmares...what do the Godspeakers want with the Words, and with you?"

When she answered me, the gravity in her low voice drew my eyes to hers, which were as dark and liquid as the water. "I can give life where it can take root, and return life to something that has died, only if that...*spark* of life is still there. The Word to create life from nothing is lost, or maybe it only ever belonged to the Gods. If there isn't a spark and I try to make something live, it's a false life. The thing lacks true consciousness, a will. You'd think this would be an undesirable trait in a living creature, but that's exactly what the Godspeakers and the City Council want." She shook her head, making a disgusted noise in her throat, and then her gaze returned to me with an even greater intensity. "The Godspeakers used the Word of Shaping, Cruithear as she's called—'shaper' in Scots-Gaelic—to create a human-like form out of simple organic material."

There, sitting in a pile of trash, I couldn't grasp the significance of what she'd just said. Like I'd often done with Drey's lectures, I focused on a smaller detail, noting that the Word of Shaping, or at least her donor parent, must have come from the United Kingdom, Scotland in particular. Even the Words' names didn't belong to them. Tavin—even Gustav—didn't sound so bad now. At least when Drey chose the name, it hadn't labeled me as the genetic contribution of some country while specifying my future job at the same time.

I wondered in what language "khaya" meant "life."

Khaya had been watching me for a reaction, then continued when she didn't get one. "This took years and years," she said, as if stressing the immensity of something that already sounded beyond believable to me. "It was the continuation of a project begun during the previous generation of Words, and it took cracking the human genome for Cruithear to have the building blocks to make a human body. But she finally succeeded, and while these things are only dolls, made out of flesh and blood, I can bring them to a sort of half-life." She took a deep breath. "At first the plan was to create an army."

"An army?" The word was a sickening reality check, like the ground hitting me after falling on my face.

Khaya's intensity dropped her voice even lower. "What better soldiers could you have—unthinking, obeying automatons with no real life to lose? But they weren't practical; they're not as expendable as originally hoped, since it takes Cruithear so long to make them, and worse, they're not as intelligent.

They're more versatile than robots, tapping into the body's natural instincts, but they still need orders. They don't have the ability to think on their feet or make decisions, which ended up getting most of them slaughtered in the mock battles the City Council staged outside of Eden City a couple of years ago. It was..."

She paused, staring into a pile of broken eggshells as if seeing something else. Then she shuddered. "It was a bloodbath. It was hard to watch, even when I kept telling myself they weren't really human, not really alive, not really dying...just sacks of meat." After a pause, she blinked, seeming to come back to herself. "So they failed as soldiers. They only work as replacements for people who don't need will, whose ability to reason is a hindrance to their function. Then they're perfect."

"As Words." I said it before I'd even realized it, as if my mind had made the leap without taking me along.

"You *are* smart," she said, a smile cutting across her face. "Without a will, we're utterly controllable. If you told the Word of Earth to make a mountain, and if it was within his power—within his programming, written on his back—then the Godspeakers or even his own mind wouldn't need to muddle through the process. He would just do it."

I pictured an army of automatons that could destroy an enemy or even themselves at a single command...and then an army of a different sort, much smaller in numbers, but with much, much greater power.

"Or at least that's what they think would happen if the Words became automatons," Khaya added. "They haven't gotten that far."

"Because you left before they could," I said, making another leap.

Khaya nodded, looking out at the shimmering water.

"Where should we go?" I asked.

She glanced at me. "I thought you might want to find the address on that postcard." She shrugged her slim shoulders. "But I don't care where I go, as long as it's as far away from Eden City as possible."

So Khaya really didn't care about herself or her future. As a tool in the hands of someone else, she was dangerous, and all she wanted to do was get away. I found myself wishing she would think about herself a little more; never mind that I had accused her of selfishness earlier.

As for myself, I didn't know where I wanted to go. All Drey had left me was an address, an escape pack, and a whole ton of questions. But maybe that place held the answers.

The city lights parted around us, dropping back as we entered Lake Eden and passed the lit-up fountain shooting hundreds of feet into the night sky. Eventually, the north shore of the city receded into an indistinct glow. We were almost out; it was the farthest I'd ever been from home. I'd always wanted to leave and see a new place, but I didn't feel as eager now as I'd imagined I would be. I felt sick.

I knew we would need energy so I tried to get some sleep, dozing on and off for a few hours. The lights on the shore dwindled to sparsely scattered clusters, while foothills rose into dark mountains looming above the shimmering black lake. I was so tired, but too scared to really close my eyes for more than a few minutes at a time.

"Why would they do this?" I muttered at one point. "The Athenaeum already has so much power."

"They want more," Khaya said simply—awake, like I was. "Just like anyone else in the history of humankind. The City Council isn't content to rule only Eden City, even though they already run the show, behind the scenes, on the world stage. They want it all outright. They want to rule the world as if they were the Gods themselves."

"Drey always said no one should have the power of the Gods."

Khaya hunched forward, hugging herself as if she were cold. There was a breeze playing over the lake, but it was warm. "He must have been wise. Whether or not the Words should have these powers, at least we're still human. It could be much worse. We were about to be the last generation of free-thinking Words. We weren't going to have children this time; we were going to pass the Words on to automatons, killing ourselves to do it. And they weren't going to wait for us to turn forty. They were going to do it as soon as they could. Then the Words truly would have become tools, no longer sustained on the breath of true life." She paused. "I'm the only Word, aside from Cruithear, who knows their plan, since we were the only two necessary to implement it. The Godspeakers didn't want the others to rebel. But a will—saying no—is what makes us alive. Even if I'm a tool, I'm also human."

"So you said no."

Khaya smiled at me, and it was so surprising I almost jumped in shock. But then I saw strange lights reflected on the water behind her, off the port side of the barge where it had been dark a second before, and I jumped because of that. Flashes of yellow and green were flickering over the waves.

Keeping low, I scrambled over plastic jugs, cardboard boxes, and other, slimier things to the gunwale, where I lifted my head enough to peek over.

The lake behind us had come alive with several speed-boats. Their green and yellow lights identified them as law enforcement. While they were too far away to tell, I guessed there were gold pyramids emblazoned on their sides.

Khaya scooted up behind me, her sharp intake of breath a hiss in my ear.

"Even if you say no," I said without turning to look at her, "I think they're telling you otherwise."

"They're only double-checking because of the barge's suspicious route. If they'd seen us board, they wouldn't have let us motor for thirty miles," she said, her voice low and tense. "Tavin, do you know how to swim?"

"Yeah." My voice came out choked, and my stare dropped from the speedboats to the wide black water, swirling and rippling around us. Drey had taught me, but I hadn't done it often. "Sort of."

Right then, the barge banked, turning slowly north from its eastern course and toward the center of the lake. For a horrible moment, I thought Jacques had decided to double back and turn us in. Then Khaya said, "He's giving us the chance to slip off the starboard side. We'll be out of sight, and the water's so dark. He'll lead them away from us."

"Oh," I said.

"Take off your pants."

"What?" I spun around. Khaya already had her shoes off and was tugging her pants down over her smooth thighs, her skin looking luminous in the night.

"Your pants and shoes," she hissed, "so you can swim. It's going to be hard enough with the backpack."

I looked away, my face burning. I kicked off my shoes and shoved down my pants, leaving only my T-shirt and boxers. She stuffed her clothes and shoes into my pack, wearing only her black tank top and underwear. With my pants and boots soon piled on top, I could barely zip the bag closed, and it felt like a lead weight when I tossed it over my shoulders.

"We can't afford to lose the pack," Khaya said, as if weighing the bag with her eyes. "Keep hold of it at all costs."

"Even drowning?" I sounded less sarcastic and more terrified than I'd intended.

"Tavin, you're not going to drown. Staying calm is the first step toward realizing that. Now follow me." She slipped over the starboard side as lithely as a dancer, as dark as a shadow.

I hauled myself over. Luckily, we weren't far off the water, and the gunwale provided a handhold that we could use to lower ourselves. I clung to it as Khaya slid herself into the lake. She let out a little gasp as she did. Somewhere in the back of my head the voice of reason was screaming. I ignored it and followed her into the black water.

My own gasp left me as if my chest had been squeezed. It was cold. Definitely cold. And the pack was already trying to sink me as it dipped in the water and caught the barge's current, almost slamming me into the algae-slick hull.

"Shit," I said, trying to kick myself away.

"It's okay, Tavin, just breathe," Khaya said in her calmest voice. She had to have been as cold as I was. "You're going to take my hand, and we're going to duck under at the same time, then swim toward shore, got it? We need to stay under as long as we can. Remember, deep breaths."

The barge was almost past us—it was our only cover, hiding us from the speedboats. The high-pitched hums of their motors was growing louder. I nodded, a bone-deep shiver rattling up my spine and out through my teeth.

"Okay. Last deep breath. Here we go." She took my hand firmly and inhaled, long and deep. I did the same, filling my lungs.

And then she ducked under. I went in after her, the water closing over my head.

The world became black and icy and muffled and pressing. With one hand I paddled like mad, while the other squeezed Khaya's hand in what must have been a painful grip. It wasn't difficult to sink with the backpack weighing me down, and soon we were well beneath the surface, hidden from anyone who could see us, kicking as hard as we could.

Thank the Gods Khaya seemed to know where she was going, because I couldn't see a thing. We could have been paddling right toward the speedboats for all I knew. Not that we were getting much closer to land even if we were on the right track, not at this pace. I'd seen how far we were from the dark shore before we'd ducked under. We'd be lucky if we could make it that far without drowning, let alone getting caught.

Water whirled by my ears as I swam, whistling a background tune to the throbbing beat of my heart. My lungs soon started to feel tight, and eventually, they started to burn. I squeezed Khaya's hand urgently in the suffocating darkness.

She squeezed it tighter, holding me down.

So I kept kicking for one second, two seconds, three seconds, four...then my chest convulsed without warning, announcing that time was up, and my hand wrenched involuntarily against hers.

This time she let me pull her, and I struggled upwards harder than I'd ever struggled for anything in my life. My chest was shivering and lurching, my lungs wanting to breathe even if they took in water, especially now that I was so close to air. I tried to keep my mouth closed, pressing my shaking lips together and clenching my jaw until I thought my teeth would crack. But my mouth opened anyway—right as my head broke the surface.

I only had time for a ragged gasp of air—the most beautiful substance on Earth—before the backpack dragged me back under. Hands seized my T-shirt and yanked me back up.

I tried to stay afloat, but my body was so heavy and numb. My hands were like rigid claws that sliced and didn't catch the water, even though I moved them faster and faster. I didn't even care that the speedboats were no longer nearby, the green and yellow lights moving after the spotlighted bulk of the barge in the distance.

"It's okay, Tavin, I can hold you up for a second. Just breathe." Khaya sounded out-of-breath herself, if not quite as bad as me. Her hand clamped around my arm, lifting me, her legs kicking in a strong, smooth rhythm. "But we need to swim for shore."

The shore was a dark line of trees and looming mountains above a vast expanse of even darker water.

"I don't think I can make it that far," I gasped, almost wanting to laugh at the realization. Maybe my panic was making me hysterical.

"Yes, you can," Khaya said, as calm as ever, and then she said something I didn't understand. Her fingertips grew warm, almost hot against my cold skin. Heat and strength buzzed through the rest of my body, like I'd tossed back a double shot of Drey's whisky but without the sloppiness. My stomach suddenly rumbled, so loud I was surprised the speedboats didn't hear it and turn around.

"I gave you energy, but it comes from your own body— I only put it on overdrive," Khaya told me. "I can't do it again or you'll be too tired and hungry to move when this is all over."

"If I'm still alive." I was able to hold my head above water more easily than a second ago. My legs and arms felt warm and invigorated, but the expanse of water was as cold and wide as before, the bag just as heavy. "If this pack doesn't kill me. I won't be able to do a crawl stroke like this."

"How do otters swim when they're carrying their young?" Khaya asked.

"How the hell should I know?"

"On their backs. Do you know the backstroke?"

My jerky nod was more like a spasm. She swam behind me, helping me slide the pack from my back to my chest, looping the straps back around my shoulders. My head only went under once during the entire reshuffle. And all the while, the speedboats were heading farther and farther away from us.

"Try that," she said. "Aim for shore."

I leaned back in the water, kicking and doing what I was sure was the lamest backstroke ever, the straps chafing my shoulders. But it worked. I kept myself and the pack afloat at a crawling pace, my breathing just short of hyperventilation. Little rolling waves washed over my face every ten seconds or so, making me sputter and blurring my view of the night sky like stinging tears.

My muscles kept working, pumping on and on in mechanical movements, and I let my brain slip into numbness with the rest of my body. I didn't think about the fact that I might drown at any second, because I couldn't think. The act of swimming became everything. I couldn't even spare any consideration for Khaya. I didn't even know where she was.

At first, I didn't recognize what had happened when—maybe twenty minutes later, maybe twenty hours—my stretching, paddling hands came up with fingers loaded with dark goop and my shoulders pressed into something firmer and more slippery than water, halting my endless backward motion.

Mud. I had reached the shore. My arms and legs gave out then and I dropped like a rock, my back sinking into sludge, the pack on my chest speeding the process. Luckily I was only in a couple feet of water; a foot deeper and I would have drowned. The ripples were already lapping dangerously close to my gaping mouth, and then a slightly bigger wave splashed down my throat, making me cough.

Khaya had washed up next to me. The pace of her breathing matched mine, and all either of us could seem to do was listen to ourselves gasp for several long minutes.

"I think we rinsed," I said eventually, my lungs heaving as I hauled myself up onto my elbows. My limbs felt like melted rubber.

"What?" Khaya gasped, dragging herself farther toward the rocks leading up to the line of dark trees. Her bare arms and legs were smeared in mud—marks on her skin that were no more comprehensible than the Words on her shoulders.

"You said we needed to rinse the smells off."

There was a pause, and then Khaya collapsed on her stomach, laughing a full, breathy laugh. It was the first time I'd heard anything like that coming from her. A grin shaped my numb face in spite of the cold—in spite of everything. I was alive, and Khaya was laughing, and that felt pretty damned good.

ten

Khaya didn't stay down for long. "We need to move," she said—her new mantra. She got up on her hands and knees, then stood on wobbly legs on the night-soaked lakeshore. I couldn't remember the world ever looking so dark; never, in the glittering spread of Eden City. "Not only will the Athenaeum be tracking us soon with all the resources available to them, but we'll get hypothermic."

She tugged the pack off my chest, helping me up as she did, even though I nearly pulled her back down.

"It's cold," I said, feeling the air on my skin for the first time. Shivers took hold of me, shaking my body like a pack of gremlins. "Weird. It wasn't cold earlier."

"We're well out of the city. Our weather pattern will no longer be regulated by Luft, so we'll have to contend with the natural climate of this area." Khaya's words wavered with her own sudden shudder.

"Luft?" I asked.

"The Word of Air."

Right. I was sure I had more questions somewhere in my numb brain, but I was too tired to dig around and find them.

"So we'll have to stay warm and keep ourselves strong—not that you'll have a problem with that," she said, turning to lurch toward the trees, hauling the pack with her. I let her carry it. It was her turn, after all. "Thank you, by the way. I'm a decent swimmer, but I couldn't have made that distance with a load like this by myself."

"At your service, my lady," I panted, stumbling after her, slipping on the rocks. We had to dash across a two-lane country highway, deserted at this time of night, and my knees buckled twice before I made it to the edge of the forest, but I managed not to collapse. So much for my strength. "You must have had swimming lessons in the Athenaeum."

"Among other lessons. All the Words are highly trained. I can also play the harp and ballroom dance . . . and kick a man's nose up into his brain." She shot a glance back at me as we stepped under the cover of the trees. "Still think I'm a lady?"

I thought she must be joking until I remembered that Khaya didn't joke.

"Why the hell do you need my help, then, if you can do all that?" A twig stabbed me in the foot, which was already aching with cold, and I tripped with a curse. I couldn't see a thing in the underbrush. "Never mind the whole Word of Life thing."

"Because I would never actually kick a man's nose into his brain." Khaya dropped the pack to the ground and fished out our sopping wet clothes and shoes. "I'm the Word of Life, not Death. And I told you, I couldn't have done any of this without you: disguising myself in trash—twice—securing passage on the barge, or swimming while holding this pack, which is our key to survival. I couldn't even walk yesterday, remember?"

I wasn't used to her compliments or thanks, so I only shook my wet pants out of the bundle and grimaced as I held them up. "These are going to be cold."

"You'll be colder without them. Your body will warm them up … eventually," she said, tugging her black, long-sleeved shirt over her head without expression.

I alternately hissed and yelped as I forced my legs into my frozen pants, not bothering to hide it from Khaya. She had seen me half-naked, crying, and now drowning, so I didn't care if she saw me whining like a baby over wet clothes. I could barely feel my toes as I crammed them into my shoes.

"Faster," Khaya said, waiting fully dressed in her black pants and shirt. "We need to find a stream. We'll be much harder to track that way. No footprints, no smell to follow."

"Right," I said, tying the final knot in my wet, gritty laces. Then I straightened and threw the backpack over my aching shoulders. More like the backpack nearly overthrew me.

"Eat this." Khaya tossed me one of the food bars from the pack.

My stomach rumbled like a truck engine as I caught it. She hadn't taken one for herself, but that didn't stop me. I ripped open the wrapper with my teeth and chewed half of it off in one bite.

"How are we going to find a stream?" I asked with my mouth full. "Just stumble around in the dark until we fall into one?"

"Basically," Khaya said, starting off through the underbrush. She moved roughly parallel to the lake, though keeping a straight line was difficult through the tangle of shrubs and fallen logs. "I can't check the map right now, because the flashlight might draw unwanted attention. But there should be tons of streams feeding Lake Léman."

Something with thorns snagged at my pants as I followed. "Ouch. Lake Le-what?"

I mostly just wanted to talk about something. Escaping on the barge had been surreal—frightening, sure—but now, on foot, this felt all too real. I couldn't let myself think about the fact that I was leaving the only home I'd ever known like a thief in the dark. A clumsy thief.

"Watch out for the blackberry brambles," Khaya said, not looking back at me. "Though I hope they stay plentiful. I can force them to grow berries, even when it's too cold and they're not in season, like now. And Lake Léman is what Lake Eden is called outside of Eden City, in both France and Switzerland. Just like the Nectar River is also known as the Rhone. We like to rename things, even change languages. Our own English-speaking Eden City was French-speaking Geneva before we took it over a couple hundred years ago, at the turn of the nineteenth century."

"Oh." I didn't know too much about what existed beyond the borders of Eden City—or even Eden City's history—aside from the fact that there were lots of other countries out there, and Captain Crunch came from one of them.

Gods, I wanted some Captain Crunch. I tried to stop thinking about all the things I'd rather be eating and stuffed the other half of the food bar in my mouth. It tasted too healthy. Drey had long ago tried to feed me stuff like this, but had soon abandoned all hope of succeeding.

"If my memory is correct," Khaya continued, "we need to hike southeast through these foothills into the Chablais Alps, then make our way back across the Swiss border, which shouldn't be too far. We'll be in the Swiss Alps after that."

The Swiss Alps. The location of the Matterhorn and Drey's mysterious address—a place of exile for Khaya and perhaps answers for me.

"Sounds like you had lessons in geography, too." I stubbed my foot on a low, rotting log that was indistinguishable from the rest of the ground and I uttered a curse. "I can hardly point to Eden City on a map." I could hardly have pointed to myself in this darkness.

"It's in the southwestern corner of Switzerland, at the far end of Lake Ed—Léman," Khaya said, her pace quickening ahead of me as if she had night vision. "It's only a few miles from the French border—46.2 north by 6.15 east."

"Way to make me feel like an ignoramus." Drey had never wanted me to sound stupid, yet I realized he could have taught me a lot more than he had. He'd talked about faraway places, ancient legends, and distant histories. But anything recent, right next to me, was like a blank spot on a map in my brain.

Khaya actually sounded chastised. "I'm not bragging. I just know."

Like she was *just* beautiful, *just* the Word of Life, and *just* knew how to kick someone's head off—though I had yet to see that last one demonstrated. I wasn't sure I wanted to.

"At least one of us knows. And while being the Word of Life is cool and all," I said with yet another shiver, "I wish you were the Word of Fire. I'm freezing my a—uh, I'm pretty cold." I censored myself, not wanting to sound more lower class than I already did.

A light drizzle had begun working its way between tree branches, invisible in the dark and misting my face like someone's lisping spit. It rarely rained in Eden City, only enough to give the city the occasional wash-down and water the planters and parks—thanks to the schedule maintained by the Word of Air, I now realized.

"Trust me, you don't wish that," Khaya said, vaulting over a log. I thought I heard a smile in her voice. "Agonya has a very short temper. She would likely have lit you on fire by now."

"At least I would be warm," I said, falling over the same log. "Okay, maybe I don't want the Word of Fire. How about the Word of Electric Heaters? Or maybe the Word of Warm Coats?"

Khaya laughed again, really laughed, her voice ringing through the trees like a bell. The sound carried me up with it, making me feel like I was flying instead of crawling around in the bushes. But she swallowed her laughter nearly as soon as it had begun.

"Gods, I'm being too loud," she said. "I must be tired."

I hoped tiredness wasn't the only thing letting her loosen up. "We could always stop—"

"No, we can't," she said, cool and businesslike once again. "Not until sunrise. We need to get as far away as possible and take advantage of the darkness to move. And we should probably quit talking. Whether or not they know how we got out of the city, they'll soon realize we're not there, and then they'll be combing the countryside for us—especially the lakeshore along the barge's route."

We stopped speaking after that, trekking in a silence that was complete aside from the occasional snapping twig or whispered curse when I tripped. Or the low growls from my stomach. The food bar only helped for about a half hour before I was ravenous again. Khaya was right—the boost of energy she'd given me in the river had definitely come from my body, and now it was demanding repayment, with interest. I didn't want to stop to unpack another bar, because I didn't know how many we had. Even if they tasted bad, they were our only food. And I was pretty sure Khaya would leave me behind at the pace she was going. I'd never encountered such darkness or silence in my life, and didn't exactly want to be lost in it.

About a half hour or so after we'd started walking, we still hadn't come across a stream but we'd nearly stumbled into the backyards of a few country houses. I was about to ask Khaya if her knowledge of geography was all that sophisticated when the sound of running water rose through the trees.

"Finally," Khaya said.

The stream appeared, a braid of shimmering darkness through the underbrush, about as wide as a street. I thought it would be easier going once we hit the stream, but when I saw Khaya go perfectly still as she stepped into the water, shoes and all, I knew I was in for some extreme discomfort. Khaya always seemed to act the calmest when things were the worst. Sure enough, when I trundled in after her, I swore loud enough to earn a glare and a finger held to her lips for silence.

"Sorry," I hissed as she stepped behind me to unzip the backpack, "but it's like ice water. Or fire. My feet are burning!"

She didn't answer, just filled the water bottle, which had a filter in the cap, then shot several blasts of liquid into her mouth before handing it to me. I didn't think I wanted any more water touching me until I sprayed some in my mouth and realized I was dying of thirst. Then I couldn't get enough. All too soon, Khaya was repacking the bottle and starting upstream ahead of me.

My shoes kept rocks from jabbing my feet, but I still slipped and staggered, hurting other parts of my body. Even though I'd rolled up my pants, they ended up soaked to the mid-thigh. Between the splashes and the ever-constant drizzle, I was nearly as wet as I'd been after dragging myself out of the lake.

Soon I could no longer feel anything below the knees. As if Khaya knew, she picked up her feet and slogged faster against the current.

"Keep your blood flowing," she said.

I was already huffing and puffing from exhaustion, so

I didn't think that was a concern. "Did you get marathon training in the Athenaeum, too?" I asked.

"Not quite," Khaya said shortly.

"Was your donor parent a triathlon gold medalist, then?"

She didn't answer. She must have known I was trying to dig for information, which wasn't as subtle as I'd thought.

"Probably," I said, when she remained silent. "All we need to test the theory is to get you on a bike, since we've got the swimming and the—"

"My donor mother was Israeli," Khaya said with a backwards glance. I couldn't read her expression in the dark. "A brilliant obstetrician. And of course she was beautiful—is beautiful. I'm sure she's still alive. I don't know much more about her than that."

I still had plenty of other questions. Khaya seemed to have forgotten her ban on conversation, now that we'd reached the stream, and talking was distracting me from the fact that my feet felt like unfeeling bricks attached to the stubs of my ankles. "The Godspeakers don't let you keep in touch?" I asked.

She shook her head. "Why would they? They're not really our parents—only our genetics. Besides, they want to limit any foreign influence on us. See, even though Eden City is trying to look inclusive of the other world powers, it's all for show."

"So, Khaya means 'life' in Hebrew?"

"Well, that's *khayim*." She sounded eager to talk about something other than her donor mother, and gave the word a harsh, hocking accent. She must have learned Hebrew, too, along with everything else on the planet. "But 'Khaya' is an established girl's name that essentially means the same thing, so the City Council went with that, since it's more feminine. They're not always so nice. The previous Word of Death, Herio's mother, was named with the Italian word *morte*. We all called her Em, anyway."

"So what's Herio? It must mean 'death,' of course, but in what language?"

"Basque," Khaya said quietly. I almost didn't hear her over the burbling water, and I wondered if she didn't like talking about him. "His donor father was French, but from the Basque region in the southwest."

"What's 'death' in French again?" I asked, for lack of something better to say. I didn't want to talk about him either, really, but it was like prodding at a wound—I did it anyway.

"Similar to Italian: *mort.*"

"That's not very nice, I guess." My words began to come faster. "Not that Herio deserves a nice name. I wish I'd had the chance to shoot him with that gun before we—"

Khaya stopped short but didn't turn. "How could you say that?"

I stopped too, the water parting around my shin as if I'd turned to stone. I felt colder than stone. "He killed Drey."

"So that makes it right to kill him?"

"Someone needs to do something." My voice rose. "Are you defending him? Why, because he's a precious Word—"

"No!" Khaya spun on me with a splash. "I hate him, do you hear me? I hate him!" Her voice held more emotion than I'd ever heard. "The Word of Death shouldn't exist—like that gun. But killing him would be a bit hypo-critical, don't you think?"

Maybe. But the thought of the gun was still … intoxi-cating, almost; heady. I'd never had something like that before, something that could kill at the twitch of a finger, like Herio could. I'd never held such power.

I shook the thought out of my head. The subject had obviously gotten too touchy for the both of us.

"Have you ever heard the name Drey Barnes?" I asked. "I mean, aside from when I've mentioned him." It was the first time I could stand asking her about him. "Or a Dr. Swanson? Drey said he used to work for Swanson in the Athenaeum."

The change in topic made her blink in the darkness, and some of the anger left her eyes. She had moved closer to me with her outburst, close enough for me to be able to lift a hand and touch her face—not that I did. As if she also noticed how near we were, she turned and continued trek-king upstream.

"I never heard of Drey Barnes before I met you," she said, "but I've definitely heard of Dr. Swanson. He's the head of the Godspeakers."

"Wait, what?" I almost stopped again. "I thought Swan-son was just Herio's assistant, part of the Athenaeum's security team."

"He might present himself as such. The Godspeakers like to lie low so the outside world doesn't get wind of how much power they truly wield. Because the idea of the divine leader-ship of the Words—the Words of the Nameless Gods Made Flesh—is just too perfect, too potent an image." Bitterness touched her voice. "If the world knew the truth, everyone might be less willing to cooperate with us. In actuality, Swanson is one of the most powerful people in Eden City."

"Wow. And Drey worked for him." I paused, embarrassed that I sounded like a pauper trying to make bogus claims to a higher stature or something—to raise myself to *her* level. But really, I just couldn't believe it. I slipped on a smooth, slimy rock and almost didn't catch myself before falling on my face. "It's just . . . crazy."

"Not really. Swanson has had many people working under him over the years."

It was probably true. I let it drop, since I didn't know what else to say. She'd likely been about to tell me to be quiet again anyway. Besides, how could I explain to her—a girl whose birth had been preordained and engineered at a precise time and location—what it was like to not know where you came from, or even know about the person who raised you?

I wanted to get to Drey's address in the Alps even more now. That place had to be filled with clues to the puzzle Drey had left me—the puzzle of his life.

When my thoughts turned to Drey, I let my mind slip into silence. I was too exhausted to think about him, worried that doing so would take up my remaining strength as I trudged in Khaya's wake, my body falling into the numb rhythm of struggling through water for the second time that night. I filled my head with the murmuring of the forest instead while the hours slipped past: the gurgle of the various streams we followed and the chilly gusts whispering through the tops of the otherwise silent trees, which stood over us like dark sentinels. We'd crossed a couple of dirt roads and hiking paths earlier in the evening, but now the forest was thick and imposing on either side of us, any other route barred by branches, the only way forward through the few icy cuts of water we managed to find. I'd thought some neighborhoods in Eden City were inhospitable, but this gave the word a new meaning. We didn't belong here.

It was less of a thought and more of a feeling that took hold of my body, along with the cold, like an icy fist squeezing my heart. Or maybe I was freezing and on the verge of collapse. Right when I was about to say that maybe we shouldn't—or that I couldn't—go on, Khaya lurched to a stop and I stumbled into her from behind, almost pitching both of us into the water.

Her hand shot back, squeezing my side in a clawlike grip, steadying the both of us.

"The sky will start getting lighter in less than an hour," she said, her voice gravelly from lack of use. She cleared her throat and released me. "And then they'll have helicopters scouting from above for movement. And dogs on the ground, of course. So here is as good a spot as any."

I rubbed my side. Squinting into the darkness over her shoulder, I saw a tangled blot marring the center of the stream, forcing the water to part around it. "An island," I said, my voice sounding even rougher than hers. "So the dogs can't track us."

It looked as if all life in the forest had fought for purchase on the tiny patch of land. Two tall, ivy-covered trees stood on either side of the rocky strip, while a mass of bushes and fallen logs stretched between them.

"Exactly." Khaya stumbled forward, falling to her knees as soon as she hit solid ground. She looked nearly as tired as I felt.

But she wasn't resting. She flattened her palms against the earth of the island, wet like us from the misting rain, and muttered under her breath.

Immediately, the bushes and then the ivy on the trees stirred. Soon they were thrashing and twisting like the tentacles of some sea creature. The ground even shuddered beneath my feet, the trees groaning and creaking. But only thirty seconds passed, maybe, before Khaya stood and absently wiped her hands on her pants. Things had obviously been rearranged, but the bushes and ivy still looked like bushes and ivy to me.

"There," she said, grabbing the pack I let fall from my shoulders. It felt heavier than the heaviest trash bag, even though I knew it wasn't that bad. "I hope the tree will live through this. I'll send its roots back down before we—"

"What did you do?" I interrupted, too drained for manners.

"Let's go see." Khaya shoved her way forward, the flashlight in her hand. I hadn't even noticed her digging it out of the pack. The world seemed to be moving in bursts, while everything in between dragged in slow motion. Or maybe that was how my brain was working.

She turned on the flashlight as she ducked into the underbrush, but the light didn't shine through the branches.

It was almost like it was pointing into an enclosed space. I followed her into a seeming hallucination—a tent, disguised as foliage from the outside. The inside had walls of woven vines and leaves, tight enough to keep out rain. And the floor wasn't covered in damp dirt, but lined like a mat made of reeds or bamboo. I realized it was the tree's roots, unearthed and laid out at her command.

"This will insulate us from the ground," Khaya said, crawling inside. She sat in the center of her small, living shelter and drew her knees up to her chest. "Don't you want to come in?"

I dove in after her, my awe forgotten in my hurry to be somewhere dry and bright and filled with Khaya. As soon as I entered, she muttered another word and the flap of the "tent" closed behind me, the entwining vines locking us in.

"Give me your hands," she said. I offered her one without hesitation and she chafed it between her own. "If I warm you, you'll probably lapse into a coma."

"Mmm, a coma sounds nice right about now," I said, too tired to yawn. Nothing had ever felt as good as her warm hands, even if hers were probably only slightly less frozen than mine. My ass on the ground felt almost as good. I'd forgotten what it felt like to not be moving.

She didn't hold my hand for long, though, letting it drop to pry off my shoes. My feet were white underneath my wet socks, my toes a pale bluish hue. Khaya frowned at them and began riffling through the pack at her side until she found the small package containing the strange silvery sheet, folded tight. I suddenly recognized it, even if I didn't recognize the words on the label.

"It's an emergency blanket," she said, voicing my realization out loud. "The metallic coating will reflect our heat back at us." Then she added softly, "Drey was well-prepared."

I didn't answer, still too tired to think about Drey. I only reached my stiff, frozen arms around my back, peeling my damp shirt off over my head. The air felt warmer than my shirt as it touched my bare skin.

Khaya stared at me for a second, then abruptly looked at the vine-woven wall of the tent.

I would have laughed if I'd had the energy. We were a lot closer and much better illuminated than we'd been over the last twenty-four hours, but she *had* either taken off my clothes or ordered me to take them off twice in that timespan.

"Take off your pants," I said, giving her a taste of her own medicine—as Drey would have called it. Khaya's eyes shot back to me before I added, "We can't sleep in wet clothes, can we? It's a basic survival lesson—even *I* know that."

Her gaze softened, her honey-toned cheeks looking warmer. "I also know that. But I'm—I'm going to turn off the flashlight."

"Okay," I said, already starting on my pants. The button and zipper were giving my clumsy, unfeeling fingers far more trouble than usual. Even if I was too exhausted for embarrassment, I wasn't about to ask her for help with that part—though I did stick out my foot. "Can you pull my pants over my ankle? It's hard when they're wet."

She complied without comment, yanking the cuffs over

my feet. She turned away after that, clicking off the flashlight and plunging us into total darkness without waiting for me to finish laying out my shirt and pants at the end of our shelter to dry.

She obviously didn't want any help undressing. I listened to her stripping down in the dark, sitting in a shivering huddle waiting for her to finish. When I heard the crackling of plastic, I knew she was unfolding the emergency blanket. The edge of it fanned me with an unwelcome breeze as she shook it out.

"Here," she said. "Take one side and get under. And you're supposed to take everything off, Mr. Survival Expert."

Even though I knew she couldn't see, I slid off my boxers only when I had part of the blanket over me. Which was doubly stupid, because she was under the blanket too.

The blanket wasn't big enough to avoid touching her. As I scooted farther under, my hand grazed what I hoped was her arm. I settled my shoulder near hers, lying on my back as far away from her as possible without edging my other shoulder out from under the cover, which was about the distance of an inch. I was too tall, as usual, my feet sticking out the bottom. I tried to tuck them under without brushing her. And failed.

She jumped next to me, rustling the blanket. "Gods, your feet are cold!" Then she sighed. "We'll be warmer like this." She sidled her shoulder against mine, her skin warm and soft. Even though our hips weren't touching, hers were close enough for me to feel the warmth radiating from her body, hovering like a whisper of breath, making my skin prickle.

And that was when it hit me. I was naked under a blanket with an equally naked Word. Not that I could have done anything about it even if I'd wanted to, but there it was. At least it was enough of a distraction to keep me from thinking about Drey.

Or maybe it was too much of a distraction. As tired as I was, it took me a hell of a long time to fall asleep.

eleven

I woke up, disoriented and insanely thirsty, to spidery cracks of light working their way through the bizarre walls of my surroundings. It was daylight, whatever time it was, wherever I was. Lately, I'd been in strange enough places to not expect to see my cot in the back room of Drey's garage as I glanced around, but I certainly didn't expect to find what I did.

Khaya lay curled against me, her head buried in the crook of my arm, her wavy hair a wild, dark storm around her serene face. It was obvious by the bare curve of her shoulder—patterned with indecipherable black script, visible above the edge of the silvery blanket over us—that she didn't have a shirt on. I didn't have one on either.

In my groggy daze, the previous night's events came back to me slowly. Once again, remembering what had happened was like retracing a dream. But this time, I wasn't as horrified by the fact that I couldn't wake up. This was much less like a nightmare, with Khaya asleep next to me, warm and soft, even though Drey was still dead and I was still running for my life.

I'd never woken up next to a girl. It was both amazing and really damned weird, two things that made it hard to close my eyes on the situation, no matter how badly they wanted to close. Besides, I could very well get killed within the next day or two and might never see Khaya like this again.

Sleep relaxed her face in a way I'd never seen before, giving her a peaceful, carefree look unlike her forced calm. Her eyelashes brushed her silky cheek in a dark, perfect fan, her full lips slightly parted. I figured she would hate being seen in such a vulnerable state, so I studied the only other visible part of her—the top of her shoulder, peeking out from under the blanket and inked with dark shapes.

Even taking my time, I couldn't make sense out of anything written there, and gradually my sight blurred, my eyelids drooping.

That half-asleep dream state crept over me, and the last thing I saw before my eyes closed was one of the Words melting down her shoulder, running along her arm and dripping like black ink from the tip of her fingers, which rested against the root-lined floor.

I saw them in my head then—the Words.

Reach, give, nurture, grow ... the succession of thoughts blossomed in my mind, leaping one to the next, wild and uncontrollable, more like images than words. They all sprang from the same seed, linking them together like a golden string, streaming through my mind and body like blood, like sunlight:

Life.

My own muttering woke me up. My eyes flew wide.

Khaya's eyes were open in front of mine, staring blankly. The Words felt like strings, stretching from where I touched her to the ground, running down her arm as if she were a puppet. On the floor, hairlike roots were sprouting, twisting and curling around her fingers.

I shouted wordlessly and wrenched my arm out from under her, breaking our contact. Khaya shot bolt upright, seeming to remember at the last moment to clutch the blanket to her chest and nearly pulling it off me entirely. She panted, looking from me down to the cluster of roots that had ceased growing in fast-motion now that she was no longer touching them—now that I was no longer speaking.

"How could you?" she gasped, her wide, dark eyes glistening with tears. "You just want to use me like everyone else!"

"No, Khaya, I promise, I—"

But she buried her face in her blanket-covered knees before I could finish, folding her arms over her head.

I scooted closer, both because I was reaching out to comfort her and because she was pulling that last, crucial corner of blanket from my lap. She jerked away when my hand brushed her shoulder, forcing me to do a seated hop even closer.

"Don't touch me!" she cried.

"Khaya, I didn't mean to! Gods, please believe me." I hovered next to her, not daring to touch her again. She looked so small, her slim shoulders shaking above the blanket. "I'm so sorry. It just happened—"

"Don't look at me—don't read them! You wouldn't if you knew how it felt, like someone slipping inside your skin, *using* your body." Her voice grated from behind the shield of her arms and hair, rubbing me raw like sandpaper.

I wanted to hug her and apologize over and over again until she stopped crying. But my touch repulsed her. I knotted my hands into fists, folding my arms and hiding them away. I'd never intended to godspeak through her—that was what I'd done, I realized—but there I'd been, watching her without her knowing, drinking her in while she'd been asleep, and that was what my semi-conscious mind had led me to. The fact that I could do this while wordless, which everyone always said was impossible, didn't even amaze me. I felt too sick.

I sat for a minute in dull, nauseated silence, Khaya crying to herself, both of us hunched and alone, until I realized I was acting like a moron.

"Khaya, come here." I unfolded my arms and wrapped them around her shoulders. She tried to pull away, but her back had already met the woven wall of our shelter. Instead, she froze, stiff as a statue.

"I'm not going to hurt you, Khaya, or do anything like that ever again. I was just seeing what the Words would look like to someone wordless. I didn't think anything would happen." I bowed my head next to hers, her hair brushing my temple and tickling my nose. "See, my eyes aren't even open. I'll never look at the Words again if you don't want me to. I don't even want to. It's not fair that people do that to you, and I want nothing to do with it. In fact, I want to hurt the Godspeakers even more now. I'm wordless and I'm happy that way. I'm sorry. Did I tell you how sorry I was?"

Somewhere amidst my babbling, Khaya's shoulders relaxed. I let my final question fall into silence.

"I didn't mean to get so upset," she murmured, her face still hidden in her arms. Her voice was audible only because I was so close. "I was only shocked, that's all. I've been free of the Godspeakers for a couple of days now, and this is the happiest I've ever been. So to be woken up like that..."

"I'm so sorry," I said, squeezing her tighter. If this was the happiest she'd ever been, things must have been pretty awful in the Athenaeum.

"Tavin, you're crushing me."

"Oh!" I released her. But I didn't go far. I was still limited by the length of the silvery blanket, and my chest was already bare from the waist up.

"I'm fine," she said, lifting her reddened, damp face. One hand rubbed her eyes while the other held the blanket nearly up to her neck. "I'm just—I'm tired."

"Here, go back to sleep." I gestured at the ground. "I can sleep outside if you want me to."

"No, that's stupid. You'll freeze, and you might be seen."

"Then I'll give you some privacy," I said, dropping onto my side, facing the opposite wall. "I'm sorry. I'll shut up now. Good night."

She was silent behind me, and I could almost feel her eyes on my back. Then she sighed and slid down next to me under the blanket, leaving at least a couple inches between us. "Sleep well, Tavin."

I didn't think I would be able to sleep again, but I did. My body seemed to have the useful ability to shut down when I didn't want to feel anything anymore. *At least I took responsibility for what I did*, I thought right before I fell asleep ... though Drey would have smacked me upside the head for doing something like that in the first place.

My subsequent dream didn't help ease my guilt.

As I slept, I could have sworn I felt someone's hands on my cheek, turning my head—then soft lips pressing against mine for a long, unbroken moment, like falling slowly and never hitting the ground. But then it ended, and a voice—Khaya's voice—said:

"Now we're even."

twelve

My lips were still burning when I woke up, and now my face was, too. The dream could have been worse—my imagination could have gotten a lot more creative—but after last night, a kiss was bad enough.

I forgot about it when I couldn't hear or sense Khaya next to me. What little daylight had been able to penetrate our shelter was now gone. I spoke into the darkness, not wanting to reach out in case I groped her by accident.

"Khaya? You there?"

There was no answer. Then I heard something else, outside in the distance, a sound like beating wings. But it was much too loud for any bird, and rapidly coming closer.

"Helicopter!" I hissed, as if anything above a whisper could actually be heard over the thrumming blades. And then the noise was right above, drowning out all other sound, and a bright beam of light was passing along the tent like a miniature sunrise and sunset. Although it only poked in through tiny, hairline cracks, I kept waiting for the spotlight to stop right over me, illuminating my face in the darkness like the fugitive I was. Me and only me, since Khaya was nowhere to be seen.

But then the light was gone, the sound of beating wings fading away as soon as it had come. The helicopter must not have noticed our shelter, otherwise I imagined I would be hearing a police squad kicking through the bushes.

"Khaya?" I said into the deafening silence.

"I'm here," she whispered from outside the tent, and I exhaled in relief. "Get dressed. We need to get moving."

Her clipped words made me nervous again. I threw back the crackly blanket and fumbled for my clothes, ignoring the protest in my limbs even though my body creaked and groaned like the tree Khaya had moved to make the floor of our shelter. My clothes felt dry enough, certainly drier than they had been, but I couldn't see enough to put them on.

"The flashlight is next to you," Khaya said, even quieter. But it wasn't out of caution, because then she spoke louder. "Have it on as little as possible and only in the tent, because of the batteries and anyone scouting for us. They were only skimming the creek, but they were smart enough to give this island special attention. They might be back."

I tugged my clothes on while she updated me, using the flashlight long enough to get my shirt and pants into position for dressing in the dark.

"The sound of the helicopters woke me up right before dusk, passing in the distance," she said through the vine wall. "We need to eat, so I risked searching for a blackberry bush, which, like this poor tree, I probably killed by forcing it to grow." I heard her sigh. "But we have berries now. I also found and grew some edible mushrooms, and I left you half a food bar."

…Berries, raw mushrooms, and half of one of those grainy bricks that tasted like it was meant for birds or, at best, for horses. As unappealing as it all was, my stomach growled.

"The food is out here, and some water."

The wall of the shelter parted when I reached for it. In fact, the whole tent unraveled around me, revealing a starry night sky and Khaya before collapsing in a tangled heap on my feet.

"It's a strain for the ivy to hold itself in such an unnatural shape," she said without apology.

I kicked free of what was now only a dark clump of vegetation, marveling at how many new vines and branches Khaya had grown into such a complex pattern, and how precisely she must have directed the Words to do so. For the few seconds I'd felt the Words raging through me, they had seemed to have a mind of their own, a wild strength that was almost impossible to contain. Khaya could control what I had to struggle to cling to like a runaway truck.

And how had I even read the Words on her back? I was wordless. But the Words weren't limited to the changing, black symbols in Khaya's skin; they were far greater. And maybe, in my semi-conscious state, I'd read the *true* Words— the ones beyond letters. The power had been unleashed, astounding, exhilarating…

I choked off the thought after remembering what it must

have felt like for Khaya to have me using her like that, especially while she was asleep.

Now we're even.

The whispered words of my dream came back to me. I let myself wonder, for a split second, if she'd actually kissed me as I slept. But why would she have? I quashed the absurd thought and, with a carefully blank expression, crawled over to where she crouched in the shadows next to the moonlit water bottle and my pile of horse fodder.

"It's all yours," she said, her face smooth. "I already ate."

Both of us seemed to be pretending that nothing had happened the day before.

"You sure you don't want seconds?" I asked wryly, then proceeded to wolf down the berries and mushrooms. I even savored the food bar, which tasted like it had more calories than the rest. "How many of these do we have left?" I asked around a mouthful, shooting glances at the sky even though I would probably hear any helicopters before I saw them.

"Four," Khaya said, then stood.

That was bad news, especially since I was still hungry. But I was more concerned by her indifferent tone.

I swallowed the last bite in a gulp. "Khaya, I—"

"Don't worry," she interrupted. "We don't have time. We need to go."

She was right.

Khaya folded the emergency blanket while I guzzled water. She repacked both it and the filter bottle once I'd emptied it. I snatched the pocketknife out of the backpack before she zipped it closed, with the intention of whittling a walking stick for easier trekking. When she tossed the pack over her shoulders, I tried to protest, but she silenced me with a lifted hand, tilting her head sideways.

Then she dropped her hand with a slight shrug. "I thought I heard something."

She started upstream without another word. She didn't even pause when her feet hit the shimmering black water, though I heard her long, slow exhale. I tugged a decent-looking stick out of the underbrush, one that actually looked like it didn't need any whittling, and followed her. Only by clenching my jaw until it creaked did I keep from shouting curses as I stepped in the stream.

"At least it's not going to rain on us," I said through gritted teeth, stabbing the stick in the water with more violence than necessary, as if I could somehow fight off the coldness gnawing at my feet.

"I wish it would," she said, ahead of me. "Low clouds give us more cover, and rain washes away tracks and smells. Luft might be behind this. He can manipulate air pressure over pretty large areas..." She trailed off, muttering to herself.

"Fine, *I'll* appreciate not being drenched and freezing... from the knees up."

"We won't be following streams for much longer." Khaya hefted the pack higher on her shoulders. "I studied the map before you woke up. We're working our way southeast, over a pass."

I waded faster with my walking stick and caught up to her. She might have been the only one who knew where we were going, but that didn't mean I always had to lag behind. Especially not while she was carrying the pack.

"We'll take one of these adjoining creeks—the next one on the left—and follow it upstream to the pass, which will drop us into a valley that will take us east into Switzerland. Oh, here's the creek."

I'd almost missed it; this one was hard to see even with the light of the moon. It was sandwiched by trees and narrower than the stream we were in, barely wide enough for us to walk through side-by-side. And the rocky bottom looked rougher—more like stairs with water running down them.

The climb had already been getting steeper, wearing on my worn legs. Now that there were no clouds, I could see the craggy hills in the moonlight, rising sharply on either side of the stream. We were miles into the mountainous terrain she'd called the Chablais Alps.

"Good," I said, trying to look at the bright side. "It'll be downhill into the valley after this."

"Actually, not good," Khaya said grimly. "The valley contains a major road heading back toward Eden City."

"Oh." The news was nearly enough to make me lose my monstrous appetite, reminding me that Lake Eden wasn't the only way out of the city; there were also dozens of highways through the hills. I hoped the roads would at least be less closely watched in France. It was no longer Eden City's territory, after all, even if they often acted like it was.

"We'll need to cut across the valley as fast as we can," Khaya continued. "We'll be safer on the other side. They likely won't expect us to have gotten that far. And once we're in the Swiss Alps, there won't be many roads for them to search for us on."

"And not much food," I said. "I don't know about you, but I can't live on berries."

Khaya continued as if I hadn't spoken. "And it will be more politically challenging for Eden City to send helicopters throughout *two* different countries ... though I wouldn't put it past—"

A howl cut the night air, rising downstream from us. It was followed by vicious barking.

For a second, we both stood frozen, the babbling creek and the barking dog making the only noise. Then Khaya was struggling toward the bank of the stream, getting herself out of the water as fast as she could.

"There's only one by the sound of it," she said, "so they're probably sending one dog up every creek." She held up a finger, testing the air. "It only smelled or heard us because we're upwind."

By the time I reached the bank I could hear it, splashing in the stream as it barreled toward us, snapping twigs and branches. The dog was gaining on us quickly. At least I couldn't hear any sound of an owner.

Khaya was looking more frantic than I'd ever seen her, giving voice to her racing thoughts while mine had lurched to a halt. "We can still lose whoever is following it. We're at a fork, and we passed quite a few along the way. Even if the dog doesn't come back, they'll have a hard time knowing which way we went."

"How the hell do we keep the dog from going back?" I

asked, glancing between her and the direction of the cacophony. It sounded more like a bear crashing through the forest. I raised the stick in my hands. While it made a good walking stick, it looked pretty flimsy as a club.

Khaya met my eyes, then grew still. "I don't know."

That was when the beast rounded a bend in the stream at full speed, growling and snarling. It was a German Shepherd, stocky and springy, white teeth gleaming in the moonlight. I turned my back to Khaya and brandished the stick at it as if I could fend it off.

I had to. It was our only hope.

The dog slid to a halt a few feet away from us on the bank, feet planted and hackles raised, its tail stiff and sticking straight out behind. The only part of it that moved was its quivering upper lip as it growled.

When I moved a step back, it went into a ferocious storm of barking that probably even the Gods could hear, so I lunged forward and took a swipe at it with the stick.

I thought it might back off and shut up for a second. It did one but not the other. It stopped barking and lunged at me, sinking its teeth into my right forearm. I almost didn't feel the pain at first—only pressure, hot and hard, and the stick fell from my numb hand. Then the dog jerked its head with me locked in its jaws, tearing deeper and yanking me to the ground. I heard my own shout of agony like it was someone else's. The dog kept whipping my arm back and forth even when it had me down, spattering me with my own blood. I swung blindly at its head with my left hand, my fist connecting with fur, but the dog didn't let go. I clawed at its nose and eyes but it would shake its head again, knocking away my hand and sending me down a red roller-coaster of pain where all I could do was yell and hang on.

At least it couldn't bark with its mouth full. And it couldn't move or dodge that well, glued to me as it was. I abandoned my forearm to its mouth and fumbled in my pocket with my left hand.

"Khaya, get the gun!" I shouted over my shoulder. "Shoot it, for the love of the Gods!"

When I didn't hear anything other than the snarling and my own gasps, I risked a glance over my shoulder and saw her standing, unmoving, with the pack in her hands. She hadn't opened it.

"I can't," she said, her eyes wide with fear.

I forgot Khaya and tried to open the pocketknife one-handed, pinching what I hoped was a blade and not a bottle opener, beating the rest of it against the ground in an attempt to spring it loose.

But then Khaya was on the dog's back, pouncing like a panther, cramming her fingers into its mouth. Its pink gums flashed as she peeled back the dog's lips and stabbed her index fingers into the hinge of its jaw, back into its throat. It made a gagging noise and couldn't keep hold of me, but then turned on Khaya, its teeth finding new purchase in her hand.

I seized the dog's neck with my freed arm, and when I squeezed, I felt pain like it was a tangible thing, as if the dog's teeth were still buried in my muscle. But I didn't think about it, didn't let my grip relax. I brought my left hand down over and over again, deep into the fur of its chest and throat, the blade of the pocketknife glinting first silver then red in the moonlight.

Snarling and biting became yelping and thrashing. But I didn't let go, not until the dog was gurgling and twitching in my arms. And only then did I stop stabbing.

I fell back on the bank of the stream, wet and burning and gasping. Everything hurt, and everywhere I was covered in blood. Mine or the dog's, it didn't matter—all I saw was Drey's blood, his shirt and stomach ripped and red like the dog's furry neck. I had managed to block out the memory until now. I rolled over and retched, lightning pain shooting up my arm when I moved.

"Don't, Tavin, don't vomit. It's okay," Khaya was saying, even though she sounded sick herself. She ignored her own bleeding hand as she groped around the unmoving dog's neck, unbuckling a thick, black collar. She twisted it around my walking stick and launched it downstream like a javelin. It splashed some distance away in the water, floated to the surface, and then sailed away.

"It likely had a tracking device," she said, turning back to me. "They can't know where we killed it or they'll know which fork in the stream we took."

"They'll know by this." I hauled myself to my knees and gestured drunkenly at the dog's corpse. My chest and arms were covered in scratches, my shirt torn in several places and looking black, not blue, through the blood and darkness. My hands were shaking violently.

Khaya shook her head and dropped down to the dog

again. "No, they won't." She twined her fingers in the blood-ied fur, and her sickened expression vanished as she began murmuring. She spoke in such a rush that I only caught part of the sequence:

"Richness, fertility, abundance, replication..."

The words sounded big, not in actual length but in concept—general, expansive, and inviting. I could hear the power in her voice—the Words. But I paid more attention to what she was doing, rather than what she was saying, when grass began to sprout all over the dog like new fur, and moss rose between the grass blades like downy fluff. Suddenly, the whole chest of the dog caved in under the new weight, send-ing out a wave of rot-filled air that almost made me gag again.

In less than a minute, there was only a mound of mossy soil and plants where the corpse had been. A trail of grass even grew toward and around me, drinking up the spilled blood, tickling against the hand that held me upright.

Now I felt cold rather than hot, and I was shaking more than ever.

Khaya was already kneeling at my side. She put a hand on my forehead, smoothing the hair out of my eyes. "Decay is part of the cycle of life, not death, contrary to what everyone says. Death is sterile."

I shied away, irrationally afraid she would turn me into a pile of fertilizer like the dog, hiding any evidence I had ever been there.

"I need to stop your bleeding," she said. "Unfortunately, I can't heal either of us more than that, or we won't have the stamina to cover the distance we need to go tonight."

Then she was speaking Words again, so low and quick I heard only scattered things like *stimulate, metabolize, mobilize, congeal.* She sounded less encouraging, more commanding than she'd been with the dog—directed, sharp as a doctor's scalpel. After all, she was filling in narrow scratches and bites in specific locations, not dissolving a body into the earth.

"Hmm," she said. "You were in shock too. But you should feel better. And your bleeding has stopped."

"Why can I understand you, now, when you speak the Words?" I asked. The world looked sharper around me, the bushes and pines dark and defined in the light of the moon. The sound of the stream rose behind me again, after it had gotten lost in the chaos. "I couldn't before."

"I usually speak them in Hebrew, but it seems fair to include you." Khaya helped me up, directing me into the stream.

Unfortunately, I felt the cold on my feet quite clearly, and even all the way up in my aching arm. It was as if my nerves were connected like a spider web—if one area was touched, I felt it everywhere else. I wasn't bleeding anymore, but the wound in my arm was deep and angry, a collection of jagged, red holes in my swollen skin.

"Why didn't you shoot the dog?" I asked.

"The noise would have been much louder than the barking," Khaya said.

"That wasn't why you didn't do it. You said you couldn't."

"I'm sorry." She stopped in the stream when we were submerged up to our knees. She sounded truly apologetic, but I didn't know if it was because of her inability to kill or what she said next. "We need to rinse off."

I knelt in the stream without hesitating, pressing my face in the water before I could change my mind and run. It was worse than dropping into the lake. My skin burned as if the Word of Fire had set me alight, and my lungs refused to work altogether. Even after I brought my head up and crouched on my knees, shuddering and gasping, it took me a few seconds to be able to see or hear again, or notice Khaya grabbing handfuls of sand and mud with her unbitten hand and scrubbing me everywhere she could reach. I hardly felt it. The pain was just another drop in the Tavin-sized bucket.

And then she was taking me by the hand and leading me on. Hurting all over as I did, her hand was the only one I would have let touch me. I wasn't even sure why, but I welcomed it. Anyone else's hand I would have bitten like a dog.

thirteen

We followed the steep creek higher into the mountains, and then I had exhaustion to compete with the pain and cold. I didn't know which one felt worse, but waiting to see which would win out in the end was the only thing keeping me going.

We didn't stop once that night, not even when we heard more barking in the distance and saw helicopters passing overhead, their enormous spotlights cutting great white swathes through the starry sky. None of them came near enough for us to need to hide, even though I began to wish they would, just for a rest. Every time I slipped, instinctively catching myself with my right arm, I felt like I was shattering. The only improvement came when we left the creek after it finally disappeared, but even that was hardly noticeable; by then, my feet had long gone numb.

The air grew so cold, I thought my sweat would freeze

on my skin. Snow glowed on the treeless, moonlit peaks looming on either side of us. All that kept me from collapsing was a combination of forward momentum and, ironically, gravity—the land had started to tip downhill. And then I saw it stretching down below us: a valley, threaded by a ribbon of moving lights in the darkness. Cars on a road.

It was funny to think I could simply flag down one of the cars heading west, get in, and be back in Eden City after a short, smooth ride. Or, not really funny at all.

After dashing across an open, brush-filled stretch of the mountain pass, we paused when we regained the tree line, stopping for a drink from the water bottle that Khaya had filled before we left the creek. Only crisp, stinging air had passed through my mouth all night—no food—so the filtered water felt like a balm on my raw throat, even if it was too cold.

"Gods," I croaked, which was about all I could say.

"We've hiked about fifteen miles through creeks and mountains," Khaya said, breathing hard. "Well done."

I didn't feel very accomplished. More like defeated.

"Here," she said, thrusting her good hand—now her right hand—into the backpack. She still had a white scar looping around the base of her thumb, but her left hand was looking as ugly as my arm. She pulled out a food bar. "Eat."

I ate mechanically, tasting it about as much as an engine tastes fuel. I barely remembered to stop halfway through and offer her the rest.

She only took a bite and said, "That's enough for me. But could you carry the backpack now?" She gave me a doubtful look.

I nodded dumbly, swallowing the rest of the food bar. I swung the bag on my back using my left arm, and Khaya helped me loop the straps over the right. Together, we seemed to make one whole, functional person, with her right hand and my left. The straps settled into my shoulder like tires in the grooves of a well-abused road, and the old aches from yesterday rose to join the general outcry.

Khaya started down the mountainside, looking a little wobbly. I tried to follow her, but I couldn't get my feet to move. It was as if they had put down roots with the trees.

"Talk to me," I said, pulling her up short. "Tell me a story or something." Only Drey had ever told me stories, but I imagined Khaya could do the same.

"I don't know any stories," Khaya said, glancing back at me, then at the ground. "I was never told any. My father ... well, he didn't have much opportunity."

"I'm sure you know all sorts of crap about the Gods—no, wait, I don't want to hear about them. So tell me about your father. You knew him, right?"

"Yes," Khaya said cautiously. "He died twelve years ago, but I knew him. He was born in the Athenaeum's hospital, like me, and lived in the Athenaeum his entire life—only forty years. When I turned five, he passed the Word on to me, like he was supposed to."

She started walking again and I followed her. My rubbery legs kept trying to fold on the downhill, but at least my feet moved when I told them to.

"You're seventeen, then," I said, doing some simple mental math. "So what was your father like?" We were about the same age, but somehow I doubted that Khaya's childhood had been anything like mine. Even if she'd had a real father and I'd had a strange adoptive one, growing up in the Athenaeum had probably been a lot weirder than the garage.

"His name was Hayat—'life' in Arabic," she said, weaving through the trees. "His donor mother was from Saudi Arabia. His father, my grandfather, had a French donor parent."

"Like Herio."

"Yes, but the French lost their place with the Words during my father's time. They'd showed too much weakness in the Second World War—or so Eden City thought. The Saudis had just discovered they held the world's largest reserves of oil, attracting enough attention to replace the French among the Words. But soon after my father turned five and succeeded his father, the Saudis felt confident enough to take part in the '73 oil crisis, refusing to sell oil to the West unless support was withdrawn from Israel. So what did Eden City do with the next generation of Words? They gave Israel the Word of Life."

"That's interesting," I lied, ducking under a branch, "but that's not really telling me anything about your father."

Khaya's steps faltered. "You're right. I'm not used to *really* talking about him. Most people don't ask about him as a person—only about the politics and power." She was quiet for a minute as she picked her way through a particularly bushy stretch of underbrush. "He was a nice man. We never lived together, but he was allowed to visit me from time to time. He always called me his little flower, even as he died to give me the Word."

Her voice was perfectly flat … a cover for her pain.

"That's so messed up," I muttered. Taking real families, kids who actually had parents, and then twisting and destroying them—that was almost as bad as all the world domination.

"What?" Khaya asked.

"Nothing," I said. But it wasn't nothing. What I'd said to Khaya in our ivy tent had been true: I really did want to hurt the Godspeakers now, and keep Khaya safe. Which was laughable, because what could I do to them? We were running and Khaya was the one protecting me. Though I supposed I'd done a decent job protecting her from the dog, even if I'd trashed myself in the process—and horrified her because I could kill when she couldn't.

Somebody had to do something against the Athenaeum. They seemed to do whatever they wanted, to whomever they wanted. They'd made Khaya into the embodiment of a battleground, by the sound of it, with an Israeli mother and a father of Saudi descent. Sure, she'd explained the political motivations behind the arrangement, but all I'd really understood was that the Athenaeum's harmful manipulations affected everything from the individual lives of the Words all the way up to the affairs of the greater world—even more so now that they were trying to replace the Words with automatons and take over the world. The thought would have made my stomach churn even if I hadn't known they were after me.

No wonder Drey no longer trusted them. Whatever he'd been doing for them, he had quit. And then the Word of Death punched a hole in his guts.

I wanted Khaya to keep talking, but I couldn't ask her to carry on about her father when thinking about Drey hurt me so much. I opened my mouth to tell her to talk about something else, anything she wanted, but she was already speaking.

"My father didn't tell me any stories, but he sometimes sang me a song, one without words. Which is nice, sometimes, when you're a Word."

She began to hum. Her voice was soft and light among the dense trees, surprisingly different from when she spoke—like when she laughed. The sound buoyed me, almost making me feel like I was floating along behind her.

It was the sweet carrot on the end of the string that kept me trotting after her in the dark, down the rest of the mountain. I wasn't even concerned we would be heard. The forest, which grew greener and warmer as the eastern sky began to lighten, felt like a magical world containing only the two of us, and her song was like a spell keeping the illusion alive.

I almost wished the mountain was taller so we could keep winding our way down. I didn't want the song to end.

But Khaya's voice cut off when the ground leveled out. We found ourselves standing at the edge of the trees, staring through the predawn light at a wide strip of highway lined with bramble-filled ditches.

"Those look thorny," I whispered, eyeing the snarled brambles.

"They're good cover," Khaya responded. Her voice was rough, ragged. She must have been singing for over an hour. "We won't have darkness for much longer."

It seemed like we'd had darkness forever. The last few

nights had stretched ages longer than I was used to in Eden City, where it lasted for precisely eight hours. There, dawn and dusk were quick affairs, bringing on full light or dark at the exact same time every day, with a relative suddenness and completeness that I hadn't seen mirrored in the outside world.

Of course, I thought. Because the outside world didn't have the Word of Darkness or Light.

Even at this early hour, cars rushed by every so often in a blur of headlights, and while we watched, no fewer than three vehicles with flashing red and blue lights streaked through the fleeing night.

"French police," Khaya said under her breath. "Their red and blue is like our green and yellow. Who knows how much the City Council has told the French government, so watch out for those colors."

After she seemed sure the highway held no other surprises, she walked alongside it in a parallel line, moving in a low crouch behind the wall of brambles until she found whatever she was looking for.

I shouldn't have been surprised. It was a stream, more like a rivulet, trickling down the foot of the mountain and into the mud of the ditch, twisting its way through the brambles until it eventually met the road.

"Water always makes a path," Khaya murmured, then began stepping along the watery ribbon as if walking a tightrope, keeping her head down. But eventually the tangle of branches closed in on all sides, forcing us lower and lower until we were inching along our elbows and stomachs in a muddy trough, stopping to hold our breath and nearly push our faces into the mud every time a car whistled by overhead.

I was so close behind Khaya that I didn't see the incline of the highway's shoulder until we'd reached it. And there, punching through the gravelly hill, crossing underneath the asphalt, was a culvert for the water to pass.

It looked about as wide as my shoulders—a narrow, dark, dank tunnel.

Khaya didn't hesitate, of course, as she wormed her way into the corrugated pipe. When I inched in after her, the sleeves of my T-shirt brushed the sides and the backpack scraped along the top. I wasn't claustrophobic, but even so, my breathing increased to a pant, sounding loud in the enclosed space. Barely into the pipe, with the highway vibrating over our heads, I lurched forward too quickly and lodged myself tight.

"Khaya," I whispered, my hand shooting out to grab her ankle—I couldn't even unfold my arm all the way. "I'm stuck!"

In place of her response, a car door slammed. The road was overhead, but the sound had come through the pipe. I craned my neck, turning from Khaya and the light ahead to the light behind, where the brambles at the pipe's mouth—just beyond my boots—were now flickering with hues of red and blue.

Another door slammed, and then footsteps crunched through the gravel of the highway shoulder, getting louder as they went.

Then a voice: "Je ne vois toujours pas pourquoi on fait ça."

"Ils ont dit de chercher dans les caniveaux, alors on cherche dans les caniveaux," said another gruff voice, both of them male.

"Ce n'est qu'un garçon."

I didn't know much French, but I knew the word *garçon*, since it had always been shouted at me by anyone who did speak French in Eden City. *Boy.*

They were looking for me.

I tried to wrench my arm around to reach the backpack. To reach what was inside.

"No!" Khaya hissed, as if she knew what I was doing. She started whispering, almost inaudibly at first, then louder and louder. I quit squirming to squeeze her ankle in warning, but she didn't stop. And then I heard scratching and squeaking behind us, as if something was moving in the culvert—something other than us. But it couldn't be the men; they were still too far away. I craned my neck again, but the light was too dim to make out anything—like it had been partially blotted out.

The steps froze. "Tu as entendu quelque chose?" one of them said.

The footsteps rushed closer, and falling gravel echoed from the mouth of the pipe. I jerked in panic, but I was wedged so tightly I couldn't flee *or* go for the gun.

Then a blinding beam of a flashlight illuminated the culvert. But it was broken now, blocked—Khaya had grown the brambles over the pipe to hide us.

There was rustling by my feet and a curse from one of the cops. The bushes were thorny, but not thorny enough.

"Eh!" There was a shout of surprise as a hand caught my ankle. I thrust backward with all my strength, kicking, and dislodged myself in the process. When my boot connected with something solid, a gruff voice shouted, "Arrêtez! Stop!"

I scrabbled at the zipper of the backpack. But Khaya was faster.

Her Words were more commanding than I'd ever heard them, echoing in the pipe and forcing me to cover my ears. The bushes responded—how could they not?—thrashing like an angry creature. I only had time to see the look of astonishment on one of the officer's faces before the branches caught him around the throat, dragging him to the ground and filling his mouth before he could shout.

"That will hold them," Khaya called. "Come on!"

It wasn't exactly a fast flight through the culvert—we were more like inchworms on the run. Khaya slid gracefully out of the other end, but I dragged myself free so quickly I scratched my dog-bitten arm, ripping off one of the fresh scabs, and then took a tumble into the thorny brambles filling the ditch along the opposite shoulder, adding yet another tear to my tattered, muddy shirt. But I didn't care.

After untangling ourselves from the hedge, we ran in a crouch, making it into the forest on the other side of the highway as the sun lit the sky a buttery blue. We slowed to a trot only after the highway had long vanished behind us, hidden behind layers of trees and hills.

"Gods," I panted alongside Khaya, barely able to talk and breathe at the same time. "That was close!"

"I almost couldn't do it in time," Khaya said, gasping. "It's difficult ... to direct the Word of Life to do something ... so unnatural."

We trekked in silence after that, both of us weighed down not only by our tiredness, but the truth about our escape: those cops, bound and gagged with brambles, would be found sooner or later, and the Athenaeum would know we'd been through there.

They would find us all the easier now.

I was more exhausted than ever after the surge of adrenaline dissipated. And with our nocturnal schedule, dawn felt like dusk, triggering an intense urge to hide away and sleep. Part of me knew we should get as far away as possible from the highway and hide. But another part of me almost didn't care if we were caught. Even surrendering—just getting it over with—almost seemed like it would be a relief.

I was about to ask if we could stop right as Khaya started humming again. It was as if the highway had only been an intermission in her performance, and now that she'd resumed, her voice was gentler and yet somehow stronger than a pair of hands, dragging my tired, aching body after her.

Not yet, her song seemed to tell me.

"Okay," I mumbled, so exhausted I was responding to what hadn't even been said.

And I followed her. I could follow that voice to the ends of the earth, even if my legs were worn down to stumps. Maybe even off a cliff. I'd as good as done that already, throwing my life into a tumbling dive at her request, without knowing when or where or how I would land.

Okay, I'd said in response to her written message—*HELP ME*—before I'd ever even spoken to her. *Okay.*

And I was still saying that.

Hours later … I wasn't entirely sure how long … Khaya stumbled up against a tree, sagging into it with a sigh of relief. It took me a second, after blinking away the seeming enchantment of her song, to notice that we were in a tight cluster of trees. They looked like they'd been competing for space. There wasn't even much underbrush between them, where they'd crowded out the sun. The ground in the center was dry, but not exactly hidden.

"Finally," Khaya said. "I've been looking for something like this."

"What do you mean?" My voice rasped like a rusty hinge in need of greasing. Khaya sounded nearly as bad.

She crouched between two trees, her hands feeling along the bark of each. "We'll be safe inside."

I still wasn't sure what she meant until she said a few words in Hebrew—forgetting, probably in her tiredness, that she said she would speak in English—and the trunks merged between her hands, not violently, but as if they had grown together naturally over a period of years and years. Then all the trunks from maybe six trees swirled around each other, becoming one in a matter of seconds, save for a crack big enough for Khaya to stick her head through.

"It's hollow," I said. The perfect hideout. A tree in a forest of trees.

"Come inside." She slipped through the crack, vanishing within.

Like the culvert, the narrow gap in the tree squeezed me more than Khaya, but I made it through by shoving the backpack in first. It was cramped inside, with a low ceiling tapering at the top like a conical hat. But there would be enough room for us to curl next each other, if not stretch out, on a carpet of soft, rotten leaves and fragrant earth. Khaya was already digging the emergency blanket out of the pack.

The tree grew warmer inside, especially after Khaya sealed the crack from the bottom up, closing the wood like a zipper and leaving only a small hole for air at the top. Our clothes had dried enough for us to keep them on, but lying next to her somehow felt more intimate this time. Our closeness was less the result of a need for survival and more a human desire to be near someone.

Or at least that was how I felt as I wrapped my injured arm around her and buried my face in her hair. I wouldn't have been brave enough to touch her if I hadn't been too tired to think about it. It just happened. And Khaya didn't push me away.

"I'm sorry," she said, halting my slow drift into oblivion.

"For what?" I murmured.

"Ruining your life," she said, as if she'd heard my thoughts in the forest. At least, I was pretty sure I hadn't said them out loud in my exhaustion. "I haven't apologized yet, and you probably think I take you for granted, but—"

"Shh," I hushed her. "It was my decision to help you. It's not your fault."

It *had* been my decision, and I'd been making it again

and again since I'd met her. And every time, it got easier and easier to make.

"I'm sorry you had to use the Words to … you know," I said. I'd seen the look on her face after she'd gagged the cops—she hadn't wanted to, but she'd done it to keep me from using the gun.

"I've never used the Word of Life like that before," Khaya said softly.

"Why not? You have the power." It definitely would have helped during the dog attack.

"Because then the Word just becomes a weapon—a tool for threatening others. A gun is a threat. The police are a threat. Even muscles can be a threat." She brushed my arm. "If all being powerful means is that you can threaten other people with violence to get what you want, I don't want that power. I want no part of it."

I didn't have the energy to argue … assuming there was anything I could argue. "Then, if it's no trouble, could I get some of the non-violent Words?"

I fell asleep to her murmuring Words of healing that didn't have a chance to take effect before I was out.

It seemed as if I had only been asleep for seconds when I felt Khaya shaking my shoulder, wrenching me out of a deep, dreamless slumber.

"Tavin, *wake up!*" she shouted, as if she'd been at it for a while. "There's a fire!"

I realized I was coughing. I had no idea how long I'd been asleep. Hardly anything was visible in the dark interior of the tree, but all around, there was the smell of burning wood.

fourteen

The air hole only provided a pinpoint of light, so Khaya turned on the flashlight and shined it around the inside of the tree. Smoke was seeping through the bark and curling up to drift against the conical ceiling. She ran her hands along the wall of the trunk while I stuffed the emergency blanket in the pack and threw it over my shoulders. My arm no longer hurt. The swelling had gone down and the teeth marks were only ridges of pink flesh, but there wasn't time to appreciate it.

"This side is hot!" Khaya said, leaping to the opposite side. She shouted some Words and the tree trunk parted before her like a curtain. Both of us went tumbling out.

Instead of the fresh air I'd been hoping for outside, smoke surrounded us, sunlight filtering through the sooty haze. And a bright red-orange glow. My first thought had been that someone had managed to track us to this exact spot and was burning us out of our tree. But instead of a small fire at the base of our trunk, a solid wall of flame blocked the way we'd come, stretching as far as I could see, bending in a ring that must have nearly encircled the forest. Even as we both watched in horror, the fire gained a few feet of ground, almost reaching the backside of our tree, which was already sizzling and smoking.

I backed away, but Khaya only stood, coughing and staring through red, watery eyes.

"They're flushing us out," she said. "And burning down a forest to do it." Her eyes weren't just watering, like mine. She was crying. "All these trees . . . how could you, Agonya?"

The Word of Fire.

"Khaya, come on!" I shouted, seizing her arm. The burning forest wasn't something to callously ignore—it was actually hard to ignore—but now wasn't the time to weep over dying trees when we were about to die ourselves. "We've got to run!"

I hauled her away without waiting. Soon, she no longer resisted and ran as fast as me. And we had to run fast. The fire spread like a tidal wave, spilling heat and flame behind us. If we tried to cut too far to either side, the wall closed in on us, forcing us back the other way.

"They're herding us," Khaya said.

A particularly wracking bout of coughing slowed me for a few seconds, but I picked up the pace again, leaping over fallen logs that wavered in the heat. "Where?"

"Probably to water, so Pavati—the Word of Water—can help protect their group. A fire this size would be difficult for Agonya to control. Fire is one of the hardest Words to manage."

So it wasn't only the Athenaeum's police squad hunting us, but the Words themselves. At least two, by the sound of it: Pavati and Agonya, Water and Fire. And probably Luft, the Word of Air, since he'd been modifying the weather, and why not Herio, too? We were being herded into a trap more deadly than the blaze.

But we had no choice. Obviously, neither of us wanted to burn to death just to avoid greater danger, and so we kept running.

Khaya was right—we did meet water. We stumbled out of the trees and down a hill into a small valley, where we found ourselves facing a stream. But no one was there and the fire was burning on the other side, so we were forced to turn and run along the bank, upstream. At least the bank was smooth and firm, making the going much easier than it had been those first couple of nights. We couldn't afford to trip, not just to keep ahead of the flames, but also the smoke, which burned my throat and lungs with each gasping breath. There wasn't even time to think.

Several times, another stream joined ours, but we could never follow them—the fire was burning so close on either side of each new creek that it nearly bridged the gap. So we passed them, running, until the walls of our valley rose steeply on either side, leaving us in a ravine with only one way to go: forward. At least the smoke was better down beneath the blaze, even if the terrain was tightening around us like a noose.

For once my legs were holding up to the strain, but my lungs were tight and burning like lumps of hot coal in my chest. I wasn't fit for marathons, as I'd told Khaya earlier. From my best estimation, we'd been running for over five miles, and I was carrying the backpack. Never mind the smoke. But I didn't need to say anything to Khaya. She probably heard it in my raspy breathing. Her hand found my shoulder, and then a lightning surge of energy, like a shot of adrenalin, crackled along my limbs and expanded my lungs. She wasn't taking it easy this time. Being depleted later on obviously wasn't an issue anymore.

Because later on I would probably be dead.

With my newfound vigor, I flipped the pack around, slowing my stride just enough to fall behind Khaya. My fingers dug through emergency supplies, down into the depths of the bag, until they felt what they were seeking: cold metal through plastic.

I had just re-zipped the backpack when Khaya glanced back, motioning breathlessly for me to keep up. She hadn't seen what I had stuffed into the back of my pants.

The stream eventually shrank into its source: a chain of ponds that we skirted, finding another stream spilling out the opposite end. And now we were running downstream through the gully, downhill and picking up speed.

As we burst out of the ravine to find a lake spreading out in front of us, I wondered if they'd planned it this way, forcing us to gain momentum to our inevitable end.

A group of people stood on the shore of the lake, the

water like a gray slate under the hazy sky. Khaya and I staggered to a halt, both of us bending over to lean on our knees, gasping uncontrollably. I kept one hand on my lower back as if it hurt. But really, I was keeping ahold of something through my shirt.

None of the people stepped forward, as if they had all the time in the world. We had nowhere else to go, after all, with the raging inferno burning nearly up to the lakeside, the trees like kindling. They could wait for us to catch our breath.

I took quick stock of the gathering through squinting, itchy eyes. It wasn't what I had been expecting. It was worse. Herio was definitely there, along with four other Words, not three. The guys were shirtless except for Herio, who was fully clothed in black, and the girls wore halter tops that left the Words exposed on their backs, able to be read. I recognized the Word of Earth, Tu, with his black hair and East Asian features, standing next to Pavati, the Word of Water, long braids sweeping over her smooth, dark-skinned shoulders. Luft and Agonya, the Words of Air and Fire, stood stiffly beyond them, as pale as ever. Luft's blond hair stirred in the breeze.

All of them were so good-looking it was creepy. I would have thought they were vain idiots showing off their bodies if I didn't know better.

Dr. Swanson and four other suits—two men and two women—stood behind the Words. Men with guns stood on either side of them, making over a dozen in all. The guns were trained on us.

Dr. Swanson raised his hand in greeting while Khaya and I stumbled closer, the smoke-filtered sunlight glinting feebly off of a gold ring on his finger. His gray-streaked hair and gray suit looked as neat as before. I wondered if he ever wore anything but gray, or if Herio wore anything but black.

My thoughts were running loose. But the rest of my body was tense and focused, my hand held ready behind my back.

"Khaya," Dr. Swanson said. "Tavin." He spoke my name as if I were a longtime acquaintance he was meeting for lunch.

Neither Khaya nor I responded. She wasn't even looking at Swanson. She was staring in icy fury at Agonya, who looked stunning with her high cheekbones and light brown hair drawn back in a tight bun. Now that we were closer, I noticed that both Agonya's hair and the exposed skin around her halter-top were shining, as if she had been greased.

"A Godspeaker didn't even force you to make this fire," Khaya said. "You don't have anyone but yourself to blame."

Agonya didn't look at her, only stared in concentration over our heads at the fire swallowing the world, though her eyes narrowed. It was probably my imagination, but the heat at our backs seemed to rage hotter. My skin felt like it was about to crack it was so dry, and I realized what Agonya's grease was: a heat-resistant moisturizer for someone who played with fire all the time.

"Agonya is a patriot," Dr. Swanson said. "She doesn't need to be forced to aid her country." He didn't acknowledge the middle-aged woman standing right behind Agonya, who was obviously a Godspeaker ready to step in and take control at a moment's notice.

Herio was standing at Dr. Swanson's elbow like a trained attack dog. He seemed to have no problems killing without a

Godspeaker to force him. I kept my sight locked on him for the most part, as though he were a poisonous snake among the group, ready to strike—a snake nearly as tall as me, with dark brown hair falling in his eyes. The eyes were what gave him away as a killer.

"A patriot," Khaya said, raw emotion shaking her voice. "And yet you'll replace her with an automaton as soon as you get the chance!" She turned from Agonya and Luft, whose perfectly square jaw was clenched as he, too, focused on the fire, to the other pair of Words. Pavati and Tu glanced at each other but didn't say anything. "That's why I ran—that's what they're doing! Cruithear made bodies, and they're going to replace us—"

"Hush, Khaya," Dr. Swanson said, signaling two of the men with guns on his right. Their focus sharpened and they took closer aim at Khaya. It didn't make sense that they'd just kill her, destroy one of the Words they'd been so desperately trying to recover, but it wasn't the time to ask questions.

"Let's not be uncivilized about this," Swanson continued. "But if you insist on spreading lies, then I'll be forced to—"

He broke off as I whipped the hidden object out from behind my back and pointed it between his eyes.

"No. If you hurt her," I said, keeping his head within the sight of the black handgun, "I'll be forced to blow your brains out."

Silence fell over the group. Most of them only stared, tense and unmoving. Khaya looked at me as if she'd never seen me before, but I'd expected that. Herio had a smile quirking the corner of his mouth. Dr. Swanson folded his arms as if he was merely disappointed.

"Obviously Khaya's lies have gotten to you, Tavin, if you're pointing that at me," he said. "But it's not entirely her fault if she didn't tell you the truth, because she doesn't know all of it herself. Drop the gun and perhaps we can talk."

"You don't want to talk; you want to kill us," I said, my arm unwavering. I had never shot a gun before, but it didn't seem so difficult. "And you pointed guns at us first, so how about you dropping yours first?"

"Tavin, I don't want to kill either of you. Nothing could be further from my thoughts." A vague smile touched Dr. Swanson's face just as it vanished from Herio's—Herio definitely wanted to kill us. "The guns aren't loaded with bullets, but tranquilizer darts. I will put you both under if I have to, but it would do well for you to come back voluntarily rather than subdued. It will be a more convincing argument against those calling for your blood... proof that this is all just a big misunderstanding."

"A *misunderstanding*?" I spat. "After what you did to Drey?"

"Drey?" Swanson blinked. "Ah, yes, Andre. He must have given you that gun and other supplies, though not possibly enough to sustain you for long." He looked us both over, almost with consideration. "I'm sure you're hungry. Come home, both of you. We can resolve this peacefully if you just—"

"Peacefully, my ass!" His use of the name *Andre* and even the word *home* threw me, especially since he was talking to both me and Khaya—as if he knew where I belonged, too. I forced myself to refocus. "If you don't want to hurt us, then why is Herio here?"

"Merely to encourage cooperation—" Swanson began.

I nodded at the gun I held. "Do I look encouraged?"

"—from the French," he finished, giving me a slight frown, as if he found my interruptions rude. Or maybe it was because of the gun I was pointing at him, though he hadn't seemed to mind much so far. "Herio is quite useful when it comes to intimidation, and he's France's representative among the Words. They didn't like the idea of us using fire in their forest to retrieve you, but with his presence, they came around."

"I'll kill him before he can kill me," I said, turning the gun on Herio. "I'll kill him like he killed my dad. I've already put down one of your dogs, so this shouldn't be much different."

Herio took a step forward—silent, swift, and smooth, like I'd always imagined Death would move. My finger twitched on the trigger but Dr. Swanson put a hand on Herio's shoulder, stopping him in his tracks.

When I realized I'd very nearly shot someone, tingles erupted across my scalp and raced down my spine, raising bumps on my scarred, dirt-smudged arm. My heart was pounding as if Khaya had given me another jolt of energy.

"Tavin, Tavin," Swanson said in a soothing tone, giving Herio a hard look. "No one wants to kill you. I wish we could talk more privately, but if you insist upon now...Luft?"

The Word of Air glanced away from the fire long enough

to nod at Swanson, then started muttering in what sounded like German. Swanson walked toward us, ignoring the gun now aimed at his heart, until he was only five feet away. The tingles had spread into my throat, giving me a funny taste in the back of my mouth, and everything was bright and loud, from the sunlight glinting in his hair to the dry lakeshore grass rustling around his shiny leather shoes. My hand was shaking.

Luft's Words fell silent even though his lips were still moving. My ears popped, like I'd undergone a rapid change in elevation. I glanced around in alarm, but my smoke-streaked surroundings hadn't changed. Khaya put a hand on my shoulder, making me jump a second time. It was the same calming gesture Swanson had given Herio, his attack dog, but at least she was no longer looking at me like I was a monster. She stood close, her dark eyes intent on him.

"Relax, Tavin," she murmured. "It's only the air pressure."

"One of Luft's little tricks," Swanson said, removing an earpiece and dropping it into the breast pocket of his gray jacket. "Now no one can hear us. Not even Luft."

But Herio could. He'd followed Swanson as silently as a shadow. His jaw twitched, as if popping his ears when he crossed what must have been the strange sound barrier. I wondered if Swanson knew he was taking part in our little gathering.

We might have been standing in the open air on the shore of the lake, surrounded by others, but the four of us were essentially alone together. And two of the four were the very last people in the world I wanted to be alone with.

Pavati and Tu watched Herio, then looked at each other

again, holding one another's gaze for longer than before. They still didn't say anything. Not that I could have heard them if they had, from within our invisible bubble.

"You must know, Tavin," Swanson said, his back to everyone else, his eyes on me, "I've only ever wanted what was best for you. I was trying to look out for you in the Athenaeum, to reach out to you. This man you call Drey Barnes—Andre Bernstein—is not your father. I know this because he used to work for me...then against me."

"Because you're evil," I spat, shaken after hearing Drey's other name again, one I'd never known. And it was likely his true name. I'd always known the last name he'd given me wasn't really mine, but now I knew it wasn't his, either. It wasn't even real.

Swanson shook his head, his eyes going strangely soft. "No, Tavin. Not because I'm evil. Because I'm your father."

Herio looked as if someone had emptied a trash can of rotting fish over his head. I hadn't even known his cold, murderous face could make an expression of such horrified shock.

Mine must have looked about the same.

Khaya gasped, but I didn't even glance at her. All I could do was stare at Dr. Swanson as the world rocked around me, my blasted mind able to hold only one thought:

No, no, no, no...

I searched his features frantically for proof. His eyes were brown, like mine. His hair might have been like mine without the gray and with more length. He was tall and broad-shouldered. But his skin was lighter; pale, even. Herio could make a stronger claim to be my father, in spite of his youth and better looks.

But what if Swanson was telling the truth?

The gun swayed in my grip, and I wondered if I was going to pass out. Then Khaya squeezed my shoulder and I realized my unsteadiness wasn't entirely my fault. The people outside the bubble were running, their mouths open in silent shouts. The earth had started vibrating.

Swanson continued talking, too focused on me to notice. "Another misconception you have about Andre is that he is dead. There is still a chance for you to—" But then he felt it. His eyes widened and he turned. "Tu, no—!" His shout died, his hands going to his throat as if he was choking. Herio's hands shot to his throat at the same time, his eyes narrowing.

"What?" I cried. "What do you mean? Drey is—"

A half second later, the earth erupted beneath our feet. Khaya and I were thrown back, away from Swanson and Herio, who tumbled to the ground and were swallowed by heaving dirt.

Tu and Pavati were the only ones still standing. Tu chanted in time with the tossing earth, as if his voice was the cause. I realized, stupidly late, that of course it was the cause—he was the Word of Earth. Half the guards had lost their guns, and all were on their hands and knees. Agonya and Luft were down like the others, half-buried in dirt.

"Go!" Pavati shrieked, her braids whipping as she spun and raised a hand toward the lake. "Run!" It was almost like she was pointing and reaching at the same time, and she began chanting, herself.

Khaya yanked me to my feet, my head spinning and ears ringing, and launched into motion, dragging me along behind her. I crammed the gun in the backpack as we ran, stuffing it into a plastic bag just as we reached the water.

Something weird was happening in the lake. A huge hole had opened in the surface, twisting down and inward. Basically, a giant whirlpool the size of a parking lot had appeared out of nowhere. Khaya kept tugging me in its direction even after we began wading, ripples from the disturbance crashing into us like ocean waves. The coldness was almost welcome after the heat, but I didn't imagine we were going for a refreshing dip.

"Khaya, what are we—?"

"Swim!" she shouted, tugging me under right as the air started lashing and howling like a hurricane. Luft's voice had risen with the wind to a volume that matched the Word of Earth's—and then the water drowned it out.

The world beneath the surface of the lake was calm and quiet in comparison, though I felt the pull of the whirlpool sucking us in. I wasn't calm. Unlike the last time Khaya had yanked me underwater, I hadn't gotten a deep breath before-hand. And yet—just like last time—she held on to me with viselike grip, dragging me into the murky blue-green depths where long strands of seaweed stretched up toward the dis-tant sunlight like reaching fingers.

It only took about ten seconds before I was no longer kicking with her but against her, my hands on her wrist, scrab-bling to dislodge her fingers. But her small hand was like steel, twisted in my shirt, and the backpack sank me like a stone.

My clothes and shoes weren't helping either. With the tug of the whirlpool, I wouldn't have made it to the surface even if Khaya wasn't holding me down. But that didn't stop me from trying. I wrenched on her hand, and the only reason I didn't jerk harder was because I didn't want to break her fingers.

She was drowning me and I didn't want to hurt her. Still, my movements were getting more violent, out of control.

It was then that she pulled up, facing me in the rippling aquamarine shadows. Her dark waves of hair floated around her face like green-black seaweed. I thought she would kick for the surface with me now, or maybe breathe air into my mouth in one of those fairytale moments, saving my life with a kiss.

Instead, she punched me in the stomach, a quick, sharp jab in my diaphragm, and my remaining air left me in a rush of bubbles.

I immediately inhaled. My lungs burned as if I'd breathed in acid, and I coughed and wretched in muffled silence, squeezing Khaya frantically, only to breathe in more water. Pain and panic blinded me. I thrashed to get free of it all, but the entire world had turned against me—along with her—to become only pressing, suffocating death.

I'd said I would probably follow her off a cliff, but I never imagined she would actually kill me.

I had nowhere to go. My movements became sluggish. Then my hand only floated in front of me, seeming disconnected, as if it was no longer a part of my body. I observed the miniscule bubbles trapped in the hairs of my forearm, then lifted my heavy eyes, which no longer seemed to belong to me either, to peer out through drifting brown hair—maybe my hair at one time.

Khaya's face was there in front of me, watching me without expression. And then I saw nothing at all.

fifteen

The first thing I felt was my lips, mostly because something soft was pressing against them, and I remembered a dream I'd had of falling endlessly with Khaya kissing me.

This felt exactly the same.

Except this time I landed—hard. Or maybe I only became conscious of my back, cold and wet and pressed against a lumpy surface. I was sprawled on the ground and my lungs were filled with bright-hot pain like I'd inhaled molten lava.

I opened my eyes. Khaya's face was inches from mine. Her hair dripped on me as she pulled away, her thick eyelashes clinging together in clumps. She wiped a hand across her wet lips.

"Oh, thank the Gods. Tavin?"

I opened my mouth to say something and water came out like I was a sculpture in a fountain—volumes of it. I flung myself over just in time to avoid shooting Khaya with the force of a fire hose and vomited again and again with a violence I had never felt before, my back arching and the blood vessels in my eyes feeling as if they would burst from the pressure. It was like the hand of one of the Gods was squeezing me until every drop of liquid was out of my lungs.

Which was probably a good thing, since I wasn't able to take a full breath until then. My first lungful of air was both the sweetest and the most painful thing I'd ever tasted. I lay on my stomach and gasped breath after fiery breath, drinking in beautiful air like I'd apparently drunk the lake. My chest sounded like a ripsaw as it rose and fell.

"Tavin?" Khaya said, hovering somewhere above me. "Talk to me. How do you feel?"

"I—" I coughed long and excruciatingly hard, spitting up more water and half-expecting to see blood. "I feel like shit."

She sighed in relief. "At least you're alive now."

"You mean I wasn't?" I coughed again, rolling on my side and cringing, then stared at her with one stinging eye. "You—you drowned me." The words managed to sound incredulous, hurt, and royally pissed off all at once, and that was after making their way through my ragged throat. I was surprised they were even intelligible.

"Yes. Your heart had stopped beating by the time I got you here. I ... " She paused, her normally warm skin going nearly pale under its wet sheen. Her voice was flat. "I killed you. You're the first living thing I've ever intentionally killed."

I sure felt like I'd died. Every part of my body ached. I

twitched my pinky just to be positive, and sure enough, it ached, too. But Khaya looked so vulnerable that I couldn't say all the things I really wanted to say, which would have involved a lot of shouting and swearing.

"Come on," I croaked. "Not even a single spider, ever?"

She frowned down at me. "I once smashed a wasp that stung me, but it was a reflex. You're definitely the first person I've killed."

Her frown was better than her blank look, which was always a mask for something terrible.

"That's one more person than me. Not a good record for the Word of Life." I flopped on my back as her frown deepened. "Though I almost beat you to it by the lake there."

The lake, where I'd almost pulled the trigger on Herio. Where Swanson had said he was my father, and that Drey was...oh, Gods, Drey. Could he really be alive, and I'd just left him?

The strangeness of my surroundings dragged my weary mind back to the present. I didn't resist, since too many things had happened that I wouldn't—*couldn't*—think about, not yet. "Where the hell are we, anyway?"

Everything was dark blue and green, like I was looking through the lenses of thick sunglasses, and the ground was hard and uneven underneath me. The light was too dim to see far, but it appeared I was lying in a dry riverbed. But that didn't make sense, since the stones covering the ground were wet and slimy. And now that I looked closer, the darkness around me seemed to be moving.

"On the bottom of the lake," Khaya said, as if it were an

everyday place to be. "With that whirlpool, Pavati opened a space in the water for us to hide, trapping air down here for us to breathe."

The bottom of the lake. So the dark, bubblelike wall that looked like shifting glass was actually a billion gallons of water held over our heads by a single girl. I was too tired and sore to be properly amazed or terrified.

"Pavati," I said, picturing the tall girl with braids. "The Word of Water."

"Yes, and you saw what Tu, the Word of Earth, did. It was too much for me to hope—but they helped us. I don't know if they got free themselves. They still had their monitor bracelets on." She looked at me, anxious. "I'm so sorry, Tavin. I had to get the two of us down here or else we would have been captured. I knew I could revive you if you drowned, but I wouldn't have been able to do anything if we were caught. And then you were fighting me so much, we both would have drowned if I hadn't hit you. Please forgive me."

"Interesting way to save someone, killing them." I looked into her wide dark eyes, as liquid and shimmering as everything else around us. I could drown in them as easily as in the lake, but I couldn't let myself, not right now. It was time to face the truth. "Khaya, I have to go back."

She blinked at me. "You must be delirious."

"Drey might be alive. If there's even the slightest possibility he is, I have to—"

"Do what, Tavin? What can you do?" She rode over whatever argument I was about to make. "No, listen to me. Swanson could be lying about Drey, but even if he's not... once

Herio touches someone to kill them, things are set in motion to an inevitable end. *The* end. He can kill instantly or by increments. You can't do anything to stop it."

Khaya could. But she couldn't go back; I knew that. Drey wouldn't have wanted it either. I could go by myself, though without her I was worthless. And yet I had to do *something*. Even if it meant I only sat by Drey's bedside while he died. At least I'd have a second chance to tell him how much he meant to me.

Khaya must have seen the desperate determination in my face, because she leaned over me and smoothed my wet hair back from my forehead. "But a cure to the Word of Death exists. I know about it. My father helped create it, instilling a carrier elixir with the Word of Life. I didn't recognize the name Drey Barnes, but I *have* heard of a man named Andre Bernstein. He used to work with my father, under Swanson, designing the cure. He would have had access to it, and it seems he was so well prepared in every other way ... do you think Drey might have hidden a vial of it?"

"The address he gave me." It was a slim chance, but it was a chance. "He told me I had to get there for a reason. He might have stashed a cure there, and I could bring it to him." It seemed too good to even be possible, but Khaya nodded as if it was, giving me hope, hovering over me, her lips so close ... and something else occurred to me. "Did you kiss me?" I asked abruptly.

She sat back, looking startled. "It's called mouth-to-mouth resuscitation. I used Words to jump-start your heart, but then your lungs still needed help to—"

"Not right now. I mean earlier," I interrupted. "The first night we slept next to each other."

Her lips had felt the same as they had in my "dream"—exactly the same, even if the circumstances were radically different. I couldn't have imagined them with such accuracy the first time around.

Her eyes widened.

"You did, didn't you?" I sat up and then regretted it. My back muscles screamed in protest and my head spun. I clapped a hand to my forehead, as if I could hold it steady, and propped myself up with my other hand, glaring at her from under my arm. "And all this time I've felt guilty for thinking I dreamt it!"

Khaya looked away, studying an algae-covered rock that had a wormlike creature wriggling along it. A blush rose in her cheeks, warming her skin again.

"Why? Why did you do it?" I didn't pause to consider how absurd I sounded.

But Khaya did. "I just drowned you, and you're demanding to know why I *kissed* you?"

Maybe I was so focused on this because I couldn't be mad at her for drowning me; I couldn't think about what Swanson had said; I couldn't do anything to save Drey right this second. Whatever the reason, I persisted. "When you did it, you said we were even. So was it only to get me back for the whole godspeaking thing? Tell me—and you owe me the truth, because we're sure as hell *not* even now."

She didn't look up. "I wanted to see what it was like. I'd never kissed anyone before. One of the Godspeakers kissed me once, when he was using me to godspeak. A young, *promising* guy," she said with a grimace. "But I hardly felt it, and I complained to Dr. Swanson afterwards. He fired him." She hesitated. "The Words aren't allowed to interact with anyone like that, even if we want to. Ever. So I wanted to try. With you." Her voice had dropped to a whisper.

She looked smaller and more lost than ever, worse off than the little creature on the rock whose lake had just vanished.

"Oh." All of my righteous indignity left me in a breath, as if she'd punched me again. I glanced away, then back at her. "Want to try again?"

She inhaled sharply. Her eyes shot to me, and she wore an expression that was more than shocked—furious, maybe.

Maybe terrified.

I didn't know what to say for about three beats of my pounding heart, astounded by the brain-addled audacity of my own suggestion.

But then she pounced on me like she had the dog. I almost thought she was going to strangle me until her hands seized my face and her lips met mine with breathless desperation.

It was nearly enough to stop my newly restarted heart. Dizziness burst in my skull like a fireworks finale, and not because she'd jostled my head. The whole world now revolved around the place where our lips and tongues met. I couldn't control myself. My body was orbiting around her, twisting, following her to the ground.

It took me a moment to realize I'd flattened her beneath me. Or maybe she'd yanked me on top of her.

She froze underneath my weight. I pressed off, holding myself above her. Maybe I'd scared her. Or maybe the rocks were jabbing her in the back. But after only a second's hesitation, she seized handfuls of my shirt and dragged me back down, biting my lip so hard it was almost painful.

Deep, full-throated laughter burst over us, dousing the heat coursing through my veins as if the lake had come down on top of us.

"Well, well, well. I don't blame you, Khaya. I can't wait to get some action, either—but with this guy?"

Khaya jerked away from me and was on her feet before I could even haul myself to my knees. Once up, she didn't move, only glared. I was ready to fly off the ground and tackle whoever had interrupted the best moment of my life—and insulted me on top of that—never mind how much my body hurt.

But then I realized I was staring at the Word of Earth.

sixteen

Tu had a smooth face so handsome it was no wonder it was plastered on so many billboards in Eden City. His straight black hair was tied in a high ponytail, but no one could possibly think it looked girly due to the sheer size of his shoulders and arms, made especially obvious by his lack of a shirt. Maybe he bench-pressed boulders in his free time at the Athenaeum. He was stocky but still taller than I expected. His dark eyes glinted at me with a mocking light as he glanced from Khaya back to me. "I mean, no offense, man, but she's a little out of your league."

The urge to attack him arose again, in spite of the fact that he was the Word of Earth. It was strange: before the last few days, I'd hardly had a violent impulse in my life. But since then, I'd stabbed a dog to death and nearly shot someone, and now I wanted to pound the smirk off this guy's face. Maybe being chased, bitten, and drowned was having an effect on me. Never mind that I wanted to keep kissing Khaya almost more than I wanted to keep breathing—almost—and this bastard had just scared her away by telling a truth I didn't care to hear:

She *was* out of my league.

I opened my mouth but Khaya spoke over me. Which was probably for the best.

"He's saved me more than once, Tu, which means he's saved *you*," she said, folding her arms across her chest. "Be grateful."

Even though Khaya was shorter, dirtier, and scruffier than Tu, he took a step back after meeting her stare. He must have known better than to underestimate her. But he still threw out a muscled arm, gesturing at me in indignation. "What do you mean, he saved me? I just saved him! If you want to repay him like that for helping you, suit yourself, but don't expect me to pucker up—"

"Tu," said a female voice. "Do me a favor and shut the hell up instead." The Word of Water walked up from behind him and held out a hand to me. Her face had an angular, carved quality to it, and I couldn't place where her donor parent might have come from. "My name is Pavati. Nice to meet you."

"Tavin," I said, taking her hand. Her grip was alarmingly strong as she pulled me to my feet. I wasn't exactly light.

She was only a couple of inches shorter than me and an inch or so taller than Tu, which put her at nearly six feet. All of us towered over Khaya, who looked uncomfortable as she stood between the three of us.

I wanted to get moving. If there was any chance that Drey was alive and I could get him a cure for the Word of Death,

I had to go for it. But that didn't change the fact that I was at the bottom of a lake, dependent on either Pavati or Tu to get me out. I couldn't start making demands right after they'd already helped us. Besides, I didn't think I had the strength to move very far.

"Nice," I said, glancing at the curved walls of water for something to say. "I imagine lakes are heavy."

Pavati grinned, a display of startlingly white teeth that sculpted her already beautiful face into something breathtaking. "It's not hard. I actually used the weight of the water to keep the air trapped. The air wants to rise, so I'm sort of leaning on the lake rather than lifting, which is a lot easier."

"Definitely," I said, as if I had any idea what she was talking about.

"How did you even get down here without being followed?" Khaya asked, shooting me a look that made me hope I hadn't been staring at Pavati. "Shouldn't Luft be sucking the air out of here and suffocating us all? Oh—your monitors are gone!"

She seized Pavati's wrist and turned over her hand. It was unmarked. No split-second thumb-chopping had occurred with either Pavati or Tu.

"Pavati was brilliant," Tu said, tossing an arm around her shoulder. "It was her idea to blast them off—though of course she needed the strength of Earth to do it." He flexed his other arm.

Khaya gave him a disgusted look that communicated precisely how I felt, while Pavati rolled her eyes and shrugged off his arm.

"You needed my strength, too, pal." Pavati turned to me when she noticed the confusion that must have shown on my face. "See, the bracelets are made out of a para-aramid fiber, as I'm sure Khaya has told you—man-made, so Tu can't manipulate them on an elemental level. And they're fireproof and bulletproof; basically indestructible. I mean, they build spaceships out of this shit. But there's a type of saw that can slice through nearly anything—diamond, titanium, you name it—using a simple jet. So I tucked the idea away when I heard about it." She raised her hand in the air, wriggling her fingers. "And it worked!"

"A jet?" I asked, thinking of the aircraft even though I knew that couldn't be right.

"A highly pressurized beam of some kind, like a laser. Tu can't pressurize solid earth to that extent, and water alone isn't abrasive enough. But together"—she swiped her hands across each other—"we cut through that crap like butter." She made a face, laughing at her own comparison. "And we even did it during Tu's earthquake, right before jumping in the lake."

She put her hands on her hips, puffing out her chest with another mind-blowing grin. I liked Pavati instantly—unlike the other Word I'd just met. And it wasn't because of her lithe, lean body, barely hidden by a midnight blue halter-top and tight pants that I couldn't help but notice when she struck poses like that. I was doing my best to ignore it, especially with Khaya eyeing me.

"Swan-man never thought we'd have the guts to work together like that," Pavati continued.

"Or the guts to chop off a thumb," Tu said, then whistled. "Man, Khaya."

Pavati's grin fell like the moon out of the night sky. "If he had, we'd probably all be like Cruithear, with the monitors lodged in our brains. If it'd been anyone other than Khaya to escape first, that's exactly how we would be."

"Why?" I asked quickly. Khaya had glanced at me at the mention of "Swan-man," and I didn't want the conversation to turn toward Swanson.

"Why is Cruithear's monitor in her brain?" Tu asked. "Or why would Khaya's escape keep our brains safe?"

"Uh, both," I said, ignoring the condescension that coated his words more thickly than the slime on the surrounding rocks.

Pavati glared at Tu and answered before he could. "Because Cruithear is the Word of Shaping. All she would have to do is give one of those bracelets a dirty look and it would fall off. But if she tries to reshape her brain to get the monitor out…"

Tu drew a finger across his neck, making an exaggerated croaking noise.

"Thanks for demonstrating," Pavati said without looking at him. "And that's why Khaya was necessary for implanting one. She had to stand by in case the open-skull surgery went awry, or else the procedure would've been too risky. Even with her there, they only did it when absolutely necessary—really only in Cuithear's case. They would probably reconsider that policy now that three Words have escaped, so it's a good thing their life-support system was one of the three. Without her, no one is willing to chance losing a Word."

Khaya winced, a rare occurrence. "And they almost caught me. Thank you, all of you. Even you," she said, narrowing her eyes at Tu. "How did you coordinate with Pavati? She was the only one I could ever get messages to."

"Right, all of your 'swimming lessons' together at the pool," Tu said with a smirk. "The only reason Swanson let you spend so much one-on-one time with Pavati was because you were so depressed. Now I know your mood enhancement must have come from secret underwater conversations and not any hot girl-bonding sessions. I would have liked to be in on those nearly as much as this jailbreak."

It amazed me to hear that the Godspeakers didn't even let the Words mingle much among themselves, let alone with the rest of society. Tu's crudeness was pretty impressive as well, enough to make even me cringe.

Pavati punched Tu's arm hard enough to send him staggering, but he wasn't deterred, grinning and deftly blocking another one of her fists. "You should see the Athenaeum's pool, man," he said to me. "It would blow your little mind. I'm more partial to the rock gym myself, but when I think about the fun I could have in that pool with these two, even I—"

"Tu, shut up!" Pavati cried. "Now that we can actually talk, it's like you have diarrhea mouth."

"Can you blame me?" Tu stretched his thick arms over his head as if he finally had the room to do so. "Gods! You're lucky I'm even here, with as little as you gave me to go off of! You were too subtle for your own good, with all your winks and hand signals. I was nearly as in the dark as Swanson when it came to your plan."

That sounded familiar. Tu must have been following Pavati with the same blind trust I had in Khaya. I suddenly noticed the change in his scornful eyes whenever he glanced Pavati's way—that probably would have been familiar, too, if I could have seen my own face whenever I looked at Khaya. I hoped I didn't look quite so...*puppylike* was the best word I could come up with.

"So," Tu said to Pavati when she only scowled at him. "What is the plan, anyway?"

"*My* plan was to help Khaya escape, then get myself gone," she said, folding her arms. "When I heard about the fire, I was almost happy. Sorry, Khaya, I know you're pissed at Agonya. But I knew water would be needed, along with Luft's oxygen manipulation, to control the fire. He's probably busy doing that right now." She glanced upward. "Anyway, I convinced Swanson to take this guy, too," she said, tossing her braids at Tu, "since he could theoretically smother the blaze with a ton of earth if it got too out-of-hand—a backup-backup to put the French at ease. But really I only wanted him along so he could help me get the monitor off."

"That's all?" Tu said. "Woman, you know you wanted me for more than that—my hot body, for one. And for two, who do you think threw all that earth around? *Him?*" He pointed disparagingly at me.

Khaya looked about ready to bite off his finger. She'd demonstrated her physical training to a small extent when she'd punched me in the stomach, which hadn't been enjoyable, but I wouldn't have minded seeing more if this guy was the recipient.

Pavati rounded on Tu. "And who kept everyone but us from uttering a single Word? If I hadn't done that, you'd be tornadoed, torched, death-touched, and probably drowned, too, since I wouldn't have been able to control myself with a Godspeaker blathering behind me." She paused. "Or maybe I would have drowned you and just blamed it on a Godspeaker later."

She sounded half-serious.

"How did you do that, anyway?" I asked, trying to prevent any more drownings—even Tu's. My own experience was too fresh. In fact, I still felt like a garbage truck had backed over me a few times; I was worn out from simply standing there on the uneven, slippery rocks of the lake bottom. But I didn't want to hear all the things Tu would say if I sat down. Nor did I want to encourage anyone else to get comfortable.

Pavati's fierce glare transformed into a mischievous smile. "What do people use to speak?"

I shrugged. "A tongue?"

"Spit!" she said with an explosive laugh. "I drew the water out of their mouths and throats. It was some fine work, if I do say so myself!" She paused, looking at me with open curiosity. "What did Swanson have to say to you, anyway? His little conference was good timing. He couldn't hear the commotion we made until it was too late."

"Not much," I said, without looking at Khaya. "We only had a few seconds before everything started shaking."

Khaya didn't contradict me. She must have gathered that I didn't want anyone else to know what Swanson had said.

I didn't even want to know. There was no way he could have been telling the truth about being my father. He'd had a gun in his face, after all. It had to have been some psychological maneuver to throw me off balance. I wanted to question Khaya to make absolutely sure, but it would have to wait until we had a moment alone—which I wanted for more than one reason. In the meantime, I didn't even want to entertain the possibility.

Then again, I was happy to entertain the possibility that Drey was alive. And that there was a cure waiting for him at that address in the Alps. Swanson being my father might be equally as probable.

Shut up, I told myself.

Pavati sighed. "To be fair, Luft knew something was up before the earthquake. He probably felt the moisture in the air as I drew it out of everyone else, then sucked up what he could and kept his throat hydrated. Sheesh, I thought the wind was about to tear my head off there at the end," she said with another grin.

Her grins were contagious. Even though my face ached, I couldn't help but grin too as I turned to Khaya. "See, I told you spit is useful in a pinch."

Pavati arched an eyebrow while Tu said, "I'm curious. Under which circumstances did you say that? Was this while you were kissing her just now, or…?"

I was trying to keep a tenuous hold of too many things at once: my thoughts, my upright position, my temper.

My anger flared, nearly blinding me. "I was cleaning blood off her face, you piece of—"

"Hey, now," Tu said, taking a step toward me. My words had wiped away his leer, but then a ferocious look appeared in its place. "Do you even know who you're calling a—"

"Tu," Khaya said. Her voice was flat; dangerous. "Pavati has already told you twice, and I'll only tell you once: shut up."

Tu actually did shut up. But his shoulders remained squared, his fists at his sides, as he tried to stare me down.

I stared back—and then burst out laughing. The accompanying pain in my raw throat and lungs made me stagger and nearly fall over, but even so, I couldn't stop.

Khaya and Pavati both stared at me as if I'd gone insane.

But I wasn't insane. I hadn't survived all of this—escaping the city with Khaya and without Drey, almost drowning in Lake Eden, fighting a dog to the death, trekking through endless forest, running from a hellish fire, *actually* drowning in another lake—only to be killed in a showdown with the Word of Earth over who was the manliest.

Quite frankly, I felt manly enough already. Enough to sink to the ground in exhaustion while laughing so hard I nearly cried.

"Are you laughing at me?" Tu said, his voice as low and as dangerous as Khaya's had been a second before.

"No," I wheezed with tear-filled eyes. "Not that I give a rat's ass what you think...it's just..." I waved around at the three of them and the suspended lake, but I couldn't finish.

Khaya glanced at the others. "He's exhausted," she

said, as if apologizing on my behalf. "You wouldn't believe what he's been through. You certainly haven't been through anything like it, Tu, so give him a break."

To my surprise, Pavati burst out laughing, too. "Gods, it is funny—you guys bickering like little boys. At least Tavin has the sense to laugh."

Both Khaya and Tu looked peeved that Pavati seemed to understand me. It was probably the only common ground the two of them shared, which made me laugh even harder.

Until a loud burbling noise overhead silenced me.

We all looked up. The top of our bubble was jiggling. Then a big piece broke away, forming smaller bubbles that flew up through the murky lake to the distant sky. The walls quivered.

"Oh," Khaya said with her usual calmness. "There's Luft now."

"I guess they saw us jump into the lake, so it wouldn't exactly take a tracking device or even much brainpower to guess where we are," Tu grumbled.

"What's Luft doing?" I asked. My laughter might never have existed.

"Sucking up our air," Pavati said. Unlike the rest of us, she sounded almost cheerful about it. "And once that's gone . . . " She made a dropping motion with her hands.

The bubble shuddered violently, as if the endless tons of dark, cold water were struggling to break through and devour us.

seventeen

I had the urge to run but nowhere to go. We were trapped, and our reverse fishbowl was about to shatter and let a lake's worth of water inside. And I didn't think I could run anyway. I was still sitting on the slick rocks after my fit of laughter, and wasn't sure if I could even stand up, never mind sprint.

"Don't look so scared, hero-boy," Tu said, smirking down at me. "We'll go earthworm on them. Got my back, Pavati? It'll be more complicated with the lake overhead, since we don't want a vacuum to draw the water in—"

I wished he would shut up and do whatever he was going to do, because our bubble was shrinking fast. Fortunately, Pavati seemed to feel the same.

"I know what to do," she interrupted, already moving to one of the glasslike walls. It rippled where she slid her hands against it. The ripples grew bigger as she started whispering in a language I'd never heard, then twisted when they hit the water's ceiling—turning it into an upside-down whirlpool that drilled a narrow hole skyward.

Tu's Words, spoken in what sounded like Chinese, bored a tunnel into the ground, tossing rocks like sand to clear a space. The entrance widened, sloping into the pitch-dark earth. It made a deep gasping noise, sucking air from the hole overhead and into its depths as if it were a giant mouth with a straw. Tu had been right—if Pavati hadn't made an opening in the water to draw air down from the sky, the negative pressure would have flushed the lake into the tunnel like a giant toilet. And even if she'd managed to keep the water out, we wouldn't have had anything to breathe.

"Quick," Pavati said, "before they realize what we're doing and Luft starts playing tug-of-war with our air."

Khaya was already slipping into the tunnel with the backpack. I dragged myself upright, sliding in mud and lake slime before stumbling into the underground passage. I tripped halfway down the slope and tumbled the rest of the way to level ground. At least I'd achieved forward momentum.

Khaya clicked on the flashlight as Pavati and Tu came dashing inside, the tunnel filling in behind them as they ran. They stopped short of us, as did the folding wall of earth. The ground beneath me continued to rumble for a few seconds.

"The lake just came down," Pavati reported.

"Whew," Tu said, stepping over me like I was a rock and dusting off his hands.

Khaya made a move for me, but Pavati was there first, helping me up with strong arms.

"He can walk, right?" Tu asked without addressing me.

"We need to get out from under the lake so I can poke some air holes for us." He pointed at the dirt ceiling of the tunnel. "And we don't want to give Luft the chance to poke them first. So the faster we move, the better."

Tu and I were actually in agreement. But I could only do so much when my body wasn't cooperating.

"You can walk, right?" Pavati said with a wink, drawing my arm over her shoulder and wrapping one of hers around my waist. "I could give you a piggyback ride if it came down to it...though your arm feels like a log, so you're probably heavy enough to crush me. Wouldn't the two of us be a sight then?" She laughed.

Pavati walked smoothly under my weight, warm and slender and solid. She even smelled good. I was ungainly and shaking, smeared in lake-bottom sludge, and my clothes were tattered and filthy even after all the dunkings underwater. Not to mention I could smell myself, and it wasn't good. I hadn't seen a bar of soap in several days of constant, sweaty trekking. At least, unlike Khaya, she was tall enough that her nose wasn't level with my armpit.

Tu scowled at us as we passed him and moved down the tunnel. I didn't even glance his way, because Khaya was standing nearby and I didn't want either of them to see my blush in the beam of the flashlight.

"Can't you just heal him?" I heard Tu ask Khaya. His motive was clear; my comfort had nothing to do with it.

"Not unless you're planning on carrying him," Khaya said. "Accelerated healing would drop him into unconsciousness at his current level of exhaustion. He needs time—and a place—to recover."

I knew I needed a break. But I still wanted to deny it, both for Drey's sake and for my own injured pride.

"I'm fine," I said. My discomfort, physical and otherwise, was audible even in those two words.

"We'll be far enough away in a few minutes," Pavati murmured. "Finding people underground is a heck of a lot harder than you might think, even within a short radius. Then we can rest."

It was kind that she said "we." She didn't look like she needed rest.

We covered ground fairly quickly, especially with Pavati half-carrying me. Tu muttered Words behind us, closing the sections of tunnel we'd come through and opening another before us. I had no idea which direction we were going, or how deep underground we were. Tu somehow knew. After more muttering and brushing his hand along the dirt wall, our tunnel began to slope upward.

It was harder going for me, but I was encouraged by the fact that we were getting closer to fresh air. What we'd taken below ground with us was already getting stuffy and musty.

Tu stopped and spoke a few sharp syllables.

The walls of the tunnel expanded at the sound of his voice, the dirt churning and grinding as if turned over by an invisible plow. Once everything quit shifting dizzily around us, we were standing in the center of an earthen room with walls as smooth as clay and several tunnels branching off. Khaya set down the backpack and shined the flashlight around. The tunnels led to adjoining rooms, making an area about the size of a small house.

"This is nothing," Pavati said. "A basic bunker. You should see some of the underground fortresses this guy can make."

I had no doubt she was right, but I wondered if she'd said it to banish the scowl from Tu's face. His smug smile was especially visible now that several beams of silvery light dropped down on us, speckling the ceiling like stars and bringing fresh air.

It was hard to tell, but it looked like it might be dusk up above—the usual time Khaya and I would be getting up. Whatever time it was, I was ready to collapse. I couldn't deny it anymore. I lumbered away from Pavati toward the backpack, falling on my knees next to Khaya. I could barely unzip the zipper and rifle through the wet contents of the bag in search of the water bottle, my clumsy fingers getting in the way more than anything. I hoped drowning hadn't given me brain damage and impaired my motor skills.

"Have anything in there I can stuff in my mouth?" Tu asked, looking down at me like he would a rat infiltrating his food supplies.

I took a drink. "Aside from the gun, you mean?" My voice sounded so innocent that it took him a second to process what I'd said.

Khaya nudged me in the ribs with her knee, probably harder than she'd intended. But it gave me a good excuse to lie down.

"Bullets are made of lead and copper, which I could blow

into dust before impact," Tu said, giving me a dark look. "You're pushing it, ass wipe."

I doubted he could spit out a Word faster than a bullet could hit, but I was too tired to test the theory. "You may have the latest fashions in the Athenaeum, but your insults are definitely secondhand," I mumbled, stretching out on the ground with the pack under my head, ready to pass out right there. A featherbed and pillow couldn't have felt more appealing. "And we aren't exactly loaded with food. You didn't bring anything?"

"Man, does it look like I brought anything?" Tu demanded, gesturing at himself. "We weren't on a camping trip in those woods; we were on a strike-mission to take you down. I don't even have a shirt! Gods, to think that I saved you only to put up with this."

"No need for a tantrum. Here's an energy bar." I fished around behind my head, then gave him a sardonic smile as I threw it at him. "Enjoy. They're delicious."

He bit into it and made a face.

Pavati snatched it out of his hand. "Don't eat it if you're going to complain. Besides, you had a fat lunch right before we were deployed. I saw it."

"And now it's dinnertime!" Tu said.

"Dinnertime?" Pavati snorted. "Poor baby. These guys probably haven't eaten a real meal in days."

She tossed the bar back to me. It landed on my chest when I made no attempt to catch it, and even then I only raised my head to bite it instead of lifting my arms, scooping it into my mouth with my teeth.

"S'true," I said around the mouthful. "Haven't had much sleep, either, in case you were concerned. So I think I'll slip into that coma Khaya was offering earlier."

I glanced up at Khaya, but she was already kneeling above me, putting a hand on my shoulder. She didn't wait to ask if I was ready. She started on a string of Words that hit me like a brick, knocking me out cold.

eighteen

One second I was staring at Khaya's upside-down face in the silvery light, and the next I was waking up in dimmer surroundings with a mouth that tasted like something had curled up in there and died. Time must have passed, but I hadn't moved an inch.

The others had. Khaya was stretched out on the ground nearby, and I could make out Pavati's shape leaning against the opposite wall in a seated position, her arms draped over her knees. I didn't know if she was awake or asleep. Tu was nowhere to be seen—in one of the side rooms, I guessed.

He proved me right by stepping out of one and blinding me with the flashlight, before I'd barely cleared my throat and rinsed out my mouth with the water bottle. The bottle was almost empty, but I wasn't too worried with the Word of Water sitting nearby.

I shielded my eyes with an arm—which surprisingly no

longer hurt. For that matter, sitting up hadn't hurt. I'd been so sore for so long that the absence of pain dragging at my limbs was strange—almost a feeling of its own. I took an experimental deep breath and was pleased to find that my lungs didn't wheeze or burn anymore.

But I was hungrier than twelve starving elephants.

"He's awake, so what's the plan?" Tu asked, just as Pavati lifted her head with a yawn.

"Feeling better?" she asked me. "Gods, Tu, give him a second!"

"He's had plenty of seconds," Tu snapped. "He's had all night."

So the light wasn't dimmer because it was dusk. It had already been night, and now the sun was rising again. Too much time had passed.

"It's okay," I said. "I want to get going too. I need to find this address—"

"Do you think I care?" Tu said. "There are way more important things for us to do than chauffeur you around."

I was afraid he'd say that. And he was right. It wasn't their job to help me or Drey. But I'd have a hell of a time getting to the Swiss Alps on my own, even now that I was healed and rested. Hunger alone would do me in. I tried not to panic as I wondered how long Drey had left to live.

By this time, Khaya was sitting up, raking a hand through her wild mane of dark hair. She looked like she needed a shower nearly as badly as I did.

Tu began pacing in agitation. "You two didn't want to talk about what the hell we're going to do while he was sleeping like a baby, but now he's up. Do you think Swanson isn't combing the countryside for us? How long do you think we have until they find us?"

"Calm down," Pavati said, then shot me a grin. "Sounds like someone could have used a longer nap himself. Did you wake up on the wrong side of the dirt, Tu?"

"It's not the time to be sleeping. It's time to be planning. I mean, we're—Gods, Pavati—we're *free*." He sounded both exhilarated and more than a little frightened. But then his tone slipped back into mockery. "So let's have a powwow, shall we?" He dropped to the ground, cross-legged, and jammed the flashlight into the dirt in front of him so it stood upright like a small lamp. "We don't have a campfire or a peace pipe or anything, so this'll have to do."

"Go to hell. In a cheap, Chinese-made hand basket." Pavati wore a sharp smile on her face. I got the inkling, then, that her grins and laughter didn't always mean she was grinning and laughing on the inside. But I still wasn't sure what had bothered her so much. She jumped up only to plop down next to Tu, splaying her legs out to either side like she was stretching. She even bent forward to touch her toes, whipping Tu in the face with her braids as she looked up at Khaya. "You have the floor, lady. What's *your* plan? As I said, mine didn't extend much beyond this point."

Khaya scooted up next to me, so all four of us sat in a loose circle around the flashlight.

In a quiet voice, Khaya repeated what she'd already told me, about the Godspeakers' intention to replace the Words with automatons—Cruithear's humanlike creations that lacked the ability to reason or disagree and were just empty vessels for power once they were brought to life by Khaya. But she filled in some details I hadn't yet heard.

"The City Council wanted to use Words against the world like never before—no more intimidation tactics, no more veiled death threats. Only fire and death." Khaya wrapped her arms around herself. "Their idea was to start with Europe, to solidify their foundation. They wanted to use these . . . golems both as Words and as a mindless, fearless army, toppling our strongest neighbors like dominoes: Germany, France, Switzerland, Great Britain. Then they planned to move against America. Certain political factions in all of these countries have already been begging to serve Eden City in a much more open way, in an effort to curry favor. So if the governments fell, the rest of the country would follow. Then Eden City would have the most powerful army in existence— and a much bigger platform from which to take over the rest of world."

Tu swallowed as if his throat was dry. "How do you know this when the rest of us don't?"

"Cruithear and I couldn't help learning what the City Council was up to, working so closely with the Godspeakers on the project. They weren't concerned that we knew so much, because we were barely allowed time with anyone else and we were about to be replaced anyway. I told Pavati what I could, when I could."

"So what do you want to do?" Tu asked.

Khaya sat back, looking mildly surprised. "I've done what I needed to do. They can't bring these automatons to life without me. I...Tavin and I...are going to Switzerland." She shrugged. "To hide. For good, in my case. I don't know about him."

She didn't mention Drey or the cure, probably because Tu wouldn't have cared. Nor did she look at me, even though I was staring at her in astonishment. She still wanted to come with me, even after joining up with two of her own kind...and even knowing that I was planning to go right back to Eden City if I found the cure.

Tu's expression mirrored my surprise, but not in a pleasant way. "You just want to *hide*?" His voice escalated. "But this is earthshaking!"

"Everything is earthshaking with you," Pavati muttered.

"Seriously—a third of the Words have escaped. Now is the time for action! Eden City only has half of the Elements left. Most of the others are still there, but among them, Cruithear is the only Word worth caring about."

Tu's terminology was throwing me. "Remind me who's still in the Athenaeum?" I asked, struggling to remember all the names and faces that I'd tried so hard to ignore on video screens.

Tu looked incredulous. "How can you not know? We don't have time to—"

Pavati smacked him on the arm. "From now on, Khaya and I field all questions from Tavin. You're fired." She turned to me, leaving Tu sputtering. "There are nine Words total. There used to be twelve, but... it's a long story."

I knew the numbers, just not the details. I hadn't lived under a rock. "I know—"

"Twelve—just like the Chinese zodiac," Tu chimed in.

"*Or* the Western zodiac," Pavati said. "But it doesn't matter, because no one really knows why there were twelve Words. Anyway, four of us are what Tu calls Elements, because he's obsessed with a more traditional, Eastern way of looking at things. We're also known as the Tangible Words: Fire, Water, Earth, and Air." She ticked them off on her fingers. "Another four are the Intangibles: Life, Death, Darkness, and Light."

"Tangible and Intangible, hah," Tu said. "More like Substantial and Insubstantial, or Material and Immaterial." He leaned forward, as if letting me in on a secret. "Immaterial means unimportant."

"I know what it means!" I snapped. "Just because I'm wordless doesn't mean I'm an idiot."

Tu leaned back and said under his breath, "Could've fooled me."

"Not that I think Life is unimportant," I said hastily, glancing at Khaya to see if she'd reacted to being relegated to the "immaterial" Words. "I can see why Darkness and Light would be less *earthshaking*"—I weighted the word with the appropriate amount of sarcasm—"but—"

"Tu's actually right," Khaya interrupted. "Life and Death are two of the most amazing, but least practical, Words to have around. The City Council likes to show us off, but aside from the occasional assassination or miraculous recall from death, neither Herio nor I are very useful on a larger scale. Well, until Dr. Swanson found a use for me," she added.

"I still have a hard time believing they want to replace us with these golems of yours," Tu said, sounding like he was trying to convince himself it wasn't true. "No one has ever even hinted at these bodies Cruithear can supposedly make. Even if Pavati's giving you the benefit of the doubt—"

"Which brings us to the Word of Shaping," Pavati interrupted, continuing with a theatrical flourish as though Tu had just introduced Cruithear, "who used to be part of another group of four: the Words of Power."

"Which, in the old days, used to be called the Storytellers," Khaya said in a soft, far-away voice.

"Why?" I asked.

"If the other eight Words are the pieces that the two Nameless Gods used to make the world, the Words of Power are *how* they made it," Khaya said. "These are the Words that gave the world shape, order, meaning, momentum. They can manipulate the world like we can do only with our individual Words. Hence, they're the Storytellers, playing with all the Words on a higher level. Shaping, Movement, Naming, Time—that's who they are. Well, were."

"What happened to them?"

"A story for another day," Pavati said, breaking the spell of quiet awe that had fallen over everyone, even Tu. "So, to answer your question, Agonya, Luft, Herio, Brehan, Mørke, and Cruithear are still in the Athenaeum. Agonya and Luft, you met in the forest. They're the two other Elem—Tangibles," she amended, glaring at Tu.

"The Blond Brigade," Tu scoffed. Apparently even his fellow Tangibles weren't exempt from his scorn. "That pansy, Luft, drives me nuts. Agonya is manlier than he is."

I remembered the tall, square-jawed blond guy that was pretty much the cookie-cutter of manliness. "What?"

Pavati rolled her eyes. "Tu is giving Luft shit 'cause he's gay. And Agonya is, well, tough as hell. Tu likes to call her the Red Menace. You know, because her donor father was Russian. And the whole fire thing. The fact that Air and Fire are our opposites, elementally speaking, might also have something to do with the childish name-calling."

"Not that Agonya *looks* manly," Tu continued in a reflective tone, ignoring Pavati. "Gods, that girl is hot. But like an explosion is hot." He fanned his fingers as if he'd burned himself, then hurried on at the unamused look on Pavati's face. "At least she matches her element well enough, which is more than I can say for some. You should see the Word of Darkness and the Word of Light! Right?" He nudged Pavati, as if trying to stir up the smile that inevitably appeared.

"It *is* sort of funny," she said in a grudging tone. "Mørke, the Word of Darkness, had a donor mother from Norway. She's so pale she's nearly translucent. White hair." Her fingers grazed her braids. "And if you think I'm dark, you should see Brehan, the Word of Light, whose donor father was Ethiopian. But it makes sense if you consider the effect of regional climate on human evo—"

"Yeah, yeah," Tu interrupted. "Still, that man is *black*."

Pavati's eyes narrowed. "No one's talking about how yellow you are."

"I'm yellow like Chinese soil and proud of it! The Chinese even named a *river* after the yellow *earth*. How do you like that, water-girl?"

"People name rivers all sorts of random things." Pavati nudged him back. "Are you sure it isn't named after that other yellow liquid?"

Now it was Tu's turn to look unamused. "Don't insult my fatherland."

"*Fatherland*." Pavati snorted thunderously. "Your nationalism is about as laughable as your machismo, since you have as little experience living in China as being a man."

"What—?" Tu exploded, but then Pavati threw a dirt clod at him. He was too indignant to block it with either hands or Words before it hit his chest.

"There's a good use for your earth." Pavati turned her laughing eyes on me, making my poor, abused heart skip a couple beats. "Sorry. You probably imagined we were more mature than this, huh?"

I had, but I couldn't help laughing.

Khaya glanced between the two of us, then back into her hands. I'd thought she'd been quieter lately because Tu was so loud, but she seemed abnormally quiet even taking that into account.

"Doesn't the city only accept 'donations' from the rich and powerful?" I asked, to change the subject in case all the bickering was what was bothering her. "And yet the Word of Light is Ethiopian?"

"You mean Edenian?" Pavati corrected with a slight smile. "Because Eden City is the only place any of us come from."

She gave Tu a pointed look. He glared back at her. "But, yes, Brehan's genetics are Ethiopian, which was Eden City making the point that they don't have to favor the highest bidder for any of the Words—that they're more powerful than the powerful."

"They did the same thing with Hayat—Khaya's dad," Tu said with almost a malicious grin. Or maybe I only imagined it was malicious because I knew how carefully Khaya guarded the memories of her father. "Even with the oil, Saudi Arabia wasn't really powerful. The City Council just likes to stir things up, which they did even more when they added Israel to the pot. Khaya isn't only a Word Made Flesh; she's the Middle East conflict made flesh."

Eden City definitely seemed to thrive on conflict. And now it made more sense that they'd want to destabilize the world—it would fall to them even more easily. I wondered how many other world events had the hands of the City Council behind them. Eden City always tried to portray itself as a bastion of culture, technology, and peacekeeping, but how many of their actions had a darker side? Probably all.

Khaya's stony expression distracted me from the bigger picture.

Pavati noticed it too. "Like you're any different, Tu. Your mother, Tsuchi—the previous Word of Earth," she clarified for me, "had a donor parent from Japan, and we all know how much China and Japan love each other."

Actually, I didn't, but I didn't say anything. The Words might be prisoners, but they had far more access to knowledge than I'd ever had. There were prisons other than those of concrete and metal bars: some were made of glass walls and indestructible bracelets, others of ignorance and wordlessness. Eden City had all three.

"Forget the Japanese," Tu said in disgust, dismissing his mother in the same breath. "The father carries on the line, anyway." He struck a seated pose. "I'm Chinese."

"Right," Pavati said sarcastically. "I'm sure you'll be singing the same tune when your kid is named after the next country in line for the Word of Earth. That's all your male 'line' amounts to."

"I'm sure China will win the spot again—well, if the Words aren't turned into mindless automatons built in a lab," Tu added. "But hey, I'm free now! I'm going to do things the old-fashioned way, with the girl of my choice."

He so pointedly did not look at Pavati that I nearly snickered. His insecurity almost made me dislike him a little less. Almost, but not quite.

Then Tu brightened. "That's what our plan should be! We should go home, support our home countries in the fight against Eden—"

"China is not your home." Pavati turned on him with a fierceness I hadn't yet seen. "Don't you get it? We have no homes!"

"Maybe that's how you feel," Tu shot back. "You just don't have any connection to the earth, like me. You're water, drifting."

She rolled her eyes. "And you're as thick as the earth's mantle. I don't have a home because my dad's ancestors were sent as slaves to America. Even my donor mom's people—

Native Americans—were made prisoners on their own land. And now America has made me a slave, like the both of them, to Eden City. Like China did to you. Like you."

Tu's face reddened and his fists clenched at his sides. "So you don't want to do anything? Just sink into anonymity and watch the world go by without you, never mind that you're a *Word*?"

"Sounds pretty enjoyable." Pavati leaned back on her hands and crossed her legs. "To complete the picture, I only need a sofa, a cup of tea, and a good book." She inhaled, as if breathing in the aroma of her imaginary tea. "Ah, freedom."

"Fine!" Tu rose to his feet in a storm of muscle. "If that's how you insist on seeing things, you can go hide in a hole like Khaya. But we were made for more than that! We have power, and whole nations that support us—*us*, not Eden City."

He stomped away from the ring of light into one of the side rooms. If there had been a door, he would have slammed it. As it was, the earthen threshold collapsed, sealing him off from the rest of us.

Pavati sighed and stayed where she was. "Let him sulk. He'll snap out of it."

"I don't think I've seen him 'out of it' yet," I said, staring at the smooth wall where a doorway had just been. I hoped Tu wouldn't sulk for too long. Khaya and I needed to move—which would be difficult, seeing as we were currently stuck underground.

"Yeah, Tu's like that. About as chill as a volcano." Pavati made a face. "Here I go, now, relating him to the earth. Gods, next I'll be talking about how I'm as laid-back as a river." She met my eyes in total seriousness. "I'm not."

I suppressed a shiver. "I believe you. So your donor mother was from America?"

"Both mine and my father's," she said, relaxing somewhat. "My donor mother was Hopi, in honor of her people—America's attempt at an apology for genocide."

That was why Tu had mentioned a powwow and a peace pipe. I vaguely recalled that those were Native American symbols.

"It's where the name Pavati comes from. You can guess what it means." She grinned. "My father's donor mother was African American. She was selected near the end of the Civil Rights Movement, so it was political like everything else. My father's name was Water. He hated it." Her grin softened to a smile, but it was somehow stronger, more real. "He called himself Walter, and it eventually caught on, like Em's name. Herio's mom."

"Yeah, Khaya told me about her," I said quickly, not wanting to talk about Herio. "So they let you do that? Change your names?"

"Not on paper. But even then, we have a microscopic amount of control ... for example, Agonya demanded that her name be written how it sounds." Pavati bent forward, scratching some letters in the dirt with her fingernail. "It's typically written without the *YA*, like this—*AGON*. The soft Russian *N* by itself has that *Y*-sound already built in. But then she complained that people called her 'Ah-gone,' see?"

"Uh," I said. "I can't read."

Pavati looked startled for a second. "Right. I forgot." She sounded embarrassed; but then, as always, she grinned and beckoned to me. "Come here, I can show you. See? *A-G-O-N*. But if you add only a *Y* after the *N*, it spells *agony*." She snickered. "Tu likes calling her that, along with 'Red Menace.' Okay, maybe I like calling her that too."

Leaning over the letters with her, I realized it was the first time anybody had ever tried to teach me to read. It didn't matter than I couldn't understand a thing. Something loosened inside of me, some frozen bit of resentment melting away.

I looked up at her. "Thank you," I said in all honesty.

But then I looked around. Pavati and I were sitting alone in the main room with the flashlight between us. Khaya had slipped away in the dark.

nineteen

Pavati must have read the anxiety in my expression as I looked around for Khaya.

"Go talk to her," she said, eyeing me. "You two have probably been through a lot in the past few days. I'll, uh, plug my ears. Seriously, I have this trick with water, and Tu shouldn't be able to hear through the wall."

I trusted Pavati and didn't hesitate, leaping up. I took the flashlight with me since Pavati had natural light, albeit only a little, shining from the holes up above.

It didn't take me long to find Khaya—there weren't many places to go in our burrow. I checked one room, didn't see her, then wandered down a short hallway into another. She was sitting in a corner, hidden from even the weak reach of the light, deep in shadow.

I pointed the flashlight at the ground so I wouldn't blind her. "Khaya?"

She blinked and looked up at me, showing nothing in her expression. "Tavin."

Her distant tone made me hesitant. "Uh, I was looking for you. You disappeared."

"What can I do for you?"

"Do for me? Khaya, I want to talk to you. I've wanted to talk to you since the lake—"

"About what Swanson said."

"No. Well, yeah, but not just about that." I stepped closer, but not too close. I didn't want her to feel like I was cornering her. "What's wrong?"

"Nothing's wrong. And I have no idea if Swanson is your father, but if I had to guess, I'd say he was lying to manipulate you."

I'd hoped she would say that, but I still had nagging doubts. "But Drey said something when he... when I saw him last... that he'd always thought of me as his son, instead of something else. Maybe *someone* else's, which makes sense when I think about Swanson." A sick, horrible kind of sense. "Drey told me he used to work for Swanson, but then went against him. Even Swanson confirmed that. What if they both meant that Drey had kidnapped me or something, to get me away from Swanson? I don't know."

It sounded absurd, like one of Drey's stories, not something he would actually do. And, of course, why would he have gotten me that job and sent me into the Athenaeum if he'd taken me away from Swanson in the first place?

Khaya wore a slight, dubious frown. "Maybe. Maybe

Swanson was telling the truth; I don't know. Maybe I just don't want you to be his son."

"Is that what's bothering you?" I said, crouching down nearby. "Thinking of me as a Godspeaker's son? Even if I am, I'm—I'm not! I told you, I could never be like that. And besides, I'm wordless. I grew up collecting trash. Even if Swanson and I share the same blood, that doesn't make me anything like him."

At least, I fervently hoped it didn't. I still remembered how easily I'd used Khaya to godspeak. As a Godspeaker's son, would that make me like a Godspeaker? I suppressed a shudder.

Khaya sighed. "This isn't about me, Tavin. *I'm* not bothered by the possibility. I was worried about how it would make you feel. Swanson isn't a good person, and from what little I've heard, Andre—Drey—sounds like he is. So I'm glad to hear your perspective on who your real father is wouldn't change."

It was a little more complicated than that—quite a bit, seeing as I felt nauseous just thinking about it. Or maybe I was only really, really hungry. I didn't like it, in any case, but I liked how Khaya was acting even less.

"So what *is* bothering you? I don't care about you drowning me or anything else that happened at the lake, if that's what this is about."

Too late, I realized she would think I didn't care about her kiss—not that I wasn't weirded out by it. I would happily do it again and again, even drown again if that meant I could kiss her afterwards.

"Good, me either," she said in a clipped voice. "I'm just glad you're not dead."

Now I knew I was in trouble. But I was never one to fess up and beg for forgiveness when I hadn't really done anything. And even when I had...

"You mean *still* dead, don't you?" I said, reminding her that she'd officially killed me.

"Not exactly. What I mean is, I'm glad you're not half-alive. If I'd been too late, the Words would still have woken you up, only..."

"With a lobotomy?"

She swallowed. "You wouldn't have been you anymore." She looked at the wall and her curt tone softened, her words running together. "Your being dead would have been preferable. Because I would have tried, no matter what. I would have brought you back even if it wasn't you, and then—"

She looked so scared, suddenly, and she was speaking too fast. I reached across the short distance between us and took her hand. Her mouth snapped closed.

"Well, I'm also glad I'm not dead *or* brain-dead," I said.

She looked down at our hands, then pulled hers away. "You and Pavati seem to get along well."

Earlier in the conversation, I'd felt like I was careening around narrow, curving streets in the garbage truck at night, but now it was as if I'd turned off the headlights.

"I like her," I said with caution—apparently not enough, because Khaya's expression went blank. "Gods, not like that!"

"It's fine," she said, her voice small and cool, her words

like little ice cubes. "You don't have to lie. I've seen how you two look at each other."

"Come on," I said, exasperated. "Pavati laughs and smiles at everyone. If you've seen me looking at her, well...yeah, okay, she's pretty. Really pretty, but that doesn't mean I feel anything other than friendly toward her. Khaya!" I grabbed her arm as she tried to look away again. She glared as if she might punch me, but I didn't let go. "Listen, there's sometimes a hell of a big difference between what my body wants and what my mind wants. If I look at Pavati, that's just...that's just biology, Khaya, something animal, nothing else." I grimaced at how bad that sounded and scrubbed a hand over my face. "I'm sure you've noticed I've been gaping at you since I met you. Gods, you're the most beautiful girl I've ever—"

"So it's just biology with me, too?"

"No! Well, some of the impulses I have are, yes." I flushed. I didn't want to be having this conversation—but hurting Khaya because of a misunderstanding would be far worse. "And there have been a few of those. But I've tried really hard to be more of a gentleman than that."

"So under the lake, when we kissed, you would have preferred to be more gentlemanly there?" Her expression had gone from cool to cold and I knew I'd said the wrong thing again. "Friendly?"

I wanted to grab my hair. "Gods, Khaya, you have to know how I feel about you! Don't make me say it!"

"Why not?" She looked at the doorway over my shoulder, impatient, like she wanted to get this over with and then go. "You don't want to hurt my feelings?"

I wanted to tear my hair out. I slammed my fist into the wall instead. "For the Gods' sake, Khaya, I'm a puppy! I'm a big damned puppy when I'm around you!" It wasn't a sappy, sweet declaration. Horrified self-disgust rang in my voice. "I'm a stray—Drey found me and then you found me. I'd follow you anywhere, in case you haven't noticed, and I'm afraid you'll abandon me, because then I'd be—I'd be lost!"

"It goes both ways," Khaya whispered.

"And I—what?" There was hope in my last word, flaring amidst what had been a tirade of increasing despair.

"I feel the same way," she said. "I keep waiting for you to get tired of risking your life for me. You should be tired of it. You've helped me so much already, in ways you don't even know about. I'm the Word of Life, and yet you've given me life. I don't want you to get hurt anymore, but then I think about you leaving me, and I…"

So that was it. Khaya didn't want me to leave her, to go back to Eden City with a cure for Drey or frolic off with Pavati or whatever else. Because I was important to her. I was wordless and powerless, and yet I was somehow worth something in her eyes.

She didn't notice the astounded look I was giving her because she was talking to her clasped hands. "I've laughed more than I have in years, more than I can even remember. This is the happiest I've ever been, but it's the saddest you've ever been. Then I see you with Pavati, how easily you two laugh together, and it's like—"

Khaya couldn't continue in that calm, agonized voice, because my hands were in her hair and I was kissing her.

For the first second or two, she was so stunned she didn't move. But then her lips responded, her arms flew around my neck and her body surged into me, knocking me backward from where I'd been crouching. The feeling of her breasts pressing against my chest made my brain go numb.

My hands moved automatically, running down her back, cinching around her waist and lifting her onto my lap. Her legs straddled me. I was happy to let my hands rest on her hips, since this was more than I'd ever touched her—my arms, my lungs, my mind full of her—but she seized my wrists and dragged my hands up her sides, planting them where her rib cage turned into the soft, outer curve of her breasts.

A lightning bolt of excitement shot through me—I could feel it crackling in my fingertips, on my tongue. My hair was probably standing on end for all I knew. Still, I tried to speak with her mouth against mine.

"Khaya, wait—"

"I have urges too, Tavin Barnes," she whispered fiercely between kisses. She almost sounded angry. "Don't think I don't."

Her fingers were dancing down my back, then slipping under the edge of my T-shirt. She started peeling it off.

"I believe you," I said, my hands finding hers. I held them still.

Her lips pulled away from mine. "You don't want—" she began in a flat voice.

"Mother of the Gods, you don't think I *want to*?" I hissed. "Look at me!" I was panting, my hair in my eyes, and nearly shaking from the effort not to tear *her* shirt off. "But we don't even have a door!"

There was more to it than that. With all of Drey's lectures, he sure as hell hadn't let me escape without hearing about all the consequences of unprotected sex—especially the reproductive consequences. And yet, while he'd prepared for my getaway by stuffing the backpack with everything I might need in an emergency, he'd somehow not foreseen *this* kind of emergency.

He'd only given me one form of protection: a gun.

I didn't exactly want to tell Khaya the truth. Even I knew that admitting I didn't want to get her pregnant would be utterly tactless.

"Besides, I haven't showered in, like, a week," I added.

"You actually care about that?" Khaya asked, but she let my shirt drop.

I had to tune out all the second thoughts pounding through my skull before I could answer. "I really smell," I said finally.

"I don't care!"

"But you would care if Tu walked in on us. Think of all the insightful commentary he would have."

"Tu doesn't have the requisite experience for insightful commentary … not that it would stop him." Khaya let her head drop onto my shoulder. "Ugh. You're right. I wasn't thinking."

"That's okay. Trust me." I squeezed her, kissing the side of her face so hard that she grunted. "You can be thoughtless like this whenever you want. It's just—maybe a little bit of thinking here or there is good. But we can stop."

She lifted her head, a slight smile on her amazing lips, and she kissed me again.

My brain definitely ceased working. I wasn't sure how long we stayed pressed together, our hands running over each other in the dark. I probably wouldn't have noticed the passage of time until I passed out from thirst or hunger.

Fortunately, Khaya had the wherewithal to stop herself, this time, when she grabbed handfuls of my shirt like she wanted to rip it from my back. Because I wouldn't have been able to resist a second attempt.

She released my shirt with a groan. "Gods, I want to."

"There'll be other opportunities." I had to fight down a breathless laugh when I realized what I was talking about—and my desire to give in. These were words I never thought I'd say to a girl, let alone to Khaya. "We only need a shower and a change of clothes and a door."

"I don't know," she said into my neck.

The feeling of her lips brushing my skin made it difficult to talk. "I won't forget, if that's what you're worried about. Gods, I won't be able to think about anything else ever again. Thanks a lot."

"No, I mean, I feel like I have to seize my chance." A laugh escaped me, and she leaned back to glare at me. "I'm serious. You don't know what it's like. Any … involvement … with the Words is forbidden. There can be no physical attachments, no loyalties other than to the City Council, and nothing to complicate the succession of the Words." She probably meant unplanned pregnancies, but she didn't say it. "That's why they fired that Godspeaker for even kissing me. There are things I never thought I would be able to do...and now I want to." Her eyes softened, heavy-lidded, swallowing me. "I want you."

I had to break eye contact. "Khaya, if you keep saying things like that, in that way...You're killing me, really. This is torture."

"Now you know how I feel."

I remembered what Tu had said when he first found me with Khaya—that he couldn't wait either. The Words were the most powerful people on the planet, but they were also a bunch of hormonal, pent-up teenagers facing a short life of celibacy. I was hormonal and pent-up too, but I'd at least lived without thinking that I would be that way until I died—at age forty, no less. If I were in her position, I would have wanted it just as desperately. I pretty much already did.

"Khaya, we've got to wait for a little bit." Forcing out the words was almost painful.

"I know," she said. And then: "Until when? When will we have time?"

I didn't laugh at her eagerness this time because the question made me pause—made me remember everything that had happened before her kiss had wiped my brain clean. "I don't know. I guess we don't have a lot of time. I need to see if Drey kept a cure at that Swiss address."

"And if he did?"

I grimaced. I already felt like I'd had to choose between Khaya and Drey when I'd helped Khaya and left Drey at the mercy of Herio. Now I was choosing all over again... except this time, Khaya's life wasn't at stake. Drey's was. Maybe mine too, but if there was a chance I could save him, I had to try. "Khaya, if there is a cure there, I have to get it to him. Whatever it takes—"

"I know. And if there isn't one?"

If there wasn't... "I don't know. I'll just have to decide what to do then."

Khaya nodded, then released me with a deep breath. "Then let's go."

She didn't sound distraught over my decision, but then, she rarely did. Maybe she was just facing reality with her usual stoicism. I didn't feel stoic. There was a sharp pain in my chest as I let her go, so strong it almost brought me back to my knees once I stood. I offered her my hand, but she shook her head.

"You go ahead," she said. "Let the others know we're ready to leave. I'll be there soon. I just need to catch my breath and"—she sounded embarrassed—"straighten my hair and clothes."

I left before I could change my mind.

If Khaya was hoping to keep our interaction a secret, it was a lost cause. When I returned to the main room of our burrow, Pavati was leaning against the wall that still hadn't reopened after Tu vanished behind it, nonchalantly picking at her nails. But there was a smile lifting the corner of her mouth.

"I thought you weren't going to listen," I hissed.

"I heard only one thing," she said, "and only because you shouted loud enough to bring the place down. I don't think

Tu heard, because I'm *positive* he would have come out of his hole to mock you by now."

I rubbed my forehead, squeezing my eyes closed. "Don't tell me. I can guess."

"Likewise . . . don't tell me *why* you're a puppy. I can guess."

"Pavati." I opened my eyes and gave her my most charming smile. "I haven't killed anyone yet, but there's still time."

She grinned back at me, flashing brilliant white teeth. Then she made a motion of zipping her lips closed. Even after she'd pantomimed locking them up and throwing away the key, she was still smiling so broadly she could barely keep her mouth closed, and laughter sputtered out.

"I don't care if you're a Word," I said. "I *will* kill you."

She had to resort to covering her mouth after that, because she couldn't stop. When Tu leapt through a widening gap in the wall a moment later, demanding to know what all the fuss was about, she only shook her head with tears in her eyes, thank the Gods.

TWENTY

Tu wasn't happy when Khaya reaffirmed her decision to accompany me into the Swiss Alps, and was even less happy when Pavati announced she would go with us "just for kicks"—which made Khaya sigh almost inaudibly. I only heard it because I was standing right next to her. I had to resist sighing myself. We definitely wouldn't have much time alone.

But it was good to see Pavati backing her friend, even if Khaya's decision seemed weird to her. Khaya had probably saved her life, after all.

Mostly, it was good to be moving. If I wasn't going toward Drey, I desperately hoped I was at least headed toward a cure for the Word of Death.

Tu agreed to go with us only because he insisted I wasn't man enough to protect the girls, never mind that Pavati turned the earth under his feet into a watery bog after he said that and Khaya's voice ripped roots out of the dirt walls to lash around his neck.

"See," Tu said, sunk up to his waist and half-strangled. "The only reason I don't have rocks crushing you right now is that I'm looking out for your safety."

"Thanks," Pavati said, leaving him to extract himself. She began marching down the newly extended tunnel that stretched away into darkness.

The earth pushed Tu back aboveground at his command, solidifying beneath his feet. He rubbed his neck after he unwound the now unmoving, limp root. "I didn't even know you could do that, Khaya."

Khaya's eyes were disturbed. "I didn't either, until recently."

"I guess they didn't spend a lot of time developing your assault capabilities at the Athenaeum. You *are* supposed to be the Word of Life," he said in a withering tone.

She looked embarrassed. "I know... it's not right."

"I wouldn't go *that* far," I said. "It sure would have been useful with the dog. It's interesting that Tu can drive you to violence but not the thought of getting ripped to shreds." I looked at Tu. "Never underestimate how torturous your company is."

"Maybe Khaya just didn't care enough to save *you*," he retorted. "You're a wordless idiot, after all."

I laughed at him. The memory of Khaya kissing and touching me made me feel like I was encased in a warm glow, almost like a force field. I nearly felt high. Khaya was blushing as if she felt something similar.

"It's the second time in as many minutes that you've shown you don't know a thing about us ladies," Pavati called from up ahead in the tunnel.

As we walked, I had to admit that traveling with two additional Words was not only safer but made for much easier going. Even though Tu made his displeasure as obvious as possible, complaining every step of the way, I couldn't help but appreciate his smooth, gently sloping tunnels in comparison to the tangle of the forest. Never mind those rough, freezing streams. The only water we saw was what Pavati summoned whenever we needed a drink, drawing it up through the ground. That was about as much as I ever wanted to see again.

We were still hungry, though—insanely hungry, in my case. Walking even made me feel dizzy, but I didn't want to say anything until Tu did. Which didn't take long.

"Is anyone else starving?" he demanded, as only the latest of his many complaints. "I am."

"We could surface to get our bearings—" Khaya began.

"I know where we're going." Tu tapped his head. "Built-in compass. I can feel the earth's magnetism."

"Or at least so *I* can get my bearings," she continued. "And while we're up there, maybe I can find some mushrooms and berries to—"

"Berries?" Tu scoffed. "What about a sandwich? And I could really use a shirt. We need to get back in touch with civilization, people. I know you're anxious to run and hide, but unless you want to weave your own clothes and starve to death on what Khaya can farm along the way—"

"He's right," Pavati said. "We need to make a pit stop. Where's the nearest town?"

"There's a small one, called Martigny, a few miles east of here," Khaya said, hesitating. "It's actually on the way, just across the Swiss border. But we were trying to avoid being seen."

"We'll be fine!" Tu said, waving a hand in the air. "No one will bother us. And if they do, we'll teach them a lesson."

Khaya's full lips pressed into a hard line that he couldn't see, since the two of us were walking behind him and Pavati. "That's exactly what we want to avoid. We're hiding, Tu."

"I think a little noise might let Eden City know we mean business."

"You can go make all the noise you want. By yourself."

"Don't worry, Khaya," Pavati said, grinning back at us. "I'll keep a tight leash on him."

Tu whooped. "Oh, baby, if *that's* how you like to play, I'll put on a leash and collar for you anytime. How about tonight?"

"In your sad little dreams."

The walk continued in a similar pattern, the tunnel opening onward, smooth and straight, even when we passed through different types of soil or rock. And the banter between Pavati and Tu didn't change much, either, with his complaints or crude advances shut down by her biting comebacks. Tu never stopped trying to change everyone's mind about going deeper into the Alps, and both sides got more and more insistent—or belligerent, in Tu's case.

Tempers grew shorter and hotter as the miles passed

underfoot, a crabbiness I attributed to hunger. We divided up the remaining two food bars, but the morsels weren't even enough to make my stomach stop aching. By the time the path began to rise upward through the earth, we were all about ready to murder Tu, and he certainly felt the same in return—at least toward me.

So when the tunnel opened up in the trees and we saw the small town of Martigny across a dying, autumn-colored valley in the late afternoon sunlight, I was almost relieved.

It was the first settlement I'd seen outside Eden City. While it was small and simple, with none of the shining glass and steel I was used to, it wasn't nearly as outlandish as I'd expected. The wood and stone buildings were low to the ground, but constructed in a predictable fashion, and there were streets, streetlights, and signs. I didn't know what I'd been expecting. This was Switzerland, after all, a not-so-distant, if foreign, country. There were, however, far more words on these signs than in Eden City, where they used a lot of pictures for the wordless.

Tu shuddered. "I take it back," he said, his breath fogging in the crisp air after the relative warmth of the tunnel. "I don't want a shirt. I want a sweatshirt. Or five."

We were all underdressed—Tu most of all, to be fair, though Pavati wasn't much more clothed in her halter top—and shivering. I wouldn't have minded more coverage myself, but those two needed it for more than the cold. The Words stamping their skin looked more striking than ever, as good as signs pointing to them and shouting, *We've escaped from the Athenaeum! Come get us!*

Khaya looked at them, obviously thinking the same thing. "You two have to stay here," she said, with only the barest hint of satisfaction. "You're way too conspicuous."

"As if you two aren't," Tu said, giving us a once-over with a contemptuous smirk. "You look like you've been running and hiding in the woods for days on end. Nothing suspicious there."

"Tavin and I are still the better option," Khaya insisted, folding her arms—to appear stern, or to ward off the cold, or maybe to cover a hole in her shirt. "They could still mistake us for runaway teenagers. You two are unmistakable like this."

"So what? I say we march right in and come what may."

Pavati rubbed her arms, which were covered in goose bumps. "Why don't we go in at night and just break into a store?"

The thought hadn't occurred to me. And there was a reason. The one time I'd ever stolen something had been one of the most shaming moments of my young life, not only because Drey had forced me to hand over the toy, along with my stammering apology, to the storeowner down the street, but because he'd bought it for me the next day, to prove I didn't need to steal. I hadn't even been able to play with it, I was so embarrassed. It just sat on the metal desk in my back room and collected dust.

"No!" I spoke louder than I'd intended. I was well beyond the shame of the incident, but I didn't want to dishonor Drey now. And besides, he'd prepared things so I wouldn't have to steal. "I mean, I have money," I said more quietly, slipping the backpack off my shoulders and digging out the envelope with the postcard and cash. "Plenty of it. And besides, we'd leave a trail for anyone hunting us if we break into a store and steal only food and sweatshirts."

"You're right," Pavati said, her eyebrows raised as if she was surprised by the fact she hadn't considered that. Or maybe that *I* had. But she blinked it away and gave me a smile.

I pulled out the wad of Swiss francs and stuffed it in my pocket, leaving the envelope with the backpack. The pack would be safer with Pavati and Tu, especially if Khaya and I needed to run for any reason. And Khaya probably didn't want the gun coming with us.

"We could always steal more to throw them off," Tu said with a wicked gleam in his eye. "Maybe wreck the place so we look like common thugs."

"You would *be* a common thug then," I said, and Pavati gave me another assessing look.

Khaya glanced at her, then took my arm—firmly. "Tavin and I are going in. We'll get the basics: food, clothes—"

"Soap," I interjected.

"Any other requests?"

"Tavin could always give me his shirt and I could go in," Tu said. "You need a man capable of reading, never mind—"

"No." Khaya cut him off.

Tu sneered. "His shirt wouldn't fit me anyway."

I nodded. "Too big, I know."

Khaya yanked me away before the conversation could degrade further and started off across the fields. My feet crunched in the shadowed patches of the grass. Frost.

"Get some chocolate!" Pavati shouted after us. "Hell,

lots of chocolate—we're in Switzerland, after all! And toilet paper!" Her shout dissolved into laughter amidst the trees.

"You know, I wouldn't mind some toilet paper either," I said as we walked. It felt strange to be out in the open, in the daylight no less, and I was talking mostly to stave off any nervousness. "I don't know why I didn't think of that earlier." I'd been making do with leaves.

"Probably because you were busy running for your life," Khaya said. "In that situation, toilet paper is a luxury. It still is. We'll need to get another backpack at this rate, maybe two. Toilet paper is light, but it takes up too much space."

"Killjoy," I said.

Khaya didn't even look at me. She had gone into action-mode—her way of dealing with nerves—winding herself into a tight coil of seriousness. Not that I was used to seeing a side of her that *wasn't* serious, but I'd been making some headway there. I wondered if it was part of her training or just part of her. Or because of what I'd confessed the night before.

"Though at this point, soap *is* a must," she said, almost to herself. She stopped and faced me. "How do I look?"

"Beautiful." She gave me a glare before I added, "And filthy."

"Be more specific."

"Well, I've always thought your hair was gorgeous, even when it's a rat's nest like now, and your eyes are the most melting shade of—"

She cleared her throat.

"Dirt smudges," I said in a clipped fashion, as if reporting to my superior. I threw in a salute for good measure. "Upper left cheek and above right eyebrow. I repeat: hair is a rat's nest."

A smile worked its way onto her face, even though she obviously tried to stop it. She buffed at her cheek and forehead and tried to run her fingers through the dark, tangled mass of her hair, then gave up and twisted it into a knot at the nape of her neck. It was so stiff with grime it actually stayed in place without a tie. "Better?"

"Nothing could make you look better than you already do—but you look cleaner," I said, before she could open her mouth. I took a step forward and rubbed at a dark spot visible above her collarbone. It didn't come off, not even when I fell back on my trusty, all-purpose solution and licked my thumb before trying again.

"Whoops," I said, the realization hitting me. "I think I did that. You know, when I was kissing your neck."

Khaya craned her neck to see, a flush rising in her cheeks. She looked warmer than sunlight, sweeter than any flower in the world. Even when she smelled like old sweat.

"Oh. Well, nothing to be done about it," she said, pulling her shirt a little higher and continuing to walk.

"What about me?" I asked, following her.

"Your face is as clean as it's going to get, but your arms are a lost cause. We'd need a stiff scrub brush. I suggest keeping them folded if we encounter anyone. Your shirt looks horrible up close, but at least it's dark—"

"No," I said. "What *else* do you see?"

Normally, I would never have asked anyone a question like that in a million years, let alone a girl. Asking someone to tell you why they like you is obviously searching for an ego-boost, not a bruising. But this was Khaya, and I still felt high, especially after seeing the reminder of our last encounter on her neck. Besides, I was beyond curious: how the hell did a guy like me matter to a girl like her? Finding out that I *did* matter to her had only left me with that burning question.

Khaya's stride faltered for a second, but then she kept going, faster than before, pulling ahead of me. I didn't think she was going to answer.

But a few seconds later, she said, "I like your hair, even though you need a haircut. Some people wear theirs messy to look carefree, but it's affected. You really don't care." I could hear the smile in her words, even though I couldn't see her face. Her voice warmed up as she spoke, flowing more freely. "I particularly like your eyes. Their color is one of the least remarkable things about you, compared to your height, your build..." She cleared her throat, more embarrassed than stern. "Anyway, it's easy to miss your eyes—they're sort of a nondescript muddy brown, but so clear. You see right through them almost. But I like looking, because of what I see."

"What do you see?" I asked, my throat tight for some reason I couldn't name.

"When you're happy, I see the laughter in your eyes, and the mischief when you're being a shit. When you're crying I see your pain, raw and bleeding, and when you look at me..."

She took a sharp little breath. She couldn't say it, because I hadn't said it yet. I hadn't even known it until then. And I still couldn't say it, because my throat seized up almost painfully.

233

But I knew what she saw.

She stopped right before we reached the sidewalk at the far end of the field and turned around. She had tears in her eyes.

"Mostly I see you," she said. "And you're good."

She looked scared herself. No, she looked...

And then I saw it, for the first time: her guard dropped, the doors of her eyes opened, and I saw *her*.

I saw something else, too, as she looked at me. Probably the same thing she'd seen in my eyes.

"Tavin," she whispered. She didn't need to say it, like I didn't have to. And that made me love her even more.

Gods, *love*. It was strange, intoxicating, wonderful... and utterly terrifying. It was like riding a roller-coaster drunk. I sort of wanted to laugh, scream, and puke all at the same time.

I exhaled, my head spinning. "So you don't just like me for my body."

She shook her head once and smiled, the motion making a tear run from the corner of her eye. I caught it, leaving a wet, muddy smear where I'd touched her.

I stared at my damp finger, trying to ground myself. "Even though I want to, I probably shouldn't touch you again until we get some soap. You now have another smudge of dirt on your left cheek."

She laughed and lifted a sleeve to wipe her eyes. "Better? Cleaner, I mean?"

"Check, captain."

"Okay." She took a deep, steadying breath, blinking away her tears. "You need food. You're about to fall over. Let's go."

Admittedly, low blood sugar was probably why I felt so dizzy, but not entirely. I felt like I was flying as I followed her down the sidewalk and into the town of Martigny. The world streamed by in a blur, as if nothing could touch me so long as Khaya felt the same way about me as I felt about her. We crossed a couple streets, hardly needing to look both ways since there were so few cars on the road, and Khaya scanned the signs on the buildings. Soon she stopped.

"This is about all I see." She gestured at the sign above the wooden siding of a storefront, then read it aloud when she remembered I couldn't read. "A *supermarché*—a supermarket. It doesn't look very 'super,' but there's not much else to this town."

I shrugged. "Sounds good to me."

A bell jingled as we pushed the door open. Thank the Gods there was no one else inside except a portly man with a beret, blue overalls, and a big round nose reading a newspaper behind a wooden counter. It amazed me that just anyone could read, especially a guy looking like that. In Eden City, I would have pegged him as wordless from a mile off. A TV was playing over his head, unwatched. It looked even older than the TV in Drey's garage that had broken years ago.

"Eh, bonjour," the man said without looking up.

We picked up empty baskets and ducked into an aisle. Khaya snatched things off the shelves as she passed, mostly dried food, a lot of which looked suspiciously like energy bars even though I couldn't read the packaging. She had to seize my arm when I spotted the candy bars. I gestured at them, hissing under my breath about how good they were, but she shook her head and added healthier-looking food to the basket. We crossed into an aisle with tools and plastic jugs that even I knew held motor oil, and that was where Khaya found some bar soap, toothpaste, and toothbrushes. She eyed a collection of bottles that looked like shampoo but passed them over with a small sigh.

In a back corner, I spotted a rack of T-shirts and sweatshirts, and Khaya sent me that way with a nudge, murmuring, "I'll look for anything else we might need."

There were different words on different sweatshirts, but I couldn't read what they said and only cared about the color, anyway—the darker the better, to hide dirt. I took four black sweatshirts off the rack. I paused, grinned to myself, and replaced Tu's with the next size down. It would still fit him, but snuggly. Like a muscle sweatshirt.

I was so pleased with my little prank that I didn't notice the TV until I'd followed Khaya up to the counter, where she had put her basket and stood waiting for me. Earlier, the screen had been showing a soccer game, but now there was an aerial view of a forest, obviously filmed from a helicopter.

The trees were burning.

I didn't need to be able to read the text flashing across the screen to know this was the forest we'd left behind. And my connection to it was especially obvious, since my picture was displayed in the upper right corner—the same photo that had dominated the giant video screens in Eden City.

Whether or not they believed I'd struck the match for the fire that nearly burned a massive swath of forest to the ground, every viewer would know I was involved. Not only was local law enforcement definitely tracking me, but I'd be hunted down by average citizens.

Like the portly man in overalls behind the counter. He was staring at the newspaper, not the TV, so I ducked my head to dig out a wad of Swiss francs. I passed them to Khaya without looking up and turned as if I'd forgotten something, hoping the shopkeeper wouldn't notice me slipping out of the store.

But I didn't slip away. I froze instead. Someone else's face had filled the screen, even though my photo remained in the corner. He was gaunt and gray with tubes in his nose and mouth and tape on his eyelids, surrounded by hospital equipment. He looked horrific, but he was alive.

Drey was definitely alive.

Swanson's voice suddenly became clear in the background, speaking English instead of French: "This is a message for Tavin Barnes, a plea. Turn yourself in. The only way this innocent bystander's life can be saved is if you return to Eden City with what you stole. There's nothing else that can save him." There was a heavy pause. "He has roughly one day to live. Your choice."

twenty-one

A day. Drey had only a day to live.

"Drey!" I shouted, startling the man at the counter. He glanced at the TV in surprise, but didn't look at the screen for long. He looked back down at his newspaper. "Khaya, we have to go now. We have to see if there's a cure—"

"Tav—" Khaya said in warning, then choked off my name. "Just be quiet."

She probably didn't want to give me away any more than I already had. I couldn't stop staring at the footage of Drey, let alone sneak away. Fortunately, the shopkeeper seemed to be more interested in his paper than either the TV or me.

Or so I thought, until he slammed the paper down on the countertop and my upside-down face stared at me from the front page.

"You are … Tavin Barnes?" he asked, pronouncing my name with a heavy accent.

"Uh," I said, right when Khaya said, "No!"

"I think you are Tavin Barnes."

The shopkeeper ducked out of sight behind the wooden counter and returned with a rifle before either Khaya or I could blink. He aimed it right at my chest.

"You think you can just come into my store and I will do nothing?" he demanded.

"No, sir!" The line of stuffed deer and elk heads above the windows was all the proof I needed. The man in overalls was not only a reader, but a hunter. Fantastic. "I mean, I'm not Tav—"

"Now, you wait here while I make a phone call." He held the rifle in one hand while the other reached along the countertop for an old corded phone. "If you do not move, I will not shoot."

"Sir," Khaya began. "Monsieur, s'il vous plaît—" she added in French. Of course she would speak French.

"Now, I do not know who you are, mademoiselle, but you are with a bad young man. He is wanted by the police and everyone in Switzerland."

So I'd been right about that at least, even if I'd been wrong about everything else—like not simply robbing the store, or Khaya and I coming into town instead of Pavati and Tu, or Drey possibly having more than one day left to live. Chilled as I was, I'd broken out in a sweat. And hungry as I was, I would sooner have ejected the acid boiling in my stomach than eaten.

Khaya looked around, as if for some sort of weapon. But there was nothing living in the shop that I could see, not even a potted plant. And I'd left the gun in the backpack with Pavati and Tu. I actually wished Tu were here in all of his earthshaking, shirtless, macho glory.

"Sir, really, you don't understand," I said, trying a different tack. "We have to—"

"Be quiet," the shopkeeper said, jerking the rifle for emphasis. Then he spoke into the phone in rapid French. All I caught was his name: Pierre.

As soon as he hung up, both of his hands were back on the rifle, which hadn't wavered from me. Perhaps I should have tried something while he was on the phone, but I hadn't been able to come up with any more of a plan then than now. Swanson was maybe my father, Khaya loved me, Drey was alive but dead in a day—it was all too much. I felt as brainless as one of the stuffed deer heads with glassy eyes. All I knew was that if I made any sudden moves, my chest would be turned to Swiss cheese.

Even if I couldn't save myself, maybe there was still hope for Khaya. Hope for the world.

"Let the girl go," I said, raising my hands in surrender. "It's me everyone wants. She didn't do anything." At least, Eden City wouldn't have told the Swiss government any different.

Pierre narrowed his eyes. "How do I know that? She could be your—what do you call it?—your accomplice."

"She's not. I—I kidnapped her. She's my hostage. But I don't want her getting hurt in any of this, and you probably don't either."

Khaya was staring at me, her eyes wide. Then she blinked.

"He's lying," she told Pierre.

"Khaya!" I cried. "Tell the man the truth and get the hell out of here!"

"I can tell the truth: I'm not leaving you."

"Stockholm Syndrome," I said to Pierre, thinking of anything and everything as fast as I could, pulling up phrases from Drey's scarier stories. *Drey,* I thought. *No, don't think about Drey. Khaya needs to run. Focus.* "She's just some girl. Please let her go."

"You're just a boy," Khaya said, "who didn't deserve to be dragged into this. If anything happens to you, it's all my fault. Hear that?" She met the shopkeeper's eyes. "This is all my doing. Your forest is burning because of me, that man on the screen is dying because of me, and anything Tavin has done is because of me."

Pierre glanced back and forth between us, as if he couldn't decide which one of us was crazier.

"You should know, Tavin," Khaya said quietly, "Swanson is right. There's only one way to save someone from the Word of Death. Andre Bernstein worked with my father, but it wasn't on a cure. Modern medicine can try to slow Death down, but the end will come no matter what. Nobody, not even Herio, can stop Death."

Khaya didn't meet my eyes at first, even though I was staring at her, everything else forgotten. There was no cure? *There was no cure.* Except for . . .

"Except for me." She finally looked at me, her eyes glazed with tears. "I made that up about the cure because I knew the only way to save Drey was for me to go back. And I couldn't do that. I couldn't let you go back, either, not by yourself. They would imprison you, and for what? Just so you could watch Drey die?" She nodded at the TV screen. "They're hoping you'll give me up, to save Drey. Maybe you *should* give me up. I'll ... I'll let you. You could get your life back that way."

And doom the world to a hostile takeover, she'd forgotten to add. Never mind dooming all the Words. Khaya's offer stunned me even more than her lie about the cure. I opened my mouth, but nothing came out.

"What are you saying?" the shopkeeper demanded. "Did you say *Herio*?"

"Yes. The Word of Death," Khaya said, and Pierre blanched. "And I'm the Word of Life."

"What?" His voice dropped in fear.

I shook my head, trying to focus on the here and now. "Khaya, you've got to leave! You're more important than me or ... or Drey," I said, forcing the words out. "We don't even know if he's really alive. This could still be a setup." I turned frantically to Pierre. "She's lying. I mean, come on, does she *look* like the Word of Life?"

Khaya turned, lifting up her ragged shirt as she did. Not all the way, but enough for us to see the Words streaking her back like black blood. They were moving, altering, as both Pierre and I stared at them. She dropped her shirt and turned back around. "See?"

"Mother of the Gods," he whispered, taking a step backward.

We all stared at each other, barely breathing. It wasn't much longer before I heard sirens approaching, then tires screeching as vehicles slid to a halt outside. They had gotten here quickly. It was a small town; they must not have had far to come.

And then everything started shaking. I thought it was the cops, bombarding the store with cannons as though their handguns and rifles weren't sufficient. But when the floor erupted, throwing shelves into each other like dominos, I realized it was someone else entirely.

Tu and Pavati hadn't had that far to come, either.

The two of them came launching out of a tunnel in the middle of the store, tucking and rolling as they hit the ground, Words flying from their mouths like bullets. The floor dropped out from underneath Pierre, but not before his rifle went off. I would have ended up like my least favorite cheese if a powerful blast of water from a broken pipe hadn't hit him at the same time, throwing his arms—and the rifle barrel—up and riddling the ceiling tiles full of holes instead of me.

In seconds it was over. The shopkeeper was buried up to his shoulders behind the counter, the earth packed tight around him as if his head were growing from some weird planter. The water from the pipe ceased flowing—or at least spraying like it had a mind of its own—but not before Pavati had washed the rifle out of sight.

Tu surveyed the damage with a satisfied smile. "We work well together, don't we?" he said to Pavati. "Earth and water: the perfect team, even in nature. You know how water always caresses the earth, and the earth holds it…" He rubbed his bare chest with a grin.

"You mean, how water always carves the earth into whatever shape it wants before leaving for the ocean?" Pavati said with a smirk.

"Cruel, cruel woman."

"Uh, guys?" I said, and they both turned to me. "I hate to interrupt, but—" I gestured at the front windows, which let in the flashing of blue and red lights. "I think we're sort of surrounded."

That was when a voice, amplified by a megaphone, shouted at us in French. I didn't understand quite what it said, but it was probably something like *we've got you surrounded.*

"See?"

Tu scoffed, helping himself to a candy bar from the floor. "I'd like to see them try—"

There was a loud pop, a shattering of glass, and the clank of something metallic bouncing across the floor. A canister. It was also hissing, spewing white gas. My eyes started to burn, my throat prickling like I'd swallowed a porcupine.

"Tear gas!" I wheezed.

"How dare they!" Tu snarled.

I ignored him, sweeping the sweatshirts off the counter along with one of the baskets full of food, giving Pierre's head a quick word of apology. Khaya already had the other basket on her arm, and as we turned to run for the tunnel in the ground, Pavati followed us with the backpack over her shoulders.

Except Tu wasn't following. He was marching the other way. It took the jingling of the bell attached to the front door to make me realized he'd walked straight outside.

"We've got to help him!" Pavati cried, abandoning the tunnel. Before I could shout, she'd sprinted through the white haze and out of the store.

Khaya and I exchanged reddened, watery-eyed glances, then went after her.

We burst out into the chilly, fading sunlight just in time to meet the firing squad. I didn't know what Tu had done or said, but he'd obviously pissed them off. Shots cracked all around us from the police cruisers ringing the small parking lot, their open doors shielding the officers while they pointed and fired at us. I would be filled with holes after all.

Or so I thought, but then none of the bullets hit. *Something* did, like little stinging pinches of sand that probably wouldn't leave a mark. Tu was standing in front of us, chanting, and I realized that the bullets were disintegrating before they reached us ... turning into particles of lead and copper. Might as well have been dirt clods fired at us.

The shots died, and the thundering echoes with them. Then Tu said a word that wasn't in Chinese, a name for the cops that Drey would have called French—as in, "Excuse my French"—except it wasn't French, and involved mothers. And then he crouched and pressed his palms to the ground.

Thunder rose again: Tu's thunder. The earth shook, then cracked and lifted, splitting the parking lot into jagged chunks of bucking asphalt. And then there was a chorus of voices— Words—all around me, not only Tu's.

Water and roots sprang from the fractured earth as if they were tentacles belonging to some wild, unleashed beast, tearing the guns out of the officers' hands and flattening others to the ground. The water moved with a life of its own, like a liquid snake, twisting around and underneath cars to strike. So did the roots, lashing like whips. Pavati and Khaya knew how to wield their Words as capably as Tu.

For my part, I watched with my mouth open.

Tu's voice brought me back to myself, where I stood next to an empty police cruiser on the only patch of ground that wasn't heaving. The engine was still running, blue lights flashing; its occupant had been pulled away screaming by writhing roots. "Tavin!" Tu was yelling. "None of us know how to drive, so you'd better be able to!"

"You want me to drive?" I asked, staring at the car and picturing a high-speed chase down unfamiliar Swiss roads. "Why don't we just duck back underground?"

Tu grinned, and it didn't look friendly. "We will. Now get in!"

I hesitated. By now, most of the officers had fled or were lying stunned, the sirens left shrieking into the oncoming twilight. Still, the Swiss police had to have notified Eden City that they'd found me. The Athenaeum's forces would be showing up in no time at all, and they had helicopters at their disposal.

After tossing the sweatshirts and grocery basket in the backseat, which I had to do through the rear door because of a metal screen between the front and back, I threw myself in the driver's seat and the transmission into gear. Alien knobs and buttons and gauges gleamed all around me and the radio chattered wildly. I ignored everything but the steering wheel and gas pedal as Tu leapt in the passenger seat and the girls slipped into the enclosed back of the car with the supplies.

"Now what?" I asked Tu.

He hadn't closed his door, and leaned to brush his fingers along the cracked ground, whispering to it as though it were a creature he was petting. The ground sure reacted as if it were alive, rearing up in front of us and opening a wide mouth down into the bowels of the earth, straight through the asphalt, broken pipes, and other chunks of what looked like concrete. The sudden movement flung vehicles and people out of the way. I hoped no one was hurt by the rolling cars. They'd tried to shoot us, but I at least didn't want to kill anyone.

The tunnel was wider than our stolen cruiser. The still-flashing lights on our car's roof illuminated the dark entrance in an eerie blue glow.

"Now," Tu said, "drive. But you might want to turn on the headlights."

twenty-two

Underground, the cruiser's radio fizzled out after we'd heard enough to know that the entire Swiss police force was in utter chaos. But I didn't need the frantic communications to tell me that. I'd seen enough.

The GPS still worked somehow. Tu claimed he didn't need it, but it helped me to at least know where we'd be if we were driving above-ground. Maybe it was only a mental comfort, but careening down a dark earthen tunnel, the end of which was always within sight of the bright headlights but never arrived, was pretty disorienting. Not that we were really careening. Tu could only open the tunnels at maybe twenty miles per hour.

Tu insisted on staying up front to "see," as he said. He kept his eyes mostly ahead, staring through the windshield at the tunnel he was opening with his Words, directing the churning and widening walls with his continual focus. Or semi-continual. He had plenty of spare brainpower to crow about the awesomeness of what he'd just done and to critique my driving, which was rich considering he didn't know how to drive. I guessed the Godspeakers didn't want to teach the Words anything that could increase their independence or ability to escape.

"If you're going to backseat drive, you should be in the backseat," Pavati said about five minutes into our joyride.

Her irritation was understandable. I sort of felt like punching something until my fist broke, and wouldn't have minded if that something was Tu. Not that any of this was his fault.

I tried to catch Khaya's expression in the rearview mirror, but all I could make out was the shadowy top of her head. And I didn't look for long, in case the tunnel changed direction without warning.

Pavati and Tu, of course, didn't know that Khaya had basically offered to save Drey instead of the world, just so I could get him back. She'd lied to me about a cure—seriously lied to me—so I appreciated her offer and the apology within it. But the apology was the only part of it I could accept.

Because I couldn't trade the world for Drey's life. Nor could I trade Khaya's life. I just couldn't do it.

Tears blinded me almost too much to drive. Drey was going to die, and I was driving away from him. This was like watching him bleed to death all over again, except worse, because I knew the exact thing I could do to save him. And I wouldn't do it.

Once again, all I had to say to him was goodbye. I couldn't

tell him how much he meant to me. And he couldn't tell me who he really was, or who I really was.

But maybe I could still find out. I hoped the address at least held some answers, even though it didn't hold a cure. Because soon—in one day—that would be all of Drey I had left. Whatever information I found there would be like his last words. And I desperately wanted to hear them.

On the upside, we were moving faster through Tu's tunnel on wheels than we would have on foot. We were already in the Swiss Alps, or under them. Whenever we next stopped for a break, I planned on asking Tu to enter Drey's address into the GPS. We'd probably reach it in a few hours—most destinations within the Alps were about that far away. And then Tu would have to decide what he wanted to do with himself, and I hoped it wouldn't involve prolonging his presence. For that matter, I would have to decide what I wanted to do with myself.

Pavati rattled the metal barrier behind Tu's head, startling me. I quickly wiped my eyes on the back of my hand.

"If I didn't know any better—and I don't—I would say there's some sexist discrimination going on here with the ladies stuffed back here with the groceries," Pavati announced. A wrapper crackled. "Though I guess that does mean we have access to all the food."

"Hey, give me something." Tu scratched at the screen.

"Sorry, won't fit through. More for us second-class citizens!"

Tu growled. Hunger didn't seem to improve his mood.

"Hey, check this out," he said a few minutes later as he

punched buttons on the GPS, only half-watching the extending tunnel. "I entered that address of yours. The GPS actually isn't working—it's only making an educated guess about where we are now, based on our direction and speed when the satellite signal was lost—but it's probably not too far off, since my tunnel is accurate. Look, it can give us the time to the destination. We're going as the crow flies, or as the gopher digs, so in about two hours—"

I glanced down at the glowing screen and the line that stretched from our current position into the mountains. "How did you know the address?"

"It was on that cheesy postcard you left in the backpack when you decided to go get yourself held up at gunpoint."

"How about you stay out of my shit next time?" The words were out of my mouth before I could stop them. I'd wanted him to enter the address, but not if he had to go through my few remaining belongings to do it.

"I just saved your ass, ass," Tu said in a murderous tone.

Pavati spoke up from the backseat. "There you go again, taking all the credit. Did you somehow miss Khaya's contribution back there?"

Khaya's silence was so noticeable it was almost loud.

Pavati added quickly, "Or my mad skills?"

Tu scoffed. "Your little tricks were nice and all, but if I hadn't gone into town like you all tried to keep me from doing, this punk would probably be dead"—he jerked his head at me— "and Khaya would be on a one-way flight back to the Athenaeum."

"Why did you go in by yourself?" Pavati asked in her

dead-serious tone. "One minute you were there in the trees with me, the next—poof."

I glanced at Tu. I hadn't known he'd left before Pavati. I'd assumed they'd come together. She must have been baiting him by bragging, so she could pounce once he touted his own actions. The entire backseat was now heavily silent, like a dark shadow where a predator crouched, ready to strike. Tu was probably grateful now for the screen separating them.

"You came too," he said, his words braced with defensiveness.

"I only made it in time because I ran my ass off, and that was only because I heard sirens and knew something was going down. I almost didn't find your tunnel in the first place, it was so well-hidden in the bushes."

"I left the tunnel open for you to follow me! Trust me, you wouldn't have found it if I hadn't wanted you to. I only went without you because I knew you'd try to stop me."

"You know what I think?" Pavati asked in a casual tone that was more frightening than an angry one. "I think you left your tunnel in place so you could come back to exactly where you'd left me and pretend you hadn't done anything."

"Done what? What would I have done?" There was an edge of nervousness under Tu's bluster. "I was only making sure these guys weren't getting themselves in trouble. I was going to help—"

"They didn't need help...yet. You were going to *make* trouble, to cause a disturbance like you'd wanted to, as a sign of defiance to Eden City. Tavin and Khaya beat you to it—

accidentally—but still, you managed to capitalize on the situation pretty well."

"So what?" Tu said. "Someone has to take some action, if none of you will." His tone was snide, but again, there was something else in it. Maybe it was my imagination, but he almost sounded relieved. Maybe Pavati had guessed wrong. "And I saved the day, so how about I get some appreciation instead of accusations?"

"You're appreciating yourself enough for all of us," I said. "We can leave you alone, you know, if you'd like some more privacy while you—Gods!"

The end of the tunnel had stopped moving forward, and I mashed on the brakes. We all pitched forward in our seats as the car screeched to a halt, the front bumper resting only a couple feet from a wall of solid earth.

Tu kicked open his door without a word, got out, and slammed it. I shot out of the car after him, into the dead-end tunnel lit by the headlights.

"Are you trying to wreck the car?" I shouted over the top of the cruiser, slamming my own door.

"I'm sick of your shit, Barnes," Tu said, facing me over the hood. He looked ready to leap over it, his bare shoulders tense, his hands balled into fists at his side.

There was a rapping on one of the back windows. Apparently the rear doors wouldn't open from the inside. It made sense, since the people who were usually back there had been arrested.

Neither Tu nor I moved.

"And I'm sick of yours," I said. "It won't be long before your drama queen antics get one of us killed."

Tu snarled. "Like I said, it's better to be doing something than nothing at all, you chickenshit waste of space. I don't know who you think you are, and I don't know why Pavati and Khaya are playing along with you like you're worth something—worth even sharing our air—but I know the truth. You're nobody. Not only are you nobody, but you're trying to drag us down with you. And I'm not going to let that happen."

Pavati smacked the back window with her palm, her muffled, angry cry barely reaching us through the glass.

"You don't have to be here!" I yelled. "Why are you?"

Tu glanced at the car—toward Pavati. We both knew why he was still here. Not even I wanted to point out the obvious, though Pavati probably couldn't hear me. Mocking him for that would be too low a blow even to give Tu.

"In fact," I said instead, "I'd rather you left me the hell alone. Go be China's boy toy for all I care. Just don't expect these two to be as eager as you are to go be tools for the rich and powerful."

Tu really looked like he was about to come at me when a sharp crack made him pause. It had come from Khaya's side of the backseat. She hadn't broken the window, but it sounded like she'd full-on kicked it.

Tu and I could fight it out without interference with Khaya and Pavati trapped—maybe they hadn't resorted to using their Words yet, or maybe they were having trouble behind all the steel and bulletproof glass. But then Tu could try to kill me without interference, as he would likely do given the opportunity. And he would likely succeed. Never mind the whole Word of Earth thing; he had the Athenaeum's training on his side, which most certainly had covered hand-to-hand combat. I still felt like fighting him, I was so angry, but it wouldn't do me any good.

I took a deep breath, then opened the nearest back door. Khaya came flying out like an angry cat, looking too infuriated to speak, followed by Pavati, whose outburst reached us before she did.

"What the hell is the matter with you two? Can we cease and desist with the peacock display? Or else the next one to leave me locked in a car will get his balls removed by yours truly." Pavati raised a hand and wiggled her fingers. "The old-fashioned way."

Tu took a step back from her. "No need to get your panties in a twist. We were just having a chat. You know—"

"If you say 'man-to-man,' you'd better be pinching those legs together as tight as you can."

Tu swallowed and shifted his feet closer together.

Khaya squeezed her eyes closed and exhaled, long and slow, her beautiful face steely. When she opened them, she seemed calmer. "Look, everyone is hungry, tired, and probably freezing now that we're out of the car. Let's take a quick break."

She held out a sweatshirt for me without meeting my eyes. Still, it was more than I'd expected after I'd taken so long to let her out of the backseat.

While Khaya doled out the rest of the sweatshirts, Pavati

tossed energy bars at everyone. Tu left his sweatshirt on the hood and let his energy bar bounce off his back as he raised his hand to the dirt wall and started speaking to it.

No small burrow formed around us this time. The walls kept expanding, more passageways branching off, spiraling staircases of earth rising and dropping to other levels. Fresh night air seeped in through hidden openings in the ceiling, which was near enough to the surface to reveal dangling roots. Tu was showing off, of course. At least building an underground mansion was a better use of his testosterone than pounding my face in.

After pulling out the backpack and clicking the flashlight on, I shut off the car, which was now parked in our spacious underground living room of packed dirt. I shined the light at Khaya's feet, about to apologize quietly to her, when she burst out laughing.

The sound was amazing, but shocking. Pavati looked at her with her eyebrows raised.

Khaya covered her mouth, still giggling—Khaya, *giggling*, as if we'd thought we couldn't be more surprised and she was proving otherwise. Maybe she'd been more affected by the battle than I'd estimated.

"Sorry," she said, tugging at the front of her black sweatshirt. She gestured at me and Pavati. "It's these."

"Why?" I asked, looking down at my own chest. The only thing on the sweatshirt that I could understand was a symbol—a red heart. The rest was thick blue lettering.

"They say *I Heart Martigny* in French."

Our souvenirs from the town we'd just shaken up—literally and figuratively. Pavati started chuckling, then burst out laughing along with Khaya. Maybe the hilarity was half due to relief over the dissipating tension. As I'd discovered under the lake during my first almost-fight with Tu, some things could be side-splitting when everything else was so serious.

Tu finally picked up his sweatshirt, as if all this time he'd wanted to prove he wasn't cold, even shirtless. He frowned at it and pulled it over his head. His frown deepened. "What the—? This barely fits!"

It was probably my laughter that did it. Or maybe when I said, "Don't worry, we can replace it with an *I Heart China* sweatshirt."

He leapt straight over the hood of the car and onto me. I hit the floor with his weight on my chest, the breath leaving my lungs like a compressed bellows. One of his fists knocked stars across my vision before I knew what was happening. Another made me taste blood.

Someone tore him off me, slammed him facedown into the ground, and twisted his arm behind his back, hard enough to make him cry out. When I could focus again—but not yet breathe—I figured I would see Pavati with her knee in his back, since she'd been the one threatening him. But no. It was Khaya. She was snarling down at him, her hair a wild mane around her savage face.

"Khaya," Pavati said. "His arm is about to—"

There was a muffled snap, and Tu screamed. Both sounds were pretty awful.

"Too late."

Khaya leapt off him, a look of horror on her face. "Gods, I didn't mean to! I was only..."

Tu rolled onto his uninjured shoulder, gripping his arm and groaning. He must have been in too much pain to say anything biting.

Pavati sighed. "At least you can heal him. Come on, let's get him into one of the rooms."

Khaya tried to help him up, but Tu batted her hand away. "Bitch," he wheezed.

Pavati hauled him upright, none-too-gently. "None of that now," she said, then half-supported, half-dragged him down one of the hallways.

Khaya followed, looking more scared than ashamed. Not of Tu, I thought. Of herself.

twenty-three

When my breath came back fully, it had to fight for room in my throat with the blood. I rolled over on the packed dirt floor of our warren and spit out as much as I could, probing for damage as gently as possible with my index finger. Tu's left hook had loosened one of my teeth on the right side, and where his first punch had nearly knocked me senseless, my cheek was puffy and excruciatingly tender. I would have a spectacular black eye in the morning. Maybe a pair.

"Gods," I said to myself from my huddle on the ground. I wanted to find a warmer place to lie down, away from the stairs leading to the surface and the colder air outside, but I didn't feel like moving yet.

"Yup," Pavati said behind me, returning from the room where she'd taken Tu. "How are you?"

"Fine." I grimaced, then winced when grimacing hurt. "How's Tu?"

"Khaya dislocated his shoulder and fractured a few other odds and ends, but she's patching him up. He'll just need to sleep it off. Ah, well, he probably deserved it."

So much for reaching Drey's address in two hours. I could have punched myself a third time.

"Then I deserved this." I reached up to touch my face, then thought better of it. "I set him off by getting him a smaller sweatshirt. I did it on purpose."

Pavati retrieved the flashlight from where it had fallen and crouched next to me. "That's mature of you to admit it, but you didn't *quite* deserve to have your face mangled over a joke, even an irritating one." She whistled after she brushed back my hair to look at my cheek. Her hand fell away and she sighed. "He's not a bad guy, really. He's just conflicted."

She looked pretty conflicted herself as she glanced down the hallway where Tu and Khaya were.

"But why?" I said, embarking on the long climb to my feet. "I mean, I see why he's pissed at Eden City, but then to want to go play the same role for some other country..."

"He can't imagine not using his power," Pavati said, looping her arm through mine and helping me up. "But as powerful as he is, he's only one guy. He wants to be a part of something. Which I can sympathize with, even if I'm too cynical to think I could ever really belong anywhere."

I steadied myself against Pavati as a surge of dizziness threatened to knock me down again. "Well, like you said, China basically sold him into slavery before he was conceived. Why would he want to go to them, in particular?"

She sighed and started walking me toward the downward

spiraling stairs like an invalid, scooping up the backpack for me and aiming the flashlight while she was at it. "It's complicated. It has a lot to do with his mother."

"The Japanese lady? I mean, the Word with a Japanese donor parent?" I said before Pavati could correct me.

"That's the one. Also known as Tsuchi. She was the reason Tu looked toward his unknown donor father from China—and China itself—for a sense of belonging. It didn't help that Japan already had such a shaky relationship with Eden City in the first place. In fact, you could say that started everything."

I winced as my foot hit the first downward step, the motion vibrating up my leg and torso and into my head. At least the air was warmer the deeper we went. "What do you mean?"

"It has to do with the Words of Power and how, these days, only the Word of Shaping is left out of the original four," Pavati said as we made our slow way down the staircase. "The Word of Movement was the first to go—vanished, centuries ago. No one knows quite where he went missing, but it would have been pretty hard to keep track of an insanely powerful telekinetic without all the modern innovations they have for us now, like monitors. Then the Word of Naming—arguably the most powerful of the Words of Power—was assassinated by an agent of the Spanish crown in the mid–nineteenth century."

We were in a hallway that would have been pitch-black without the flashlight. Pavati steered me toward the closest doorway, which opened up to reveal a smallish room with a raised dirt platform in the middle—a bed.

I didn't have the wherewithal to ask her why the Word of Naming had been so powerful before she continued.

"That was what inspired Eden City to make other countries feel invested in the Words, with the whole donor-country scheme. It kept jealousy of Eden City's power to a minimum, if the whole world was busy vying for their favor."

She paused the story to let me drop onto the bed and busied herself pulling out the emergency blanket and water bottle for me. It was amazingly nice of her, and I didn't have the energy to protest.

"That leaves the Word of Time," she said, shaking out the silvery blanket. "Japan was a rising star after they opened their borders to the West and secured their country's contribution to the Words near the turn of the century—the first non-European country to do so. The future Word of Time was born in 1895 as a little boy named Toki, and all seemed to be going pretty swell until ... well, until Toki killed himself after the First World War, taking the Word of Time into oblivion with him."

"Why'd he do that?" Running away was one thing, but suicide was a pretty extreme form of escape. I eased myself onto my back with more winces—or maybe it was one prolonged wince.

Pavati tossed the blanket over me. "My theory is that time is probably not a thing that many people can mess with and stay sane. The Words of Time had been notoriously nuts throughout history, and this was probably just another expression of that insanity. It's amazing Time wasn't lost sooner that way."

She took a seat on the edge of the bed, her grim smile illuminated from below by the flashlight in her lap as if she was telling a spooky story. She must have noticed, because she said, "Sorry, this isn't the most comforting bedtime story. Anyway, Eden City, of course, opted for the racist theory and blamed Japan, calling Japanese stock unstable and weak. Ritualistic suicide *does* have a history in their culture, with the *hara-kiri* and stuff like that. It's still a problem today—but it's not exactly weakness, and Toki wasn't even raised within Japanese culture. He was born in Eden City like all of us. But the City Council didn't care, and Japan was banned from contributing to the Words.

"That pissed the Japanese off big time. Some people think it encouraged them to act the way they did in World War II, making them go all imperialistic and invade anyone in the vicinity to try to prove their strength and save face." Pavati shrugged. "Who knows—maybe it worked. Because Eden City accepted Japan back in '65. But the Godspeakers were careful. First of all, they only allowed a girl to be born, thinking she might be less prone to suicidal samurai tendencies—which is sexist horseshit, but that's another discussion. Secondly, they raised her to have ultimate control over her emotions. This woman—Tsuchi—was a stone. Fitting, I guess, for the Word of Earth. But not so good for a mother."

Pavati hesitated, her eyes drifting to the floor. "We only have our one real parent until we're five, but that's more than enough time for them to help shape what we become before they die. And Tsuchi...well, she ignored Tu. Didn't let any attachment form. With such a cold and unloving mother—

never mind the stigma still surrounding the loss of Time—it's no wonder Tu clung to his donor father's heritage."

"China," I said. "So that's why he wants to go wave their flag for them."

Pavati nodded. "You know, Khaya and I were lucky to have at least one parent so caring. Tu and Herio... not so lucky. That's probably why Herio turned out the way he did, too. Next to him, Tu's not so bad."

"What do you mean? Em didn't love Herio?"

Pavati continued staring at the floor, twisting the flashlight in her hands and sending shadows skittering across her face. "Em had a premature stillborn the first go-around. She wasn't ready to carry again so soon, and yet each generation of Words needs to be born within a short window. So the doctors used the same donor material from France, extracted some of Em's, and used a surrogate mother. Herio didn't come from Em's body, and she never really tried to make that connection, you know? She never loved him like a son, even though he had her genes. So Herio basically had two donor parents, nothing more than genetics."

I wasn't quite sure how the conversation had switched from Tu to Herio. Neither topic was really comfortable, but together, they were enough to make my head start pounding like a drum.

Pavati must have noticed. "Go to sleep," she said, and did something even nicer and more surprising than tucking me in. She bent over and kissed my forehead, right at the hairline. Then she stood, taking the flashlight with her. She paused before she walked through the doorway. "Try not to judge him too harshly."

I wasn't quite sure if she meant Tu or Herio. She probably meant the former, since no one seemed to feel too kindly toward the Word of Death.

I did sleep. And I slept pretty well, aside from the fact that whenever I rolled over, the sore parts of my face—which was basically all of it—came into contact with the unyielding surface of the bed and I woke up. At one such point I realized Khaya hadn't joined me. A hollow pang of disappointment rang in the pit of my stomach like a gong, but I didn't have the flashlight to go find her. I would probably walk face-first into a wall, which was the last thing I needed.

Then I woke up when I rolled over and my face *didn't* ache.

Her voice came out of the darkness nearby: "I want to hurt people now, for you."

I reached toward the sound of her voice, over the side of the bed, and my fingers encountered her sweatshirt-clad shoulder. She was sitting on the ground next to me.

"Khaya? Why aren't you sleeping?"

"I'm frightened."

It took me a sluggish second to process what she'd said before that. And then a few more seconds to remember everything that had happened: her attack on Tu to defend me; her recent, arguably violent, uses of the Word of Life; and, most shocking of all, her near-surrender in the supermarket to save Drey and give me my life back. Which, needless to say, would have hurt a lot of people, including herself. Honestly, I didn't know how I felt about any of it. It wasn't what I would call frightening, exactly, but it was certainly something.

If I couldn't articulate the thought in my own head better than that, I didn't have any business saying anything out loud.

But I was grateful, and probably would have done all those things for her if I'd had power like hers—maybe even something as foolish as condemning the world. At least I would never be faced with that kind of decision, because her well-being happened to coincide with everyone else's.

Everyone's except for Drey's.

As if she knew what I was thinking, she said, "I'm sorry I lied about there being a cure. I didn't want...I didn't want you to..."

"I know why you did it," I said. "You were trying to give me hope and to keep me from turning myself in, or turning you in and messing up our lives and the whole rest of the world while I was at it. It's okay."

"Is it?" Her voice broke.

I wrapped my arms around her shoulders and buried my face into her neck. It was nice that it didn't hurt. "Shh, don't cry. It is okay. And thank you for healing me." I took a deep breath and noticed something odd. "You smell good."

"Pavati drew enough water for me to have a bath. It was chilly but worth it."

"I need to do that tomorrow. Desperately." I couldn't remember the last time I'd had a shower—it felt like years ago. I shouldn't have been hugging Khaya with how I smelled, but I didn't let her go.

"You still want to go to that address?" she asked.

"I need to know who Drey was…who I am."

"I understand. I'll follow you, if you'll let me."

It struck me, the sudden sense that we were both lost and following each other nowhere. Drey had always quoted that saying about the blind leading the blind. He'd been talking about Eden City and the rest of the world, but it applied equally well to me and Khaya.

I wasn't even sure what I hoped to find—a recording from Drey, or maybe even a journal that Khaya could read to me, telling me the truth? Something.

"Then you'll just have to follow me this one last time," I said, speaking into her neck. "After that, whatever I find, I can forget about all of it and just…be with you. We can both be anonymous nobodies together and go wherever our feet take us."

Like the cure for Drey, it sounded too good to be true. But I could always hope.

"Okay," Khaya said softly.

Eventually she shifted and slid onto the bed next to me, and I tucked her under the blanket and re-wrapped my arms around her. I couldn't wait for the day when we'd have real blankets and beds that were soft and not made of crackly plastic or dirt. In the meantime, I supposed these would have to do.

She fell asleep, and I must have followed shortly, because then Pavati was waking us up, shaking our shoulders, a faint, natural light illuminating the doorway behind her. I knew it must be morning.

"Tavin, Khaya." Pavati sounded more distressed than I'd ever heard her. I understood why when she said, "Tu is gone."

Twenty-four

My drowsiness dropped away as if Pavati had slapped me awake. Tu was gone?

"Where'd he go?" I asked, sitting bolt-upright.

"I don't know," Pavati said, clutching her elbows through her sweatshirt and looking vulnerable for the first time.

We were all up and moving in about two seconds, searching through every hallway and room in the mazelike underground mansion Tu had built for us, calling for him and hearing our shouts fall dead, muffled between the earthen walls. The place was empty of everything but us, our few supplies, and the police cruiser. At least the car was still there. It wouldn't do us a fat lot of good underground without Tu, but it meant he hadn't gone far.

Hadn't I wanted him to go away? But not leaving us stranded, not leaving Pavati looking as crushed as she did, not leaving Drey dying and me so far from his final answers. I'd been a short-sighted idiot, telling him to get lost when we all relied on him so much.

And maybe I felt bad for reasons beyond losing his usefulness. He was more than a tool, after all. Maybe I felt bad for being a jerk. And maybe, just maybe, after everything Pavati had told me, I even felt bad for him.

So when Tu suddenly came walking down the stairs that dropped from the morning light up above, I felt overwhelming relief rather than disappointment that he wasn't gone for good.

"Tu!" Pavati cried from where we'd been aimlessly standing in the center of the main room. "Where have you been?"

Tu looked taken off guard by her worried tone. He also seemed hesitant, as if he didn't know if he was welcome or not. It must have made him forget to be sarcastic. "Getting gas." He hefted two red jugs in either hand. "I don't know if anyone else noticed, but we were low."

I hadn't noticed. I had been too busy trying to drive in a moving tunnel.

Pavati only stared, her mouth open.

"Where did you find gas?" Khaya sounded reserved—not exactly cool, suspicious, or timid, but somehow all three.

"A nearby town. I saw it on the GPS last night. After I brought us closer to the surface, it started working again. It was part of the reason I decided to stop here, aside from...you know." Wanting to strangle me. "I didn't want to wake anyone this morning. I was, uh, rested up sooner than you guys." Probably from Khaya's healing that had knocked him out before the rest of us went to sleep. He was being remarkably tactful for Tu.

"Did you steal those?" Pavati asked, finding her voice—and with it, her equilibrium. She arched a dark eyebrow at the jugs of gasoline. "If someone saw you, they could have followed you."

Tu finally scoffed—he'd held out for a while. "Followed me underground? Please. And Khaya left the Swiss cash in the car last night. I used that."

Pavati's second eyebrow shot up with the first. "Huh. Amazing. I didn't know you'd had it in you." Her face broke into a grin. "I thought you'd abandoned me."

Her cheerful expression seemed to be hiding something darker inside, but for now it was nice to see a smile back on her face.

"Never," Tu said, so seriously that Pavati looked away from him.

"Shall we eat breakfast and get back on the subterranean highway?" She headed for the car and our store of food, but then she stopped. "First things first, Tavin. Good Gods, you need a bath."

As if on cue, a fierce itch attacked my scalp. "Yeah, I agree."

An hour later, we were back on the unnerving subterranean highway, as Pavati called it, and I felt more gloriously clean than I'd ever felt in my life. In one of Tu's many rooms, there'd been an indentation in the earth, the surface hardened nearly to stone, which Pavati had filled with the warmest water she could find. It wasn't very warm in this neck of the woods—she'd lamented not being near enough to any hot springs—but it had been good enough for me. Ice water, or maybe even acid, would have been good enough. I'd waged war on myself with the soap we'd taken from the market, and was now feeling more refreshed than I had in days.

We covered miles quickly, and even managed to pick up a crackling radio station for a few minutes, long enough for a song to make us feel like we were as carefree and happy as a bunch of kids on a road trip.

But I wasn't carefree or particularly happy as we neared Drey's address, and my disquiet increased when we actually arrived.

Resurfacing in the mountains was a blinding experience in the veiled late afternoon light, even though it wasn't bright outside. It was cloudy, but the snow reflected what little light there was from every surface. The troubled sky lurked behind it all like a dark shadow.

We had to take a few seconds to blink and squint, waiting for our eyes to adjust. Especially me, since I was driving.

I hadn't seen snow that often before. In Eden City, it only snowed on national holidays, thanks to Luft, when the city was already half closed-down and Drey and I didn't have to go out in the truck. Snow was a special occasion, which only added to my sense of expectation.

When we reached a wide, pale clearing surrounded by trees, I stopped the cruiser. The road was buried in snow, and I didn't know where it lay across the field. I didn't want to get our only means of transportation stuck in this icy wonderland.

"This is it?" I asked, looking at the GPS. Tu nodded, unusually quiet.

A small cabin sat at the opposite end of the clearing, reminding me, absurdly, of a cupcake with white icing, the thin chimney sticking up like an unlit candle on top. The Matterhorn, the crooked peak I'd seen so often on the postcard, rose hazily in the distance through the clouds.

Everything was hushed as we opened the car doors, as if a blanket had not only settled on the ground but also overhead, muffling the world. The cold air felt like a held breath, like something was about to happen. Or like something was waiting. Before I got out, I slipped the gun and pocketknife into my pants, just in case.

Our voices fell quiet with everything else. Tu looked around, almost like he was expecting someone, too. But there were no tracks. That should have helped alleviate the—apparently shared—feeling that something was waiting, but it didn't. Maybe the cabin itself was what was waiting.

There was nothing else to do but go check it out. We trekked across the clearing in silence, my feet growing numb in my boots. The sweatshirt was no longer enough to keep me warm, and my foggy breath drifted around my face with the light snowflakes that began to fall.

The tiny, sheltered porch creaked when we stepped on it. The door was locked. I had an inspiration, right when Tu was about to break a small window, and checked under a frosted, snow-filled pot, its previous contents long dead. That was where Drey had always kept a key next to the back door of the garage. I had to kick the pot to dislodge it from its frozen resting place and ended up breaking it, but it was worth it. There was a key underneath, glinting gold under a thin sheet of ice. I used the pocketknife to chip it free.

The door creaked even louder than the porch when we opened it. We filed quietly inside, as if trying not to wake someone. Tu stood in the entryway, his formidable arms folded against the cold. Pavati crossed the room to a small iron stove with split wood stacked nearby, located some matches, and started building a fire. Khaya followed me as I looked around.

The only furniture next to a small kitchenette was a table with a single, rickety chair. A threadbare plaid couch sat beside the stove. There were no pictures on the walls, because the walls were lined with bookshelves. There were more books in that tiny cabin than I'd ever seen in my life.

A narrow staircase ran up the back wall, and I dashed up it when I didn't see any immediate answers to my questions in the main room. I had to duck so I didn't smack my head on the ceiling, now the floor, as I came up into a small loft with a low, slanting roof. There was a musty-looking bed and a single nightstand. A quick search yielded nothing under the bed, nothing in the drawer of the nightstand but another book.

No device with a recording. No letter. No pictures. No nothing.

I rushed back downstairs, scanning every nook and cranny, opening every cupboard and drawer. I found nothing except utensils, tools, dried and canned goods, and books, everywhere books, shelves and shelves of books. But not a word, not even a whisper, from Drey. Maybe the books could somehow tell me Drey's secrets, but I couldn't read them. I picked up one from a shelf, hoping to see handwriting—a journal of Drey's—and then another and another as I found only typewriting, until I was tearing books off the shelves and hurling them in a pile on the ground—the dumb, infuriating things, keeping their damned secrets locked in their pages.

"Tavin," Khaya said.

"This *was* only a place for me to escape to." To escape even from the truth, apparently. All that hope, that anticipation, and yet... "There's nothing here," I said more loudly.

"I told you," Tu said from the entryway. "This is the sticks. Just a place to hide under a rock."

I spun on Tu with a rage I'd never felt before, and he took a step back.

I moved toward him and accidentally kicked up the edge of a ratty rug, uncovering a line in the floor: a trap door. My hope skyrocketed. I dropped to my knees and wrenched it aside as quickly as the rug. But all hope came crashing back down when it only revealed refrigerated packets of money and another gun, this one a six-shooter that looked too rusty to use.

A gun. All Drey seemed to have left me was guns.

Khaya put a hand on my shoulder. "What do you want to do now?"

I wanted to scream. But instead I stood and walked over to a window. I leaned my head against a freezing pane of glass, looking out into the world of tumbling white. The sky was falling.

Drey was dying. He might already be dead. And I would never know his secrets.

A tear splashed on the dusty wooden windowsill. Mine, I supposed.

Maybe this was for the best—not knowing. I took a deep breath. I'd said I would be satisfied to remain a wordless nobody, whatever I found here. And I had Khaya. She was enough—more than enough, more than I'd ever hoped for or deserved. I had an indefinite future with her to look forward to. I didn't know who I really was, but we had each other, and that was okay. The world would be okay.

Drey ... Drey wouldn't be okay, but I couldn't do anything about that. I could ruin my life just to say goodbye, but I knew Drey wouldn't want that. This place was the proof. It held no cure, no answers ... it was only a place to hide, to be safe. That was all Drey had wanted for me.

I would just have to accept the fact that I was powerless, keep the guns under the floorboards—just in case—and stop pretending I was something I wasn't. I didn't want power anyway, if all it meant was what Khaya had said: that I could hurt people. There had been enough pain already.

My hand found Khaya's, where she had come up behind me. She was an anchor, grounding my thoughts, my emotions.

"Maybe we should rest here for a while," I said. "Get warm, regroup." I glanced up at Pavati and Tu. "You don't have to stay if you don't want to, of course."

That was when we heard a noise outside. The low hum of engines.

I spun toward the door, and all of us scrambled out onto the porch in a stampede. For a second, the cloud of our combined breath made it difficult to see across the snow-filled clearing. But the air cleared except for the snow, which wasn't dense enough to hide the line of black SUVs approaching across the field.

"Tu," Pavati said, realizing the truth before the rest of us. "You didn't..."

"They'll help us!" Tu said, but he couldn't say anything else before I tackled him, my anger resurging in a blinding wave. Both of us flew off the porch and into a deep drift of snow. The cold was shocking, the white powder in my eyes and down in my sweatshirt, but that didn't keep me from hitting any and every part of him I could reach, as hard as I could. My knuckles split but I didn't stop, not even when flecks of red began to stain the snow.

Pavati and Khaya dragged me off of him, and only then did I realize he hadn't been fighting back, only holding up his arms to protect his head as best he could. Which hadn't been very well, while lying on his back in a snowdrift. His nose and lip were bleeding profusely from both sides, and the white of his left eye was a vivid half-red.

The sight of his blood only made me want to see more, and Pavati and Khaya both had to use their full weight and strength to hold me back, the three of us slipping and staggering in the snow. My control was so far gone I didn't know if it would ever return.

But it did, slowly. Especially after Khaya twisted my arm behind my back like she had Tu's the night before, if not as far. The sharp pain brought me to my knees and pulled a gasp from my throat, cutting through the red haze and clearing my head rather remarkably.

"Okay, okay," Tu said, his words thick through all the blood, holding up one hand in a gesture of truce while the other clutched his nose. I'd probably broken it.

The SUVs had parked in a loose semi-circle in front of the cabin.

"Not okay, Tu," Pavati said, no longer holding me back now that Khaya had me subdued. Her tone was so dangerous I wondered if she would charge him next. "Not okay."

"Look, you're right, I called someone. When I did that publicity visit to China a year ago, the president slipped me this number when he shook my hand. I've called it twice now, once in each town, and gave them the address here. This is them—the Chinese, not Eden City!" Tu clarified as Pavati took a threatening step toward him. "They just want to help us."

"*Use* us, you mean," Pavati said, casting a narrowed, sideways glance at the surrounding vehicles. Doors were opening, people in black suits were getting out. "This is going to be bad, Tu. I'm not going without a fight."

"Just hear them out! They're not here to hurt us."

"I have no doubt they're here with our best interests at heart." Pavati spat at his feet in disgust. "Grow up, Tu."

Khaya released my arm and helped me to my feet as the men approached. About half of them looked Chinese, and the other half were white. All of them looked strong, trained, and armed, though I couldn't exactly see any guns or muscles beneath the suits.

"Why are the Swiss here?" Tu called, as loud as he could through his battered lips. "I thought I said no one else."

A Chinese man with streaks of gray in his neatly combed hair stepped forward. He started speaking in Chinese, but Tu interrupted him.

"English, please, so my friends can understand."

So we could understand that he wasn't betraying us, his so-called friends? But he had betrayed us.

The man's smile never reached his eyes. "Of course," he said. "And of course you understand the Swiss have to be here. We had to give them something to fly into their airspace, land on their soil, and borrow transportation from them on such short notice." He gestured at the hefty vehicles. "That is simply how it's done. Protocol—"

"I don't give a rat's ass about protocol," Tu said. "And what do you mean, give them something? What do they want?"

The Swiss representatives didn't say anything. The Chinese man—probably some high-up dignitary or diplomat—clasped his hands in front of himself and said, "As you come from China, this young woman here"—he held his hand out to Pavati—"comes from America, and the Swiss have promised to take care of her until she can be safely returned to her rightful place."

Take care of her, my ass. They were either going to keep her or sell her to America—or the highest bidder—for an obscene amount of money.

Pavati snarled at the man, wiping the sleek smile off his

face. "We come from nowhere! It's only Eden City's clever illusion that makes you think we have shit to do with any of you."

"But Tu knows it's not an illusion," the man said. "He knows where he belongs."

Tu shook his head. "I'm not going if Pavati doesn't come with me. That was the deal."

"But, young man, deals must be made with others as well, not only with you. You see, we are on Swiss soil." The man raised his hands as if to say, *What else can we do?*

I was about to tell him what he could do with himself in no uncertain terms, but Khaya spoke next, her flat voice carrying. "And what happens to Tavin and me?"

"Well—" the man began, but a man from the Swiss side stepped forward, interrupting him.

He was the kind of man who wore sunglasses so his opponents couldn't see where his eyes were directed. Or to look like a badass. Either way, he succeeded. "Eden City has agreed to let the Chinese have the Word of Earth and the Swiss to have the Word of Water, without a fight, if we hand you—both of you—over to them."

Surprise flickered across the Chinese man's face, but then it was gone, wiped away as if it had never been there. He hadn't known about this Swiss agreement with Eden City. Whatever he'd been expecting to be done with Khaya and me, it wasn't this.

I barked a brief, bitter laugh. "You're all making deals behind each other's backs—more like stabbing each other in the back! Tu, you did it to us, the Chinese did it to you, and then the Swiss did it to China. And you know what? Eden City is going to do it to you," I said to Mr. Sunglasses, "when they invade your country. You think you're snuggling in bed together, sharing pillow talk? You're wrong. Eden City shares with no one, and you'll be the first to fall. She can tell you." I pointed at Khaya. "They didn't say *why* they wanted her, did they, why they would be willing to trade two of the most powerful Words just for the Word of Life and a wordless nobody like me? They don't want you to know what she can do, or what we both know. When they have Khaya again, getting Pavati and Tu back will be easy for them."

Even drawing attention to Khaya would be worth it if I could get them interested enough not to give us up, or at least stall for time. I seemed to have gotten the Chinese man's attention, but Mr. Sunglasses shook his head, a cold smile barely moving his lips. "The decision has been made. Representatives of Eden City will be here shortly to collect you two. Now, if you would all come quietly—"

"Are we being welcomed home or imprisoned?" Tu demanded.

"Same thing," Pavati said. "Always has been and always will be, for us."

Tu took Pavati's hand. She broke off her stare at Mr. Sunglasses to glance at him in surprise.

So Tu wouldn't let Pavati go without a fight either, even if that meant he had to turn on the Chinese. The two of them looked like regular teenagers, standing in their matching sweatshirts in the snow. Abnormally good-looking teenagers, but still—the world knew of the power of the Words, but they hadn't witnessed it firsthand in a while. My only hope was that these guys would underestimate Tu and Pavati and what the two of them could do together. They were only men with guns, like in Martigny; there were no Godspeakers or additional Words here to interfere.

Then we heard the helicopter, blades beating the air. It flew over us, coming from behind the cabin and sweeping low to touch down in the middle of the clearing in a swirl of white. The black of the helicopter looked sinister against the white backdrop, like a giant raven perched in the snow.

I would have recognized Dr. Swanson and Herio from a mile away. At this distance, they were close enough to meet my eyes as they stepped out of the helicopter, and for Swanson to raise a hand in greeting.

twenty-five

Swanson and Herio weren't approaching through the snow. They were waiting—for us to go to them, likely.

Mr. Sunglasses surveyed them. "See, they stuck to the agreement," he said, in a fair imitation of a reasonable tone. "No betrayal. They brought only a few men and one Word, like we each have." He peered over his shades. "Looks like Herio."

He was certainly well-informed, and it occurred to me that this man probably knew all about Eden City's plans. Maybe he was one of those in the Swiss government waiting for it to fall, so he could be the first to catch the spoils.

Tu and Pavati still had time to act. I was about to signal them when someone else—and something else—disembarked from the helicopter. The man was dressed in the white, doctorlike garb of the Athenaeum and might actually have been a doctor, or at least a medic, because he was pushing a gurney. Someone was on it, swathed in blankets and IV tubes.

"Oh, Gods," I said.

It was Drey.

I took a step forward without thinking, then stopped, my teeth grinding so hard they creaked. Swanson called across the open space.

"I, too, want Andre to live, Tavin. Khaya can heal him, no strings attached. I only want to talk. Come, we'll meet in the middle."

He motioned for his two uniformed men to stay near the chopper with their guns while he and Herio advanced with the medic, who was pushing the gurney through the snow. The wheels on the bed had been replaced with a gliding, sledlike base. How well-planned.

It had to be a trap. But Drey…Drey was right there, and we could save him. The delegation from Eden City was small, exactly half the numbers of the joint Chinese-Swiss delegation, which might make them easier to take on. Eden City did have Herio, but the guys surrounding us had more guns, especially since Swanson had told the two security guards to wait by the helicopter. We probably stood a better chance against Swanson.

But only if I thought it through. Swanson was smart. I understood why he'd brought Drey, as well as the small security force. He wanted to put the Chinese and the Swiss at ease, and to lure Khaya and me in before we had a chance to flee. But why Herio? Swanson didn't want to kill us—or at least, not Khaya—and besides, he could kill us in all sorts of ways without Herio. The Word of Death was supposedly useless in any tactical, large-scale way, so why hadn't Agonya or Luft come instead? All Herio did was make me insanely edgy…

Which was why Swanson had brought him, I realized. To distract me, to keep my eyes nailed to Herio whenever they weren't on Swanson.

The medic. The medic would have the tranquilizer gun. He was the real threat. Herio was probably under orders not to do anything; just a phantom to frighten us, a diversion.

Knowing all this—and this time I didn't need Khaya or Pavati or anyone else to tell me I was right—I made a final decision.

"They're never going to let you have her, Tu," I murmured, glancing at Pavati. "Earthworm on my signal."

I didn't say *or else*, but it was obvious in my tone. And I meant it. If my plan went awry, Tu would be the one I came after if I wasn't dead. He knew it; I could see it in his eyes.

"Let's go," Khaya said, calm as always, and we started through the snow toward Swanson.

I had a diversion of my own, something for them to look at while Tu and Pavati worked their magic. I pulled the gun out of the back of my pants and held it at my side, in plain sight.

"I see we're both armed," Swanson said when we drew nearer, shooting a meaningful glance at Herio, as if the Word was a weapon—his only weapon. "But this doesn't have to come to violence. We each have something the other person wants."

I halted well away from their group, and Khaya stopped

with me. "I thought you said we could heal Drey, no strings attached. Khaya and I aren't going to trade her life for his."

"I spoke the truth," Swanson said, motioning the medic forward with Drey. "What I want is to talk, only."

I couldn't look at Drey's face for long. It was so good to see him alive, even looking as ghastly as he did—which made him yet another distraction.

Swanson and Herio hung back about twenty feet while the medic stopped, with only the gurney between us. We faced him over Drey's still form. The medic's eyes were placid, expressionless, but his act didn't fool me. He looked as if he were made of steel.

I chanced a glance behind us at Pavati and Tu. They stood uneasily in front of the Chinese and Swiss delegation. All of them were quiet, watching us, waiting to see what would happen.

Khaya laid a hand on Drey's pale ankle and began muttering a string of Hebrew Words under her breath, her eyes closed. I would need to keep my eyes open for both of us.

"So." I forced myself to look at Swanson so he wouldn't think I suspected the medic. "Talk."

"Andre is my friend," Swanson began.

"That's why you sent Herio to kill him."

"Herio was a little"—Swanson glanced at him, while Herio stared at me almost hungrily—"overzealous. We thought you would bring Khaya back to the Athenaeum if you knew we had Andre and that his life was at stake. But it didn't work out that way, and you thought he was dead after you found him at the garage. We recovered him and have cared for him. We never meant to kill him, or let his pain last this long."

"Still, that's some way to treat a friend."

Swanson took a deep breath, as if trying to calm himself, but he already looked calm in his gray suit beneath the gray sky. "Andre has done more for me than anyone I know. You have no idea—but I will tell you all in due time. As I've already told you, he eventually decided to work against me, and both the Godspeakers and the City Council have no tolerance for traitors. I had to act, even though I regretted it."

He sounded sincere, but I couldn't believe it.

"What did he ever do to you?" I demanded. "Aside from get me away from you? Not that I can believe that you're my…" I swallowed.

"Your father. Yes, Tavin, I am, and Andre took you away from me because I told him to do so, as a favor to me—one that I can never repay."

My mouth opened. Then closed. I tried again. "What?"

"Yes, Andre gave up a brilliant career as my assistant—a junior Godspeaker who showed talent like I have not seen since—to take you out of the Athenaeum and live a life of ignominy, to raise you in ignorance of the Words and their politics. But I feel this favor, while not repaid, was somewhat nullified when he had you abduct Khaya, risking your life to do so."

"What?" I said again, stupidly. "He didn't tell me to abduct Khaya! That was all me. And I thought—" All this time I'd thought Drey had somehow saved me from Swanson.

And yet, Drey was a Godspeaker just like him? Had Khaya known this? "I thought he turned against you back when—"

Swanson shook his head. "Not when he took you years ago. Oh, he wanted to resign before he left with you, disagreeing with the City Council's use of the Words. But he never acted on those beliefs, other than to obey my wish for him to vanish when he did. He never acted against me. Until now... and yet you claim he didn't instruct you to abduct Khaya?" Swanson actually sounded confused.

"No, he didn't. But why did you want me to vanish with him? Are you not allowed to have kids or something?"

And then it hit me, like one of Tu's fists. Swanson might be allowed to have kids, but not... "Oh, Gods," I croaked. "Which one was it?"

Swanson glanced back at the guards and pitched his voice lower. "I—I wasn't careful," he stammered, his cool composure ruffled. He looked uncomfortable in his perfectly tailored suit. "She was the Word of Death. An unwanted pregnancy shouldn't have been a problem. But that was the catch: she wanted it. She wanted you. And Tavin, when I saw you, I wanted you too. But for both of us, that meant giving you up."

"Em," I said.

Herio's eyes were now on Swanson. He made no pretext of seeming uninterested, unlike the medic. Khaya's Words over Drey even faltered for a moment, then resumed in an intense whisper as her eyelids squeezed tighter together.

"The stillborn..." I said.

"Was no stillborn." Swanson nodded. "Smart boy. When

I realized Em was pregnant, we sent for the donor from France. It was easy to call you premature when you were born—the date was far too early, if one assumed that the Frenchman was your father. And it was a simple matter for Em to bring you so close to death that no one would be able to tell the difference... except for the Word of Life."

"Hayat," I said, glancing at Khaya. But she didn't stir from her chanting this time.

"A loving man," Swanson said, sounding far away. "He said he would want to do the same in my position. So he helped. He publicly announced that you were too far gone to bring back, and then revived you in secret. That was when Andre left the Athenaeum with you. Afterward, we used the Frenchman's genetic material along with Em's to replace you. Herio is your half brother."

"But why?" My voice sounded lost, helpless. Like a child's. "If you're telling the truth, why send me away?"

Swanson was looking at me with a strange intensity. "We wanted to save you. We didn't want you to become a weapon, a killing machine that would be discarded when you had exhausted your usefulness. As a child born of one of the Words, you would have succeeded Em."

"But why care about *me*? You treat all those other kids like tools!"

"You are my son. You wouldn't understand the feeling. I lost Em to that fate, but neither of us could stand to lose you."

Herio was staring at Swanson with an expression I'd never seen on his face—not that I'd seen all that many. He looked surprised, of course, nearly as shocked as I was. But there was something else … a look of betrayal.

Lacking parents, Herio had obviously turned to Swanson as some sort of father figure. Never mind that Swanson made him kill. And yet I'd ruined even that twisted relationship for him, now that he knew *I* was Swanson's true son—the son both Swanson and Herio's own mother had loved enough to save from his fate as a Word.

I'd be pretty pissed myself. I was already pissed. My entire life was a sham. I was supposed to have been the Word of Death until someone else was sacrificed in my place. And then I was raised wordless, with garbage. No, I was raised by Drey. But was Drey's love for me a lie too, like everything else? Whatever moral qualms he had, he'd still been a God-speaker … someone who'd used people like tools.

I looked at Drey, whose color was already improving, but then my eyes shot to the medic. I was letting myself get distracted.

Khaya's low murmur tapered off. She pulled her hands away from Drey, stepping back from the gurney. "I've done what I can, for both his stomach wound and the lung cancer. He's not fully healed, but he should be able to recover on his own now. He's sleeping peacefully."

I couldn't tell what she was thinking. How, if at all, the revelation that I should have been the Word of Death affected her.

"So what do you want?" I asked Swanson, my hand tightening on the gun.

Swanson obviously knew our meeting was winding down. I expected an even greater diversion, and he didn't disappoint.

"Come with me," he said, lifting a hand in invitation. "You will find protection and power in the Athenaeum. I'll give you whatever you want—a life of luxury and knowledge. I won't tell anyone about your heritage, as far as Words are concerned, only that you're my long-lost son. Enough time has passed that no one will question who your mother was."

I tossed my head at the medic. "He just heard the whole story."

"He is an automaton, one of the first few prototypes brought to life. Khaya and Cruithear made him. He follows every order to the letter, and I told him to disregard whatever he heard me say to you."

That explained the blank stare—the medic wasn't faking. But that didn't make him any less dangerous, and my eyes returned to his involuntarily. It made him more dangerous, if he was designed to be a super-soldier. I wondered what other orders he'd received.

"Herio knows," I said, trying to change the subject.

Khaya shook her head. "It doesn't matter what Herio knows, because if I go back, he'll be replaced with an automaton." She turned her ruthless words on Herio. "You've served Swanson so willingly all this time, more obediently than any of us, and yet he's still going to make you die to give up the Word of Death."

Swanson stood in silence without contradicting her. Herio really didn't have much time left, if he was being exposed to this truth that was as deadly as poison. It was a truth I already knew, and still it was cruel to hear it spoken aloud.

Herio's face showed no sign of registering it, no disturbance, not since he'd looked so betrayed. He only shot a quick glance at Swanson, as if trying to base his reaction off the older man's. Which meant there wasn't much reaction of his own.

Khaya shook her head in disgust. "Swanson won't need to make you into an automaton. You already are."

Swanson didn't look at Khaya, only at me, probably to avoid showing interest in her. Not that I doubted he was telling me the truth—too many pieces fit. But I knew he still wanted Khaya.

"If you come back with me, Tavin," he said, "*no one* you care about will have to worry. I promise."

Herio shot another glance at Swanson. He must have known what Swanson was offering, even though the words were vague: Khaya wouldn't be replaced if both she and I cooperated.

But Khaya would never cooperate, because if she did, the world would fall under the direct control of Eden City. She would rather die than let that happen. Even if she'd somehow managed to trade the world's future for mine, giving me my life back by surrendering, she could never have lived with herself afterwards. Or at least that's what I told myself as I turned the gun on her.

Everyone froze: Swanson, Herio, the medic—though, admittedly, he was already motionless—and Khaya. Her dark eyes were wide and afraid as they met mine.

"If you shoot a tranquilizer into her," I said, "I will shoot her. Same if you shoot one at me. I don't know how fast they work, but the second I feel a sting, I'm pulling the trigger."

Only Khaya's freedom, not mine, coincided with the world's. And as Toki, the Word of Time, had proved, death was a means of escape. The horrible decision I never thought I would have to face was staring me right in the eyes: Khaya or the world?

It was a choice I couldn't make. I couldn't shoot her *or* doom the world. But a nagging voice in the back of my head said that by doing nothing, by not pulling the trigger, I was making a choice.

I ignored the voice, because there was still a chance for both Khaya and the world … if I could trust Tu. *Hah. Trust Tu.* I supposed it was fitting that the hope of the earth rested with the Word of Earth.

I was trying to decide what signal Tu would best understand when Herio took a step forward, away from Swanson.

"What are you doing?" Swanson asked.

"Calling his bluff," Herio said simply, taking another step.

I realized it was the first time I'd ever heard Herio speak. His voice sounded sort of like mine did when I heard it played back at me as a recording—off, somehow, but frighteningly similar.

"Stop," Swanson said. When Herio didn't listen, taking another slow step, Swanson signaled the two men with guns.

They moved out from the helicopter and marched up behind Herio. I thought maybe this was all still part of Swanson's plan, a way to get the guards closer to us … until Herio turned with a disarming smile on his face and put a hand on each man's shoulder, like they were friends. He leaned forward to whisper something in their ears.

Then they collapsed at his feet, crumpling in the snow as if they had been deboned.

Swanson cried out in shock and the medic whipped out the tranquilizer gun I'd never doubted he had under his white jacket. But Herio's boot was there to meet it. The Word of Death moved in a dark blur, kicking the gun in a spiraling arc into the field, where it vanished beneath a sheet of white.

Automatons had instincts, I remembered when the medic dodged fast enough to avoid Herio's viperlike hand—and his sharply spoken Word. Otherwise, the medic would have hit the snow too, like the two guards. But he rolled out of Death's way and came up in a sprint, heading toward his lost weapon.

Which left no one to stop Herio from reaching us except Swanson, and Swanson was staring at Herio as if he'd never seen the Word of Death before.

I froze, too. If I aimed at Herio instead of Khaya, my bluff would be called. They would know I couldn't shoot her, and chances were Herio would death-touch me anyway even if I *could* shoot him—unless my aim was spot-on and I killed him instantly, which was unlikely because I'd never shot a gun before. And then the medic would be back to drop Khaya with the tranquilizer gun. The world would belong to Eden City. Unless I could make good on my threat and actually find it in me to kill her.

I didn't know what to do.

But Khaya didn't hesitate. She snatched the gun from

me just as Herio lunged for us, pointed it at him, and pulled the trigger. The shot exploded into the cold air.

As I'd feared, the bullet didn't stop Herio's forward momentum. He hit me around the knees, taking me down with him. I tried to lift a leg to kick him in the face, but he had my legs held tight, even though the snow turned red around where he lay, the stain spreading out from his stomach.

Khaya had shot him in the gut. Maybe it was poetic justice, since that was essentially what he had done to Drey. But I didn't feel satisfied, only horrified.

"Move again," Herio panted at me, "and you die." He smiled at Khaya with bloody teeth as she kept the gun pointed at him. "You weren't made for killing. Only I am."

"I aim for your head next." Khaya's voice quavered but her hand was steady. "Even if I do nothing, you're dead with a wound like that." Her tone became pleading. "But if you let him go, I can heal you—"

"No!" I said, raising myself on my elbows to snarl at Herio. "Good riddance to a bad Word. Go for it, *brother*. Kill me." For a crazy second, I meant it. I wanted to spite Swanson and foil his messed-up plan. It would all be for nothing if I died.

But I didn't really want to die, nor did I want Khaya to become a killer. It would kill *her*.

Herio smiled his red smile. "For once I have something better than killing. A way to kill your soul. All of your souls." He looked from me to Khaya to Dr. Swanson, where his eyes lingered. "Tavin was born for it, after all."

"No!" Swanson cried, pulling his own gun out of his jacket. Not a tranquilizer gun.

I couldn't believe it. Swanson was going to kill Herio—and lose the Word of Death forever. But I could believe what happened next even less.

Before either Swanson or Khaya had the chance to shoot, Herio spoke in what must have been Basque. The Words ran over his lips like ink, black mixing with his red blood. They poured out of his mouth and dribbled onto my legs, feeling like acid eating into my skin once they soaked through my pants. The burn spread, not only along my skin but as if it had entered my circulatory system and was now fire pumping through my veins. I howled, and kept howling as I thrashed, even kicking free of Herio's now-loose grasp. But that didn't help. He'd already set one of his fatal chain-reactions in motion. I was dying.

Except the pain faded—after seconds, maybe, but it felt like minutes. I didn't die.

Herio was staring up into the darkening sky, a slight smile on his face, snow falling into his unblinking eyes. The gun dropped to Swanson's side, unfired.

"No," Swanson said. But he wasn't looking at Herio, who was somehow dead, I realized. He was looking at me. So was Khaya. Both were wide-eyed.

Then a commotion drew both their gazes behind me, back toward the cabin. I now noticed that the ground was shaking, and there were screams. The gunshot had probably been enough of a signal for Tu.

I looked over my shoulder long enough to see Pavati raise

a wall of solid ice, several feet thick, in front of her and Tu. Bullets cracked against it while Tu launched SUVs and men into the air with the bucking earth.

I turned back to Swanson just in time to see his hand signal … and then Luft, Agonya, and a pale girl—Mørke, the Word of Darkness—slip out of the helicopter with three Godspeakers behind them. They'd been there all along, hiding. I should have known. Swanson had probably been too shocked to remember them until now.

Mørke instantly cried out a Word, and blackness extended from her like tentacles, crawling over the field and covering everything in night.

The only light came from the Word of Fire.

Air and Fire worked together as well as Earth and Water. At a few muttered commands from Luft and Agonya, the air sparked into liquid flame that struck at Pavati's ice wall like a giant snake, melting it within moments and burning everything else in its path—including several of the Chinese and Swiss delegates. Pavati and Tu dove for cover as an SUV exploded and the cabin went up like a bonfire. Then I could no longer see them, only flames in the darkness.

But a wave of snow and earth rose like a tsunami and came crashing down over Luft, burying him in an instant. Agonya managed to dive out of the way, sending up several geysers of fire, but she didn't have as much precision without Luft. Not that her flames would burn any less.

My limbs weren't responding normally. I tried to tell Khaya to go without me, to run, but *go* or *run* weren't the words to come out of my mouth.

"Quit, depart!" I shouted at her. Even weirder, the strange words weren't meant for her, but only a part of her—a vital part that was being told to leave her body behind.

The feeling of the words, their intention—as if they had a mind of their own—was so terrifying it froze my mind solid, far colder and darker than the field of snow I was lying in, than all the fields of snow in the world put together.

Khaya looked at me in what I could only imagine was horror, firelight flickering across her face. Then she ran, almost like she wasn't running because I'd told her to but to get away from me. At least she was going.

Something was wrong with me. I tried to ignore the realization that was scratching at the back of my mind, trying to get in. No. That would be worse than being Swanson's son, or the Word of Death's brother. Because that would make me...
No.

The medic was finally sprinting forward with his retrieved tranquilizer gun. How he'd found it in the snowy darkness was beyond me. He slid to a halt nearby, taking careful aim at Khaya's back. Maybe he didn't realize how long my arms were, or maybe he figured I was down for the count.

My hand shot out and caught him around the ankle. But, like before, what came out of my mouth wasn't *stop*, the word I meant to say.

"Falter, seize, cease!"

That stopped him. It also stopped something else.

His body went rigid. He fell to the ground without taking his shot, like a toppling tree, just as Khaya vanished, her dark hair trailing above her as she dropped into the earth. Tu had done it. He'd gotten Khaya away, and I hoped Pavati, too—I didn't see her among the tossed, blackened earth and SUVs in front of the burning cabin, though it was hard to look anywhere other than right in front of me. I knew what I had done; I could feel it through the man's ankle and in my hand, where the Words held him in a grip far more powerful than mine.

His heart had failed so suddenly, he hadn't even had time to scream.

I screamed—louder when I met his staring eyes above the pillow of snow, glinting in the flickering light. It didn't matter that he'd been an automaton. Herio was lying on the other side of me, the faint smile frozen on his face. He had died to do this to me. I was surrounded by death—death on either side, at my fingertips, in my mouth, in my head.

My screaming continued, but not for long after a tranquilizer dart hit me in the thigh. Swanson had shot me with the gun from the dead medic's hand. I was almost glad, since I didn't know what I might have eventually screamed—what Words. Swanson's pale, sickly expression was the last thing I saw.

The sound of my own horror lingered in my ears even after my eyes closed, a dying howl in the darkness. A darkness I now belonged to.

twenty-six

The trip back to the Athenaeum passed unnoticed behind a thick veil of mental fog. The tranquilizer and additional drugs kept me under, for the most part, but I remembered screaming as they transferred me from the helicopter to an ambulance, on a gurney like Drey's. His hadn't had as many leather straps as mine did, though.

I didn't see Drey again until a while later.

In the interim, I either babbled or shouted Words of Death at anyone in the vicinity of my hospital room, trying to grab them at the same time. I needed to touch them to kill them. And that was all I wanted to do.

Swanson tried to explain to me that this was what happened when a Word passed to someone later in life. "The body isn't used to it," he said, sitting at my bedside, the leather cuffs on my wrists keeping him safe from me. "Words have to be trained—both the person and the power. Right now, only the Words are controlling you—and to a lesser extent, the drugs. Nothing is controlling the Words. They're like a speeding car without a driver."

It was hard to hear him over my death threats. Yet even then he didn't try to shut me up; it wasn't until a nurse tried to give me an IV—to feed me, she said—and I nearly killed her when I lunged at her and brushed the skin of her arm with mine. She fell to the floor, but the Words didn't fully take and the doctors were able to get her heart beating again. Shortly after that, I was injected with something strong and lost consciousness.

When I woke up, I noticed a few new additions to my outfit, which had previously only consisted of a hospital gown, padded leather cuffs on each arm, and numerous straps across my chest and legs. Now there was also a strap around my jaw, which kept my mouth closed and the Words inside, and familiar black bracelets on each wrist.

Monitors. Two of them.

There was no way I'd be able to chop off *both* thumbs to get rid of the monitors, as if I would ever in a million years be able to free myself from all the straps—never mind the drugs inside of me—and then go find an axe. Khaya's escape route from the Athenaeum would be impossible for me to take.

No, I wasn't going anywhere.

I wasn't even sure if I wanted to. All I could see, over and over again, was not the white walls of my hospital room and the glowing machines and the doctors and nurses and other Godspeakers trying to talk to me; it was the look of horror on Khaya's face before she'd run from me.

It had only been a week since I'd first met her. It had taken seven days for the two Nameless Gods to create the world with their Words, or so the stories said, and seven days for the Words to destroy my life. Maybe creation and destruction came in weekly doses.

Sure, I'd saved Khaya, and the world would be all right. But I wouldn't be. Not ever again. I was Khaya's opposite now. She strengthened and built; I weakened and destroyed. She was the Word of Life, and I was the Word of Death. I'd been searching so intently for who I was, but now I would have given anything not to know.

It was funny, and I laughed for a long time: since Dr. Swanson was born and raised in Eden City, and Words were named in the donor parent's language, my name technically wasn't Tavin anymore. Nor was it Herio from Basque or Morte from Italian, or whatever. Just Death, plain and simple. It didn't really have a nice ring to it.

Most people still called me Tavin. Swanson did, during his regular visits, looking more and more haggard. But I ignored him, listening instead to the beeps of the machines, the dripping of the IVs, and the Words raging in my head.

And then...

"Tav."

That was a voice I couldn't ignore.

Drey sat, leaning forward in a chair next to my bedside, his elbows on his knees, hands clasped in front, head bowed. He looked a hell of a lot better than he had the last time I had seen him, though he was still too thin and his eyes had a hollow look they'd never had before.

He stared at his hands for a while before he spoke. "I'm sorry, Tavin. I'm sorry I never told you the truth. But I wanted to raise you with humility, not power. I wanted people to respect you, not out of fear but admiration. I tried to keep you from this life and I failed, Tavin. I failed." For a second, his voice broke. He looked broken. But then he squared his shoulders and straightened in the chair.

He stared at me with eyes the color of a sky I would probably never see again—a wide, free sky.

"I took a risk, sending you back in here so your real father could see what you'd become—what wonderful adults could be made of all these children he treats as tools. Powerful tools, but disposable nonetheless. And they got you; they've tried to make you into a tool. But you're still the man I raised."

Drey stood, looking down at me as if I were lying on my cot in his garage, my arms folded lazily behind my head, not on a hospital bed with padded leather cuffs strapping down my straining hands.

Hands that would kill him, given the opportunity. How could I be anything but a tool? A gun? At best, an attack dog?

"I gave you a name and it doesn't mean death, no matter what those marks on your back say—no matter what you say." The tone of his voice left no room for argument, as if I could have argued instead of only making strangled noises or screaming ways for him to die. "I marked you, and they've marked you. So in a way you're both my son and the Athenaeum's. Mine and Swanson's."

Anger, disgust, and sadness warred on his grizzled face when he said that name, but he swallowed them all, his voice hardening once again. "But even more, you're your own person. And now that you have both humility and power, I guess we'll see what the result will be."

He reached out to put his hand on my head, but pulled away at the last second. Then he moved toward the door and had to rap on it before it opened—it was locked, of course. His eyes held mine before he stepped through.

"Admiration or fear," he said.

He left me in a fortress of a room with leather straps across my chest, cuffs on my arms, and unbreakable bracelets around my wrists, bound like a deadly animal being trained.

I was an animal. I was deadly. And they were trying to train me. But his words reminded me of something else.

I was still Tavin.

Acknowledgments

Several people were so crucial to this book, with their loving encouragement and attentive feedback, that without them I wouldn't even have a functioning draft. So first and foremost I want to thank my personal superheroes: Lukas, my amazing husband, who has encouraged, prodded, and supported me every step of this journey; my lovely mom, Deanna, who has read a billion drafts with never a complaint and always the same amazing attention to detail; Pam and Dan Strickland, who slogged through my earliest work and yet, in spite of that, still continue to read and believe in what has come after; and Chelsea Pitcher, fellow author, critique partner, and wonderful friend, who kept me company and offered stellar advice (and margaritas!) along the way.

After the book left my hands and flew out into the world, several more people kept it from crash-landing: Sandy Lu, the agent who tirelessly represented it; Brian Farrey-Latz, the acquisitions editor who loved it and helped shape it into something better; Sandy Sullivan, the production editor who polished it until it shined; Mallory Hayes, the publicist who told everyone about it; Katie Kane, an account manager who's selling it; and the rest of the Flux team working behind the scenes. Without all of you, my little manuscript wouldn't be a book. Thank you so much for making my dreams come true.

I also want to give special thanks to my critique partners in Alaska—Amy Sandbak, Monica Millard, and my awesome friend Michael Miller (where is *your* book?)—and the Alaska community for being so supportive. If I hadn't had such a nurturing and inspiring environment, I don't know how I would have been able to keep writing.

Last but not least, a nod to my brother, Daniel, whose personality I may have "borrowed" somewhat for Tavin.

Much love to all of you.

© Lukas Strickland

About the Author

AdriAnne Strickland was a bibliophile who wanted to be an author before she knew what either of those words meant. An avid traveler, she spent two cumulative years living abroad in Africa, Asia, and Europe and now shares a home base in Alaska with her husband. While writing occupies most of her time, she commercial fishes every summer in Bristol Bay, because she can't seem to stop. Visit AdriAnne online at http://www.adriannestrickland.com.

Watch for Book II of Tavin's adventures,
coming Summer 2015.